Total BULL

A Romantic Comedy by
TIFFANY ANDREA

To my fellow Bookstagrammers,
a sense of community and belonging is not easy to come by in this
crazy world. I thank you all for continuing to motivate and inspire me
with your creative work, kind words, and love for books.

TABLE OF CONTENTS

Believe Me

"You've *got* to be kidding me, Angel."

I'm not sure if Hannah is asking me a rhetorical question, or if she wants me to answer, so I stare at her, awaiting clarification. None comes in the following seconds. "No, Hannah, I'm not." Add in an eye roll for emphasis. "He complained the pasta was overcooked, and the shrimp was rubbery."

The overworked sous chef, who has just arrived for her shift, sweeps her sweat-soaked hair from her forehead and resigns herself to the reality that she'll have to remake another screwed up dish. "I'm so sick of redoing other people's work. I swear, their heads are up their—"

"Incoming." Fellow server, Vida pushes through the kitchen entrance carrying a tray of more returned food. "Sorry, Hannah. Steak is way overcooked, but the potato is hard."

Hannah grumbles and mutters some NSFW words, which, anyplace other than a restaurant kitchen, might be frowned upon. Here, the colourful language is readily embraced. She works quickly to replace the rejected food, and I head back into the dining room to check on my customers.

On the way past, the restaurant's owner glares at me in warning. I've been told that if I continue to "over-share" with my customers, I will be without a job. That's a politically correct way of saying "honest," which is not embraced here as easily as vulgar language. Makes one wonder.

"How is everything?" I ask the three-person family seated in my section. The mother, father and teenage daughter are all picking at their food, but none of them have any complaints. Their reluctance to eat it tells me I'm in for another sub-par tip. Awesome.

"Fine, thank you," the father replies without looking in my direction.

I take my cue to carry on, making a sweep of my other tables to ask the same thing. Get the same answer. Everyone else is just as enthusiastic. Thankfully, Hannah's shift has started, so we can have some happier customers.

The kitchen and dining room are buzzing for the next ninety minutes as we tend to the lunch rush. Our customer base is varied and often eccentric, but they all have one thing in common: they eat here because it's in their price range. No one in their right mind who could afford to eat somewhere else would choose *Harvest*. This is the type of place that doesn't get repeat business. People come for the atmosphere, assuming they'll get a meal to match, and leave wishing they'd gotten fast food. This is the reason my boss hates me. I warn people away from buying things when I know the chef on duty doesn't make them well. I caution people not to request the daily special, knowing it's sat under the heat lamp a little too long. Apparently, this isn't good for business, but I'm less concerned about his bottom line than I am with the truth.

Honesty is something I value above everything else. Turns out, I'm in the minority there, because other people I've come across would prefer to be told lies to spare their feelings. Get real. I'd rather someone have the *cojones* to tell me I have spinach in my teeth than let me walk around with it. Why is it so uncomfortable for people to speak the truth?

Now that the lunch rush has died down, the other waitresses congregate in the hostess area to chat and regroup before the early dinner crowd appears. This reprieve never feels long enough, but it's always welcomed.

Same as every other day, when I make my way over to my co-workers, including two chefs who should be in the kitchen, the audible grumbling begins. Way to make a girl feel wanted. Though, I'm not their biggest fan either.

"Hi, Angel," our hostess Alex seethes.

If I was insecure, I'd take it personally, but I know she's just upset because I told her the latest tattoo she got was misspelled. That's not my fault. Maybe she should have checked with someone who had basic grammar skills before she got "Live you're life" tattooed on her shoulder.

"Hey, Alex. How are the reservations looking for tonight?" I try to shift the conversation back to work because I guarantee if someone asks me about their personal life, they won't like what I have to say. And, to be clear, I don't set out to be mean, or say things out of spite. In today's world, honesty is evidently not the best policy. Not when it comes to building a social circle, anyway.

"Big party coming in that Vida is going to handle, and other than that, just a few couples."

"Perfect." The tension in the hostess booth is uncomfortable, so I decide to go find Hannah instead. She's likely elbow-deep in dinner-rush prep, but I can help her out instead of standing around here dodging the flying daggers being shot my way by people who should actually be helping.

I arrive in the kitchen to find Hannah being chewed out by our head chef, taking the blame for all the returned food earlier in the day.

Nope, I'm not going to stand back and allow that to happen. "Excuse me, Chef?"

Norene turns to glare at me with more hatred than any of my other coworkers were able to generate. "What?"

"Hannah wasn't to blame for the errors earlier. She only arrived as they were brought back, and *she* fixed them." In moments like these, I'm happy that I've built a reputation for honesty, because no one questions what I'm saying.

"Why would you stand there and let me yell at you for five minutes if you weren't the one responsible?" Norene glares at Hannah, now with a new reason to be angry. But believe me, she is not short on supply of harsh words or heated stares. She has plenty on reserve to address the offending parties.

"I'm not going to pass the blame to anyone else. In this kitchen, we're supposed to be a team. If one of us fails, we all fail." Hannah never breaks eye contact with Norene, appearing confident and determined.

"How noble of you. Well, if you'll excuse me, I have other people to talk to." Norene steps forward, turning back to address me with a nod. "Angel."

I return the gesture, and as soon as she's out of earshot, I speak to Hannah. "Why would you stand there and face her wrath? I understand not wanting to rat everyone else out, but at least tell her the truth. If she doesn't know who is screwing up, she can't work to fix it."

Hannah continues chopping produce for future orders. "It won't win me any favours if I'm pointing fingers. Plus, like I said, we're supposed to be a team."

"Stand up for yourself, girl. You are great at your job and don't let anyone else pull you down."

"Thanks." Hannah pauses her task to give me a genuine smile, and I hope she knows I mean every word. I always do.

By the time our dinner rush is waning and I'm given the green light to go home, I'm exhausted. Also relieved I held onto my job for another day. I should start looking for a backup plan somewhere that doesn't get turned off by brutal honesty. Maybe there's a daycare hiring—kids are brutally honest too. No, that would be disastrous as soon as mention of Santa Claus or the Easter Bunny came up. Not to mention, that's not my area of study, so I'd be clueless around kids.

A doggy daycare I could handle.

I open the door to my two-bedroom condo, which I've called home since I turned twenty, and I'm greeted by my sweet American bully, Genie. No less than a hundred people flash a smile at me each day at work, but coming home to see a bully smile warms my heart like no one else ever could.

"Hi, baby girl. What have you been up to all day?"

Genie's stocky build has her entire body shuffling on the parquet flooring, wagging her tail with zeal. Her caramel-coloured fur with white patches and pink nose make her look like a squishy little ice cream sundae. Her cropped ears stand at attention, and while that's not a choice I'd make for a dog myself, when I spotted an ad for her online earlier this year, needing to be re-homed, I couldn't say no to those soulful blue eyes. She quickly became the best part of my day.

Before I take my shoes off, I grab her leash to take her for a short walk. The temperature has dropped since mid-day, but it's still an assault to the senses walking from an air-conditioned building onto the streets of Toronto. The humidity is stifling.

Genie and I walk around a city block, then return home for a quiet night in, being comforted by modern climate control. Time with Genie is always time well spent. She's the most stubborn creature I've ever known, but she accepts me for who I am.

In the human world, few people have the same appeal.

DAMIAN

Change

'm so sick of this. Day in, day out, everyone around is eager to please me, jumping at the chance to earn my favour. Why is that an issue? Because no one challenges me. I could say I wanted to fly an inflatable gorilla across the Don Valley Parkway, and no one would bat an eye. They'd say, "yes sir," and get out an air pump. I could suggest using Webdings as a billboard font, and someone would make it happen. It's a remarkable feat for a twenty-seven-year-old to be at the top of his game in the advertising industry, but if this keeps up, I'm never going to be any better. I don't want to peak at twenty-seven.

Frustration breeds tension in my head and I'm desperate to distance myself from my brown-nosing co-workers. I tell my assistant, Paxton, that I'm taking an early lunch, and not to call me unless there's an emergency. That's a ridiculous notion—emergencies in advertising—but according to some clients, they happen.

I walk north from my office, which is the opposite direction I go most days. Today, I want something new. I need to distance myself from this life I've become accustomed to but will never grow comfortable with. That's why I left the jacket of my stupid-expensive suit behind—that, and the fact it's so humid, it feels like I'm walking through soup.

I turn onto King Street, heading west, and a simple, cozy-looking restaurant called *Harvest* draws my attention. Aside from the immediate notions I have about their terrible signage and advertising material, it's just what I need right now. Comfort food.

The hostess is a slender redhead with blazing blue eyes and freckled cheeks. She smiles as I approach her station, which isn't unusual. But when that smile turns from friendly to predatory, it makes me uncomfortable. A lot of guys would revel in the attention, but I hate it. Sure, physical attraction is important, but I've dealt with my fair share of disingenuous women trying to use me as arm candy or a meal ticket. Neither of which appeal to me. I want to have an actual conversation with someone that doesn't involve net worth or how we can be "mutually beneficial".

"Good afternoon. Table for two?" the redhead asks with a gleam in her eye. The not-so-subtle attempt at questioning if I have a partner joining me.

"Just myself. Somewhere quiet, please," I snap. I'm not in the mood for this today. Or any day, for that matter.

"Absolutely. Follow me." She directs me to a section with only one other couple seated in it, and places me at a table near the window. "Angel will be your server. Take a look at your drink menu and I'll send her right over." If I'm not mistaken, the woman, whose nametag says "Alex", is suppressing a smirk.

With narrowed eyes, I reply, "Thank you."

Seconds later, another woman says, "Hello. I'm Angel, and I'll be your server today. Can I start you off with a drink?"

I stare down at my menu, not looking up at the woman, though I'm impressed by her promptness. "Just water is fine."

"Sparkling or flat?"

My mistake for assuming this place wasn't pretentious. "Flat. No ice. Just water."

"Very well. I'll get that for you and give you a few moments to browse the menu."

When she turns to walk away, I lift my eyes to glimpse the most incredible head of curly hair I've ever seen. It's a combination of dark at the roots with blonde throughout, but not like a neglected dye job. It's more an intentional creative decision. I'd like to say I stopped perusing her back at her hair, but I'm a red-blooded male and couldn't pass up the opportunity. The woman is curvy and strong. Instead of browsing the menu, I keep my eyes lifted, waiting for Angel to return, because I want to see the other side of her. Perhaps I should have put more effort into not being a jerk while she was standing in front of me.

The woman returns carrying a lone glass of water on a tray, manoeuvering through the space with an elegant grace. Her facial features are gorgeous. She wears little makeup, if any, because I can't pinpoint anything specifically. Her skin is a gorgeous light gold, telling me she spends time outdoors away from her job. She's no more than 5'2", but my mother always said, good things come in small packages. What appeals to me the most is that she's not wearing a fake smile. She makes eye contact with me as she returns to set the glass on my table, but she's not sickeningly sweet like most waitresses are.

"Here's your water. Have you decided what you'd like to order yet?"

I spent her entire absence either looking at her from afar or wondering about her, so I'm left unprepared to order. "What would you recommend? This is my first time here."

"It's everyone's first time here." Her eyes shoot wide when she catches herself, and I notice they're a remarkable shade of brown, like black coffee. They are captivating against her light hair. "We don't get a lot of repeat customers." A blush creeps up her cheeks, and I resist the urge to smile.

Cool it, Damian.

"And why is that? I can see myself coming back." If not for the food, for the service.

Her blush deepens, and now I can't stop the smile from spreading across my face. You can fake a smile, but it's a lot harder to fake a blush, and there's something about a genuine reaction from her that gets my blood pumping.

"Wait until you taste the food. As for what I'd recommend, based on the cooks in the kitchen, I'd go for something they can't screw up."

I tilt my head to look at her, curious about her comments. "What can't they screw up, then? A sandwich?"

"Mmm... I wouldn't be so sure. If you're up for it, go with a salad."

I glance down at the menu, taking in the options available. The salads are the cheapest things on offer, but I don't think she's trying to save me money, and she's obviously not trying to make more for herself. "Okay. I'll get the tex-mex chicken salad."

She grimaces. "Are you sure?"

"What's wrong with that one?" That's the most expensive salad option, so I figured that was safe.

"Uh. Nothing is wrong with it, in theory. It's just not a big hit... with these chefs in the kitchen."

"Okay, well, you tell me which one I should get then, since you seem to know it all." I flash another smile, hoping it's clear I appreciate her input.

The sound of a throat clearing behind Angel distracts us both. An angry-looking bald man leans around her shoulder, but he's about her height, so she closes her eyes and shudders. I assume she feels his breath on her neck.

"Is there a problem here, Miss Blake?"

Blake. Angel Blake.

"No, sir. I was just discussing lunch options with this gentleman."

"And I hope you're letting him choose for himself." The man's tone is threatening, and it makes the hair on my arms raise.

"She's been nothing but helpful. Now if you don't mind." I wave him away like the pest he is, and the gesture makes me cringe at myself. I'm not this person. Waving people away is not something I do. Act natural. Own it. "I'll have the steak salad, medium. Dressing on the side."

Angel's lips form a terse line as she nods and rushes off. What was that about?

The pest strides back over to my table. "I apologize if your service isn't to your standards. I can have another server tend to you."

I'm caught off guard by his suggestion, but so far, Angel has been the most forthcoming server I've had to date, and I've eaten at a lot of restaurants. "The service has been phenomenal. I'd say the best I've ever had."

His bushy eyebrows draw together, giving him a frazzled unibrow. Why does he seem surprised? Is she normally a troublemaker? I don't see that being the case.

The short man sets his jaw and speaks through clenched teeth, "Very well. Enjoy your meal."

Angel spends the next fifteen minutes tending to the couple on the other side of her section and performing various tasks. She seems like a hard worker, and I'm not sure what the bald man's issue with her is. I watch her elegant movements across the space, mesmerized by how she does simple things like wiping tables, or tucking in chairs neatly. I've never been so captivated by a person in my life.

When she brings me my meal, she sets it down in front of me, and it smells edible. I thank her with the brightest smile I can, which has her blushing again.

The food could taste like cardboard and I'd still come back tomorrow to see that sight.

3

ANGEL

Tell Me

Of the three people in my section, one was placed there to sabotage my job. Alex snickered as she seated the well-dressed, devastatingly handsome man at table twenty-six, no doubt hoping I'd screw it up and he'd report me to the manager. The scowl on his face when he first sat down had me concerned that would be the case.

When Mr. Harrington walked up behind me, breathing his hot whisky breath in my ear, I was afraid I'd be packing my stuff and joining the line at the unemployment office. The handsome stranger waved off my boss like a peasant, and in any other circumstance, I would have berated him for being a pompous jerk, but in that case, I appreciated it.

Now, trying to keep myself busy while the man's meal is being prepared is difficult. I can feel him watching me, which doesn't give me a chance to return the favour. I perform mindless tasks like arranging chairs that are perfectly fine and wiping down already clean tables. As luck would have it, Hannah's shift started right as I placed the man's order, so when the time comes, I deliver it to him with some confidence.

He thanks me and smiles, and I can barely withhold the school-girl giggle threatening to escape. I nod, tell him to flag me down if he needs anything else, and walk away before I combust. What has gotten into me? There's never been a customer in the history of time that's drawn my attention like he does.

I position myself at the edge of the bar area, hiding behind some fake plants so I can watch him. His medium-brown hair is styled in a textured crop cut with very little product—*au natural*. His beige skin has olive undertones, largely covered by a short, well-manicured beard, and his forehead has creases suggesting he's got a lot of stress in his life. He doesn't look much older than me, but he seems the type to have his life together.

A man like him—confident, gorgeous, expensive clothing, mischievous brown eyes—no doubt has a gaggle of eager women trailing behind him. I don't belong in a gaggle.

He appears to be enjoying his meal, but I can't stop myself from going to check on him. Check on him, check him out; tah-may-toe, toe-mah-toe.

"How is everything?"

He clears his throat and takes a sip of water, his eyes wide in surprise. "You snuck up on me. Last I saw, you were peeking at me from over there." He gestures toward the bar.

My face warms again, but there's no point in denying it. "Servers are supposed to be ninjas. Walk around, accomplishing our tasks without being seen. Apparently, I need to work on my camouflage some more. Sorry if I made you uncomfortable. I was just... curious."

He places his fork beside his near empty plate and focuses his eyes on me, which sends butterflies flurrying in my belly. "What are you curious about?"

I blow out a breath, not wanting to lie, but not wanting to admit the truth. A half truth still counts as a lie, though. "You intrigue me. And not because you're good looking." I shrug, trying to play off my growing embarrassment.

A smug smile tugs at his full lips, creating faint creases around his eyes. "Is that so?"

I nod, not wanting to beeline from awkwardness to full-out mortification that would happen if I tried to speak.

"Are you always so honest?"

That's not what I was expecting him to ask. I'm a bit relieved to move on from talking about his attractiveness. "Yes."

He tilts his head, still focused on me. "That was a very confident yes."

"Because I'm always honest. I can't lie."

His eyebrows dance upward, deepening the existing lines on his forehead. "You can't lie?" He leans toward me and whispers, "Did a wizard cast a spell on you?"

I chuckle, but quickly compose myself. "No wizards. No magical spells. I can't lie because I made a promise to myself I never would. It's really that simple."

"That's admirable."

My hands are laced behind my back, wringing each other to distract from the anxiety pooling in my stomach. This is not me. I don't get nervous around people. But I've never had butterflies, either.

"Would you mind getting my bill?"

My facial expression falls. Everyone is put off when I admit the truth. It will never make sense to me, but I'm used to being dismissed. "I'll be right back."

The poor computer is the recipient of my frustration as I tap the screen harder than necessary to print the handsome man's bill. The small ribbon printer shoots out his receipt, so I grab the credit card terminal and return to his table. He's likely another customer in a long line of them who come here once and never again. I hand him the black bill folio and ask how he'll be paying. He responds, gesturing to the credit card machine in my hand. I set it up to receive his payment and walk away to give him privacy. No one enjoys hemming and hawing over how much to tip someone when said person is standing overtop of them.

When I hear the receipt tear, I return to thank him for his patronage, scoop up the folio and Point Of Sale device, then scurry back to the computer to input the information. I assume I'll never see the man again. Not going to lie—because I never do—that realization fills me with disappointment.

I pull out the receipt and drop it when I see the error he made. I scramble to pick up the paper but turn around to discover the mystery man is gone. A quick shout to Vida to cover my remaining table and I'm running out the door in search of the man who is evidently terrible at math, or he has bad eyesight… or really fat fingers.

"Sir. Wait!" I shout as I see his retreating head walking down the sidewalk. "Wait! You've made a terrible mistake."

He halts his steps, turning to look at me. He is even more handsome in the midday sun. "I don't think I did."

"You definitely did. You accidentally put in $1000 for the tip on a twenty-two-dollar meal."

"And?"

I stare at him with my mouth gaping open before I clamp my jaw shut. "That's a 4500 percent tip. That's not industry standard."

"That's what I thought the service was worth. There's no mistake."

The man in front of me looks dead serious, but I don't want this. I refuse to accept an insane amount of money for bringing him a salad and making him uncomfortable. It wouldn't feel right even if I believed I did a good job. "I can't accept this. Please come inside so I can refund your card. I'll even pay for your meal to make up for the hassle."

His expression doesn't falter. "No."

"No?" I shout, attracting the attention of people walking by. I drop my voice to a reasonable volume. "Please. I can't accept this."

He stands in front of me with a hint of a smile and questions dancing in his eyes. I brace myself for whatever is about to come.

"Why don't you let me take you out for dinner instead?"

It wasn't my intention to ask her out today. If I'm being honest, I don't usually ask women out, so I'm a little rusty in this department. But standing here on the sidewalk, having her refuse my money, tipped me over the edge and I went for it. No one has ever refused a handout from me before, aside from my mom or brother. It's a battle to get them to accept anything, even when I make it clear I want to give it. That's what makes asking Angel out a no-brainer.

Not to mention, her promise to herself has my curiosity piqued. She's intriguing in a way no one else has been for as long as I can remember. My job is based on deceit and getting ahead. No one stops to consider telling the truth. They flat out tell people what they want to hear. The people-pleasing and brown-nosing intensified to a new level when I was catapulted into my new role in management. Now, more than ever, I crave people in my life to tell it like it is. No pretense. No games. No ulterior motives.

Angel's pink cheeks in the sunlight make her appear ethereal—angelic. Until her shoulders slump. "I can't go out with you."

Her abrupt answer yanks me back to Earth, rather than in the clouds where I was clearly daydreaming about something she doesn't want. I shouldn't have been so stupid to assume she was single. She finds me attractive, but that means nothing. "Why? Are you seeing someone?"

She stares down at her feet, kicking a pebble onto the road with her generic black sneaker. "You're a customer and I don't know you. It would be inappropriate."

Despite her lack of eye contact, her voice is clear. Confident. She's sure of her decision.

"You're not a therapist. I don't think there are any laws against it. And that's the point of a date. To get to know each other." My response is just as determined.

"You've obviously never served alcohol to people after a long day at work. Therapist is part of the job." She keeps her head down, but I catch a hint of a smile. "It's not a good idea."

"What if I promise to never come back? As a customer."

"Then I'm not sure how I'll pay your ridiculous tip back. I was hoping you'd return at least forty times so we can break even."

I step closer to her, unable to stop myself. She has a delicate button nose. Her dark eyebrows set over her deep brown eyes are mesmerizing, and her narrow lips create a perfect picture that is equal parts feminine and fierce. She's nothing like anyone I've ever dated—most notably because they were all lying socialites looking for a merger—and I don't want to miss the opportunity to learn more about her. "I can come back a hundred times, if that's what it'll take."

"Maybe I'll see you again next time, then. Have a good day." She spins and runs back toward the restaurant without sparing me a glance.

The instant she's gone, I regret how our interaction went down. When I initially walked out the door, I was kicking myself for leaving abruptly, so when she came running after me, I thought it was my lucky day. But instead of capitalizing on that fortune, I'm left with more questions.

Guess I'm going to be her first repeat customer.

I walk past Paxton, who asks if I'm okay when I return to work. A simple nod is all I can manage because no matter what I say, he'll start spitting out ideas to get me whatever I want. Like I'm some spoiled rich kid who can't handle being told no. Then I realize, it's been so long since anyone told me no, Angel's rejection stung more than I remember. Have I become that demanding rich guy who I despised my entire life? I don't want to be that guy—the one who uses his money and perceived power to manipulate people into doing his bidding. It makes me nauseous thinking of anyone seeing me that way.

My mother raised me better than this. I might be in charge of this department, but that means failures are my burden to bear. That means I'm the final say before a project goes out, but that doesn't mean I'm the only say, or even the best one. Somehow I need my staff to see that too. I need them to see me more as an equal and less of a dictator.

I bet if Angel were here, she'd tell me exactly what she was thinking without fear of consequences.

My phone rings on my way home and I groan when I notice the number. In my last few encounters with the woman whose face lights up my bluetooth screen, I was bored to tears as she talked about her pedigree and why we'd make an excellent partnership. She is the type of girl looking for a business deal along with a marriage certificate and a prenup, not a relationship.

I press the end call button on the steering wheel, not in the mood to deal with her, but she calls back seconds later. If I don't put an end to this, she's going to keep calling.

"Hello."

"Oh, Damian, hi! I'm so glad you answered."

I clench my teeth to resist saying, 'you didn't give me much choice.' I go for a more civil approach. "Hi, Serena. How are you?"

"Better now. I was worried you'd lost my number." Her sing-song voice makes me grind my teeth harder.

"No, just busy. You know how it is. Can I help you with something?" If I keep this business casual, maybe she'll take a hint.

She giggles in the phone, making me roll my eyes. She has one of those manufactured giggles that silver-spoon fed people tend to employ when they want to sidestep an uncomfortable situation. It's condescending, without appearing rude. "You can help with a lot of things, Damian."

I've never heard my name purred before, but Serena Horvath has gone and done it. I'm not a fan.

"Why don't you pick me up for dinner tonight?"

Not happening. Not tonight; not ever. I resent ever being introduced to her at a snooty fundraiser. People show up to those things just to have an excuse to spend a fortune on new clothes and donate the bare minimum to have people buzzing about how generous they are. If my boss didn't insist on me attending, I'd give my donations anonymously and be on my way. In my opinion, it cheapens the gesture if you're doing it for clout. Serena lives for clout.

"Serena, I can't tonight. I've got…" A lot of work? Another date? No. "Food poisoning." I add in a groan to make my point. It can't be too far from the truth after my lunch destination if Angel's reaction to ninety-nine percent of the menu says anything. Nothing puts the kibosh on a date night quite like a bout of diarrhea and vomiting.

"It sounds like you're driving."

I'm too far down this path to turn back. "I had to run out to get some stuff from the pharmacy."

"Aw, baby. You could have called me. I would have brought something over."

I almost do retch all over the leather interior of my SUV after hearing her call me 'baby'. Someone could cut off both my legs and I'd still drag my bloody stumps to the nearest pharmacy before I'd call Serena. Our encounters have been *that* intolerable. "Thanks. Almost home now. We'll talk soon." No. Why did I say that? I disconnect the call before I can say anything else stupid.

My thoughts land back on Angel. I should just take a page from her book and be honest with Serena, but it's not always so straightforward. Is it? The few women I've been out with in recent years are eager to date or marry someone who fits in their ideal tax bracket, rather than someone who loves them. That doesn't appeal to me. I watched my mother spend years recovering from a relationship with a man who chose his bank account over his family. Angel is different, though.

Why did she really turn me down? It can't just be because I was a customer. If that's her only reason, I'd have no issues with never returning. Was she put off by the tip I left? If it was something else, wouldn't she have told me? Whatever her justification is, I want to respect it, but I also want to know why.

I just might end up with food poisoning in my endeavour to find out.

5

ANGEL

Move It

When I return home from work, I walk Genie, have a shower, and climb into bed. The air-conditioning is running, but the space still feels warm. Genie's body heat doesn't help, as she insists on sleeping right up against my side and I don't have the heart to push her away. I've been working such long hours lately, she's spending way too much time home alone. I feel guilty, but some reasons I settled on her breed, aside from her adorable face, were because I knew she wouldn't require a lot of exercise, and she's content being alone.

That won't be the case tomorrow, though. I've got my first day off after working six days straight, and I intend on taking Genie to visit my sister, Dina. Our parents thought giving us virtuous names would make us virtuous people, so I became Angel and she's named after the angel of learning and knowledge. Dina always has been the good kid, but I took a lot of trial and error. I hope if my parents could see me now, they would be proud of me, at least for my work ethic. Sure, I didn't land the big successful job as a nurse that they'd always hoped for—blood and other bodily fluids are not my jam… ew… not my thing—but I'm still doing okay for myself.

Dina is three years younger than me and is working on her Masters in Library Sciences; it was news to me that being a librarian is a science. Aside from that, she spends most of her time with her nose in books, ignoring the fact there's a world outside her fourth-floor condo.

I lie in bed thinking about what life used to be like when we were kids—before we were forced to accept the fact humans are mortal and our world came crumbling down around us—and slowly, thoughts of my past are replaced by ones of the handsome patron I served earlier today. His angular jaw, accented by his neatly trimmed facial hair, and rounded masculine nose make him the picture of perfection.

The fact he asked me to have dinner threw me off. Once I returned inside, I felt as if he was trying to pay me for my time, and I wasn't okay with that, so my decision to turn him down was the right one.

I split the tip amongst my co-workers since, like Hannah said, we're a team, and it didn't feel right to hoard a customer's generosity. I was fine with splitting it, but it stung a little to dish over eighty bucks to the kitchen staff who can't fry an egg, and Alex just for seating the man in my section. She probably saw him walk in wearing his well-tailored, expensive shirt and tie, hoped he'd be stuck up or difficult, and I'd end up losing my job. She's petty. So it's possible my intentions were less altruistic when dishing out equal portions of the thousand dollars the man left. Not that I expect us to become friends, but it would be nice if I didn't have to worry about her vindictive streak. I still refuse to admit pointing out a spelling error was that offensive, though.

At the end of the day, I was left with around ninety-six dollars from the one thousand he left, but that's still excessive. If he comes back again while I'm working, I'll figure out a way to even the playing field. It may be the first time in history waitstaff will tip a customer, but I'm fine with being a trailblazer. I don't like owing someone.

My mind is reeling, replaying our conversation, each glance or smile in my direction, his mannerisms and tone of voice. I snuggle into Genie, hoping for a reprieve, and eventually doze off to sleep.

Thursday morning, it's another scorcher outside, and since I wanted to take Genie with me to my sister's, I'm regretting my decision to delay our departure. We should have left when the temperature was lower and the humidity hadn't yet reached its peak. Humidity plus curly hair is a look I'm not too fond of. For that reason, I wet my hair and pull it back into a sleek ponytail—as sleek as tight curls can get—throw on a coral tank top, khaki shorts, and a pair of comfortable sandals. I pack up some water for both Genie and me, and text my sister that we'll be there within the hour.

A quick check of the weather app on my phone says the temperature is twenty-eight degrees now, but a high of thirty-four is expected and the humidity index is high. Stupid Angel. I hope Genie will be okay walking the distance to Dina's house.

It's 11:48am by the time we exit the elevator and walk out of the lobby. The hot air hits me like it does each time I walk into the restaurant kitchen. The thickness of the air feels like trying to breathe through a wet towel. We'll take things slow, and I'll monitor Genie's paws to make sure she doesn't burn herself. I'm not sure what I'll do if that happens because she's fifty pounds of muscle and not cooperative being hauled around. Not to mention, I'd look like I was participating in an atlas stone carry. Someone should invent dog sandals.

The walk is about three kilometres, which isn't terribly far on a normal day, but the heat will have us relegated to the shade as much as possible. With a plan in mind for which streets we'll take to maximize shade availability while the sun is directly overhead, we venture off.

With one kilometre down and two to go, Genie is struggling. Her pace is slow; her breathing is heavy—heavier than normal. I decide to stop for a moment so she can rest and get some water. We move out of the way of foot traffic by tucking into a shaded alley beside a nail salon. Genie lies on the ground with her legs stretched out behind her, exposing her belly to the cooler pavement. I'm kicking myself for dragging her out during the midst of a heatwave. She's an October baby. This is her first summer, and she's not cut out for long walks or extreme heat.

We'll stay in the alleyway as long as she needs to recover. My sister sends a message to ask me to stop and pick something up for her, but I remind her I have a dog with me, so I can't go into any stores. She concedes and agrees to run out and get the items herself. She'll meet us at her place when we get there. *If* we get there.

Twenty minutes later, Genie pops up, poised to continue on our journey. She drank all of her water and some of mine, so I hope we'll have enough to survive the arduous trek.

Our next half-kilometre is slow but steady, sticking to the shade whenever possible and me hauling Genie across any sunny stretches to keep her paws from getting hot. But by the second half of our journey, she refuses to move any farther.

A distinguishing feature of any bully breed is their hard-headed nature. You can't convince a bully to do something they don't want to do. Genie has quit, and despite my pleas, she's not changing her mind. I need a wagon.

My work is a few doors down, but I doubt Mr. Harrington would be pleased if I walked in with my dog. What would I even do if we went there? Ask for a table and take a seat like that was our intended target? I wouldn't even feed Genie the food there.

I crouch down on the ground next to Genie and beg her to walk the rest of the way. She looks at me with an expression that says, "Not happening." I groan in frustration—not with my dog, but with myself for bringing her out today—and squat down beside her. "What are we going to do now, huh? We're closer to Dina's than we are to home, but I can't carry you that far."

As I pour the last of our water into the collapsible bowl for Genie, I consider our options. I hate feeling stuck, and beyond that, I *hate* when I make epic mistakes. This situation encompasses both things.

Other people stroll by, some with umbrellas for shade, others in full business suits sweating profusely.

I mutter to Genie, "I'd hate to be that guy."

While I'm crouched in the mouth of an alleyway talking to my dog, another suited man stops in front of us. "Angel?"

5

DAMIAN

I Come Undone

Crushing defeat doesn't encapsulate how I feel when I walk out of *Harvest*, having eaten the world's worst chicken burger and been served by a stoic, unfeeling robot waitress in her late fifties. Angel was nowhere to be found, and now I feel like I ate a lead brick. Safe to say, my mood for the rest of the day may be touchy.

I drove to the restaurant today, not wanting to get myself sweaty in the scorching heat, but more so because I was trying to get here quickly. It never occurred to me that Angel would have a day off or work a different shift. I can't eat this food again in my attempts to run into her by trial and error, though. Her warnings are necessary to survive a meal at *Harvest*.

My bloated stomach and I walk back toward my SUV, parked a few hundred metres away, when I see a small woman with an adorable American bully puppy crouched in an alleyway. The woman is talking to the dog, which makes me chuckle. My laughter must be louder than I intended because the woman looks up and I'm drawn in by intense dark eyes.

"Angel?"

"Oh, hi… I'm sorry, I never got your name."

Before I can reply, the dog pops up and jumps up at my legs.

"Genie. Get down," Angel scolds, making me halt my plan to pet the sweet little thing.

"Genie?" The dog looks at me with a tilted head, still resting her front paws on my thigh. Her expression makes me laugh because she has an obvious smile and it's the cutest thing I've ever seen.

"I'm so sorry. She knows better, I swear."

"No, don't be. I'm flattered *she* likes me." I look up at Angel and take in her casual appearance. She's obviously not coming into work with her dog in tow. I shake my head to stop myself from raking over her body with my eyes. "Damian. My name is Damian Taylor. I'm sorry it took me so long to say that. Terrible manners."

She chuckles, and it's the first time I've heard her laugh. Hopefully not the last because that sound is like a sweet melody I want to hear on repeat.

"In all fairness, it's not common practice for customers to introduce themselves to their server by name."

"True. Still, I normally have better manners." My stomach gurgles, and I pray she didn't hear that.

"You and Genie both. She's getting your suit dirty. I'm so sorry."

I shake off her comment, unbothered by a little dirt. "What are you doing crouched in an alley?"

Her facial features twist, making her nose wrinkle. "We're in an alley because I'm an idiot. That's the short answer."

"What's the long answer?"

"Genie and I were supposed to spend my day off with my sister. She lives a few kilometres from me and it's too hard to get a cab or a ride-share with a dog, so we always walk. But it's too hot, and Genie has given up."

The heavens have parted and placed an angel before me. I gesture to my SUV. "Hop in. I'll give you two a ride."

"Damian, no offence, but I don't even know you. Just because you took my advice and ordered a salad doesn't mean we have some sort of connection that's going to make me hop in a car with you."

"You would have gotten in a car with a stranger if you could take a cab or a ride-share. At least you know my name."

She stands silent for a moment. "True, but still…"

"Take a picture of me and send it to your sister. Tell her if you go missing between here and there, I'm suspect number one."

She chuckles again. "Fine. But don't try anything funny because I have my attack dog."

"Wouldn't dream of it." I stare into her eyes, not wanting to look away.

She holds her phone up to take a photo, so I pull a silly face. It feels both juvenile and natural with her because I'm rewarded by her laugh again. She sends off a text before asking, "So, where's your car?"

"Here." I nod toward the SUV that I know I already gestured to.

Her lips form a perfect O. "That's your car? I thought you were just showing off. I can't put my dog in there."

"Why not?"

"Because she's a dog—one who sheds and slobbers… a lot. And that's a… that."

My face forms a hybrid only described as smirking confusion. "A Range Rover?"

"I don't know what it is, but it looks expensive, and I can't afford to have your car detailed *and* dry-clean your suit. I appreciate the offer, but we'll be fine."

"Get in the car, Angel." Before she can argue any more, I scoop up the exhausted dog from the sidewalk and struggle to open the back door to place her on the seat. She immediately flops on the cool leather, panting. "Well, are you coming? Or am I just going to dognap Genie?"

"Oh no you don't. That's my baby. Where she goes, I go." Angel opens the passenger door and eases herself in, glancing back at her dog. When I walk around the back of the car and climb into my seat, she continues, "I'm so sorry. She's drooling everywhere."

I look over at this woman whose hair is pulled back in a ponytail, but the short hairs around her head have puffed up like a humidified halo. She looks casual in her orangey-pink top and shorts, exposing much of her beautiful tan skin. I have to force myself to look ahead so she doesn't catch me gawking. Again.

"Don't worry about it. It cleans up easily." I raise myself in my seat so I can look back at Genie, perplexed by the weird name. "So, where to?"

"Fort York Boulevard. Honestly, we're almost there. It will probably be faster to walk."

"Angel, that's assuming Genie is willing to walk, and besides, she's already slobbered all over. Might as well finish what we started."

"Ugh. I'm so sorry. I'll pay to have your car cleaned. Lucky for me, I had a good tipper yesterday, so I've got some extra cash." Her face curls up into a crooked grin I can only see from the corner of my eye once I ease into traffic.

I wish we were driving somewhere quiet right now so I could at least sneak a glance at her, but busy city streets don't allow for casual looks elsewhere. "I'm glad someone acknowledged your stellar skills and showed their appreciation."

"Well, the rest of the staff sure appreciated the bonus."

I tap the breaks, because my instinct is to look at her to see if she's being serious, but then I remember her confession about never telling a lie. I don't know what her policy is on little white lies or less-than-truthful joking. "What do you mean 'rest of the staff'?"

"Everyone else working was entitled to their fair share. A thousand dollars was way more than I deserved, and they all work hard too."

I sit silently for a moment. Not only did she try to give the money back to me, but when I refused, she divided it up with everyone else? That's the complete opposite reaction to any other person I've given money to. As far as I know, anyway.

Before I wrap my head around what she said, we arrive in front of the condo building. It's about half as tall as mine and is surrounded by other buildings obstructing the view of the water, but it's a nice place.

I pull to a stop in front of the entrance. "Where did you walk from?" Somehow, that feels like a natural thing to ask.

"I live at College and Palmerston. In the condo complex."

"That's quite a hike. What time are you going back home?"

She eyes me while keeping one hand on the door handle. "I'm not sure."

"Well, take my number. Why don't you call me when you're headed home, and I'll pick you up?" I nod toward the back seat. "She already claimed that as her spot."

"I... uh... I can't ask you to do that. It will be cooler later. We'll wait until after the sun goes down to walk home."

Oh no, she is not walking home in the dark. Alone. I'm not one to go caveman and beat my chest, but my mother raised me to be a gentleman. "Either you let me pick you up, or I'll wait here until you leave."

She furrows her brows at me, and for the first time since I met this woman, she scares me. "Who do you think you are? Was that your plan? Try to pay me off, then give me a ride that *you* insisted on and now you think I have to follow your orders? Like you own me now?"

"That's not what I—"

She steps out of the car, then opens the rear door for Genie to jump out. The dog refuses to budge. Air-conditioning is magical.

"Genie, come."

Before Angel can run off, I throw the car in park and hop out to intercept her. "That's not what I meant. I'm sorry if I came across that way. You don't owe me anything, but I'd worry knowing you were walking home alone after dark."

Her head is inside the back door as she scrambles for Genie's leash and tries to coax the dog out. "You don't need to worry about me, Mr. Taylor. I've been on my own for a lot of years and I've managed just fine."

Ouch. Mr. Taylor.

"I'm sure you're very capable. I was trying to be a gentleman."

Angel straightens and glares at me with renewed intensity. "Maybe next time, try not to sound like such a controlling jackass!"

Genie jumps out of the car, and with a slam of the door, Angel walks through the front doors of the condo building with her stubborn bully trailing behind.

'm waiting in the lobby after reading a text from Dina that she's ten minutes away. She assumed Genie and I would take a little longer because we were walking, which is what I should have done.

First the man leaves a thousand-dollar tip, then insists on giving me a ride, and now he thinks I owe him something by offering my whereabouts because he said so? Nah, I'm not okay with that. He's not going to buy a date with me, and he's certainly not going to become my keeper just because he would "worry". It's been a long time since anyone worried about me, and I'm holding up fine.

Genie is snorting with excitement, sniffing the lobby furniture. She seemed enamoured with the control freak. First guy to let her drool on his leather seats, and she's ready to abandon me. So much for the loyal love of a dog.

I'm so blinded by my unadulterated rage, I don't hear Dina approach until she places a hand on my shoulder and says my name.

"Sheesh. What's gotten into you?"

I huff an exhale, pulling my little sister in for a hug, even though her hands are full of shopping bags so she can't return it. Her dark curls fare much better in the humidity than mine do, but along with her personality, her curls have always been better behaved.

"Sorry. I was distracted."

"Anything to do with that fine gentleman you sent me a photo of? Even with his tongue hanging out, I could tell he was a good-looking guy." She turns toward the elevator, gesturing for me to follow. "You can tell me about it upstairs. Come on. I bought ice cream."

"Not chocolate, I hope."

"Wouldn't dream of it. Nacho wouldn't let me live it down."

Nacho is Dina's seven-month-old Chihuahua. Ever since I started college, Dina has had a habit of trying to do everything I do—except get a job. That part she's dragging her feet on. But once I adopted Genie, she got a dog two months later. One who's suffering from an identity crisis and thinks he's a black mamba. He gives merit to the term ankle-biter, but Dina loves him.

Dina opens her condo's door and Genie zooms ahead inside to greet the epitome of little man syndrome.

I spend the whole day at Dina's, and she asks me at least fifty questions about Damian. Most of them I don't know the answer to, so her incessant whining tells me our dish sesh wasn't as informative as she was hoping. Basically, I know what he drives and that he has money to burn, leaving excessive tips for unsuspecting waitresses. The more I think about it, the more irritated it makes me because he's probably some nepotistic rich boy who dishes out thousand-dollar bills like breath mints and tries to buy people's servitude. Not this girl, Mr. Damian Taylor. Not for any dollar amount.

Had I not come to my sister's today, I wouldn't have run into Mr. Money Bags, and wouldn't be furious with him right now, but I also wouldn't have gotten to spend much-needed time with Dina, and for that, I'd suffer a hundred ill-fated encounters with handsome rich guys.

After we consume enough junk food to have us on the brink of descending into a sugar coma, the sun has gone down, and I realize it's time to head home before it gets too late. Walking home at night isn't unusual for me. In all fairness, a few months of the year, it's dark by 5pm. Sure, there's always the risk of something happening, but the city is pretty safe. I wouldn't go snooping down any back alleys, but sticking to the main streets has never caused an issue for me.

Genie trails behind me, attached to her leash as we exit the lobby. The temperature has dropped significantly. There's even a nice breeze coming off of Lake Ontario that makes not being in air-conditioning tolerable. With water refills and a route mapped in my head, we set off for home.

By the time we reach the intersection at Bathurst and Dundas, which has taken forty minutes on account of Genie's refusal to walk when asked, my dog has given up on moving an inch. She's parked her chunky butt on the sidewalk and told me with her eyes she's not taking another step. At first I'm concerned her feet are hurt from the hot sidewalk, but I feel the concrete with the back of my hand, and it's barely warm. She's not injured; she's stubborn.

"Genie, please. We're almost home. Less than a kilometre to go. I promise, once we get home, you can lie on the couch and not move a muscle."

She's not responding to my begging.

I refuse to cry. I'm frustrated, but she's just a dog. She has short legs, and this was a long walk for her. Maybe if she rests for a bit, she'll be able to continue the remainder of the way. I resign myself to sitting on the stairs in front of a marijuana dispensary and wait for my dog to decide she's ready to carry on.

Twenty minutes later, she still refuses to budge. I stand beside her, taking a few deep breaths, then squat down, wrapping my arms around her robust middle. I swear, half of her weight is in her head, but I think her brain is only full of manipulation tactics.

After a little over a hundred yards, I need a break, so I set Genie on the ground. Again, I plead with her to walk on her own, but she's not having it. A few minutes of rest gives me the energy to travel another hundred and fifty yards before stopping again. I imagine the sight is comical to anyone watching. I'm not a big person and Genie is awkward to carry, so with each stretch, I'm taking short steps with my back arched, trying to hold some of her weight on my torso, rather than my arms.

Why did I get such a stubborn dog?

I look down at her little strawberry nose and she has the gall to smile at me. She's enjoying this.

"Is this payback for not letting you ride home in the air-conditioning? Hmm? You wanted me to bend to the whims of the man with the leather seats and killer smile? Well, no such luck, girlie. We're strong independent women, and we can get home on our own. You don't need a carriage to get there."

I'm standing on the street speaking to my dog. It's one quick step from here to the loonie-bin. A cursory glance around my surroundings confirms that a frizzy-haired woman talking to her dog is *not* the weirdest thing happening around here. That's not comforting.

Miraculously, Genie decides she's had enough of playing the atlas stone, so she starts marching home.

Somewhere along the remaining distance, I regret not taking Damian's number. Not because I'm annoyed that I had to carry my dog. Not because I wish we took a ride instead. I don't care about that. I hate to admit it to myself, but I think it's because the few minutes we spent together, I enjoyed his company. The idiot just had to be a misogynistic jerk.

But is it such a bad thing if he worried about me? As far as things to be offended about, that hardly qualifies. I've become so used to functioning on my own, that split second, I felt he was trying to control me made me lash out more than I should have. Rational Angel has had time to think about it, though, and it's hard to be upset with someone for caring.

Lost in my thoughts, we finally arrive at the six-storey brick building I call home. Walking into my condo is a relief. We made it. Even Genie is excited to be home. The second we walk through the door, she runs straight to her water dish. I eye her slurping up her drink as if she just carried something more than a third her size a quarter kilometre.

No matter what that dog puts me through, I'll still love her. I laugh at how easily she managed to wrap me around her paw as I walk into the bathroom to shower. Back to work tomorrow, and my spine is going to need some rest.

I climb into bed a short time later, pull out my phone to text Dina that I arrived home safely, and stare at the photo of the man who keeps popping in my head. Unwelcomed.

8

DAMIAN

Cease fire

Eight days have passed, and I still haven't worked up the nerve to go into *Harvest* to see Angel. The way I came across was too much too soon, and she was obviously not a fan. Neither was I, to be honest, but the thought of her walking home alone at night worried me. Instinct took over before logic. I'm forever a small-town guy at heart, so the big city still makes me nervous.

Regardless, she has survived this long without having me around, acting like a barbarian.

Considering her schedule last week, I'm operating under the assumption Thursday is her regular day off. So here I am, Friday afternoon, walking through the doors of *Harvest*. I'm greeted by the same redhead who was here the first time. Today, the place is busy. There are several casually dressed families and couples, with the odd single person sprinkled around the sections. I'm the only person who doesn't scream 'tourist'. The redhead, Alex, grins at me, and I wonder if she's as happy to see other customers or if she's recalling the tip I left Angel, which she apparently got a portion of. Probably the latter. Everyone always wants money.

Before she can speak, I ask, "Can you seat me in Angel's section if she's here today?"

Her smile falters for a second, but she pastes it back on. "She is here, but I'm afraid her section is full. Rolanda will be happy to serve you."

No, thank you. Rolanda served me last week, and I suffered the rest of the day. Plus, I came here to see Angel. I'm not sure how to get that point across without sounding like a possessed stalker. "There's nothing in Angel's section? Are you sure?"

Alex looks down at her seating plan, but I'm looking at Angel's section with my own two eyes. I see a handful of empty tables surrounded by unoccupied wooden chairs with tan vinyl seats.

"The same table I sat at before is empty. Would you mind?"

Alex glares at me, but once again paints on her fake smile as she grabs a menu and gestures for me to follow her. She seats me where I was the first time I was here, and my anxiety ratchets up a notch when Angel comes through the door from the kitchen carrying a large tray of hopefully edible food.

She caters to two other tables before she walks toward mine. Unlike last time when I didn't look up, this time, I watch her every movement.

"Flat water, no ice?" She asks with no preamble.

"Angel, can we—"

"I'm sorry Mr. Taylor. I'm not upset with you, but I am busy, so if we can keep things moving along, that would be helpful."

She's not upset with me? I guess that's something. "Can we talk later?"

She taps her pen on her notepad, delaying her response. "If later is outside working hours, I'd be amenable to that, but for now, just your order."

Amenable? Who says that? "Okay. Flat water with no ice would be great, thanks."

"I'll give you some time to look over the menu."

"No, just order whatever you recommend. I trust you."

She gives me a tight-lipped smile and walks off to the next table where I hear her ask if everything is to their liking. Our interaction went so much better than I imagined it going, even if we resolved nothing. Hearing her say she's not upset with me eased some of my frayed nerves.

I can't tear my eyes off of Angel as she moves from one table to the next, offering friendly smiles and stellar service. Maybe I'm biased because I'm fascinated by her, but she's incredible. Her no-nonsense personality. Her gorgeous curls and smooth, sun-kissed skin. Her obvious work-ethic. Everything I know about her so far, which isn't much, makes me want to know more.

When she returns ten minutes later, she places an appetizing dish of chicken, roasted vegetables and a rice pilaf in front of me.

I glance up to make eye contact. "This isn't a salad."

Her head jerks back an inch, and she lowers one of her perfectly curved eyebrows. "I didn't realize you wanted a salad. My mistake." She reaches down to retrieve the plate, but I place my hand on her wrist. She freezes under my touch, so I release my gentle hold.

"No, this is great. I just thought salads were the only edible option."

"Lucky for you, Hannah is in the kitchen, and she doesn't screw anything up. I thought I'd bring you something more substantial. Since you're a growing boy and all."

A roaring laugh escapes me before I can reel it in. "Growing boy? I left that stage a few years back."

Those rosy cheeks I've come to daydream about for the past nine days reappear. "It seems so. I've got other tables to check on, so signal for my attention if you need anything." She walks off, making her rounds again, and like a love-sick puppy, I watch each move she makes with rapt fascination.

I'm drawn to her like most men watch waitresses at *Hooters*. The uniforms the staff here are wearing are terrible, with plain black slacks, a white button-up shirt with a high collar and black buttons, and the most obnoxious bow tie I've ever seen. However, Angel wears it like she's walking the runway in New York Fashion Week. Her ability to wear such a modest outfit and make it look attractive has me wondering how she'd look dressed up for a date. I'd be lying if I said I hadn't thought about it more than once, even though she declined my request.

My meal is delicious, so I clear my plate, wanting to send my compliments to the chef.

Angel returns when she sees my empty dish. "Can I get you anything else, Damian?"

Most of the day, I hear "Mr. Taylor" countless times, despite my preference to be addressed by my first name. None of my staff break from formality, though, so hearing Angel call me Damian is refreshing. It makes me feel like a person. Not a boss.

"That was delicious. Thank you. Just the cheque, please."

"Already taken care of. Have a good weekend."

Before she can walk too far away, my brain catches up with her words, so I call, "Angel, what do you mean, 'taken care of'?"

She turns her neck and replies over her shoulder, "I owe you for having your car detailed. I figured you won't take my money, so this was my solution."

Words elude me for far too many seconds. "You don't need to do that. Please, let me pay."

Now she spins herself to face me, her facial expression giving off a businesslike vibe. "Am I wrong? If I were to give you money for you to have the dog slobber cleaned off your leather seats, would you take it?"

"No, never."

"That's what I figured. So, if you don't mind, I've got a lot to catch up on. Bye, Damian."

Without a backward glance, she saunters off to carry on with her work.

I'm baffled. When she mentioned paying to have my car detailed, I thought it was in jest. I didn't think she was serious.

To remedy the situation, I return to my vacated table and leave three twenty-dollar bills as a tip, hoping that more than covers the cost of my meal. Given the average price on the menu, it should, but I don't want her paying for my food. Or my car.

Before I leave, I send a smile her way, which she returns from her spot beside a couple's table where she's jotting down their orders. My lunch hour is running out, but I realize we didn't make arrangements to speak afterward, so again, I walk back to my table and kick myself for not having a business card on hand. What kind of self-respecting businessman doesn't have a card on him at all times? One who doesn't want the job. Instead, I scrawl my name and number onto a loose receipt I had in my wallet. At least now she'll have my number.

The ball is in her court.

Empty Words

After I tend to my customers, I walk over to Damian's table to clear away his dishes to ready it for the next guests, only to discover he left sixty dollars in cash and a piece of paper with his phone number. I tuck the money and paper into my apron, not wanting to think too much of it, but a little irked he insisted on paying. Is it so much to ask to pay for what I owe him and call ourselves even? I don't want to live in this never-ending cycle of owing him for something.

I survive the rest of my shift, but by the time I walk home, I'm running on what's left of a pack of skittles and too much espresso. Genie needs a walk, and since the forecast is calling for rain, I decide to take her out right away and try to beat the bad weather. It's about time we got a storm to cut through the humidity we've been suffering through. Hopefully my hair will shrink back to normal size.

When I return home, I take the rolled-up piece of paper with Damian's phone number and stare at it. I have no intention of calling him because that seems desperate. While I do find him interesting, the thought of going on a date is overwhelming. I'm not a fan of the fake personalities people wear on first dates to impress another person. That's not me, and in the past, my not-fake personality hasn't won me any second dates. Not only that, but I don't want to go out with him, feeling like I owe him. So dinner together will never happen until we wipe the slate clean.

I can appreciate in his mind he was trying to be a gentleman, but there are acceptable and unacceptable ways to do that. Open doors, by all means. Pick up the tab? Sure, but it's not expected every time. Hold my arm when I'm trying to walk across cobblestones in stilettos? Yes, please. But between his *orders* the day he dropped me off at Dina's, and his habit of overpaying for mediocre food, his gentlemanly ways leave a lot to be desired.

Yet, here I am, lying in bed at the end of a long day, *desiring* to see him again.

I worked the entire weekend and, given that it's summer, I had a great weekend for tips. No one else left me $1000, but I'm not complaining. More importantly, Mr. Harrington didn't take issue with my customer service, so I'm still employed.

Lately I've been having a nagging feeling to pursue more options in my field, though. Maybe it's time to look outside the city. I can apply for freelance gigs and work in my free time to build up my portfolio. My degree in graphic design has largely been unused aside from a few art pieces I made for my condo, which I only made because I was too cheap to buy anything. That's not going to pay the bills, and waitressing isn't something I want to build my career on, either. It's been great for the past few years, but I'm ready to pursue something that sparks some passion—delivering food that barely meets edibility requirements doesn't.

Until now, I've hesitated to pursue a job in the graphic design field because marketing is a shady industry and I couldn't justify willingly participating in some of the questionable practices used. So if anyone calls me back for an interview, I'll just have to tell them where I stand and hope they'll appreciate an employee who has a strict moral code.

One can only hope.

After three long days of rain, I return to work on Tuesday, grateful for the sunshine. My hair is being cooperative and no longer feels as if it's trying to overtake my head, so that's always a plus.

I'd be lying if I said I wasn't thinking about the possibility of seeing Damian today. Or maybe he'll be upset I didn't call him, so he'll find somewhere else to eat. I couldn't blame him for that, because there are plenty of better options around and he can obviously afford to eat in a nicer spot. That realization leaves a funny feeling swelling in my chest, because he could eat somewhere else, but he came back to see me under an actual risk of intestinal distress.

As I walk into *Harvest*, my boss, Mr. Harrington, who is very much a hands-on owner, with bad breath and no concept of personal space, greets me at the door. "Good morning, Miss Blake. We're expecting quite a bit of foot traffic to come through in about an hour on account of some events happening, so be on your best behaviour."

Most people would smile and appease their boss. I reply with a neutral expression that hopefully relays my feelings about the matter. "I'm always on my best behaviour, Mr. Harrington. We just disagree on what that entails."

"Miss Blake," he says, a tone of warning in his voice, "let people order for themselves and don't cause any problems. It's really a simple task. A chimpanzee could wait tables."

I'm not going to touch that one because I still need this job. If I had the tiniest bit of confidence I'd be able to find a job in my field, I may feel otherwise. Must. Resist. I take a breath, destroying my reputation as queen of the clap back, but it's not worth it today.

When I enter the kitchen, Hannah is nowhere to be found. I check the schedule and today is her day off. She worked yesterday, so that makes sense, but I hate being here without her. Not only because she's the only one who can turn out decent food, but because she's one of the few people I can talk to who doesn't get offended by everything I say.

I greet the line cooks on duty, suppressing a groan because each one of them possesses the most lascivious looks when they stare back at me. I don't know how Hannah works in here with them. They're lucky they haven't caught a frying pan to the side of the head if they look at her the same way.

Pushing away the image of Hannah weaponizing cast iron, I head back into the dining room to get myself prepared for an influx of guests.

Influx doesn't describe the deluge we face. There was a lineup out the door for three straight hours and never an empty table to be seen. More dishes than I can count had to be sent back for one reason or another. Each time it's embarrassing, and I feel guilty charging people for food that they barely choked down. Mr. Harrington is very anti-complimentary meal, though. Probably because if he had to comp a meal each time it was sent back, he'd be shut down within a week. Any logical person would do something about that, but Mr. Harrington is content having onetime guests who never return and leave scathing online reviews.

Speaking of guests who haven't returned, Damian didn't come in today, and I wonder if it's because he had a finite amount of time for his lunch break and was deterred by the crowd, or if he stayed away because I haven't called him.

I finish up the last of my tasks and walk out into the warm summer air.

The humidity has nothing to do with the air being zapped from my lungs.

10

DAMIAN

Come ON Over

My lunch hour sped by today while I was stuck on a phone call with a chatty client. Whoever decided "the customer is always right" is an idiot. I can assure you, they are not, as evidenced by the ninety minutes of my life I wasted discussing the health benefits of trans fats and hydrogenated oils. Spoiler alert, there are none. Try telling that to a man determined to market his brand of oil as a health food.

The rest of the day didn't go any better, and I was disappointed I didn't get to see if Angel was working today. She hasn't called yet, so I just hope she's not avoiding me. My method of letting someone down previously has been to string them along until they give up. I hate confrontation and don't want to cause professional ripples by upsetting anyone who could impact my work life. For Angel, the options are to tell the truth or avoid me for as long as possible. But I'd rather hear the truth. Perhaps this is some karmic life lesson.

I shut down my computer at 7:00pm, grab my suit jacket and rush out the door. There's only one way to know what she's really thinking, and that's to find her and ask.

The street is busy, but there's a parking spot available thirty feet from the front door of the restaurant. I'm assuming if she started before the lunch crowd arrived, she should be getting off around now, if she hasn't already. Not like I'm rushing home to anything; an empty forty-fourth floor condo with nothing but a TV to keep me company. It's hardly a sacrifice to lean against my car and people watch for a while. Sure, I could go inside to see if she's there, but I don't want to eat anything from the *Harvest* menu. Especially if Angel isn't there to warn me off of what's awful.

No more than ten minutes after I arrive, Angel walks around the side of the building. I can't stop a smile from forming when I spot her. I didn't think about what I'd say to explain why I'm here, but her facial expression tells me she doesn't mind.

"Hey."

"Funny seeing you here, Mr. Taylor. Were you waiting for me?" She raises one eyebrow and scrunches her face. She looks beautiful even with a confused expression after a full workday.

"I was. I missed lunch today."

"You haven't eaten?" Her eyebrow raises even higher.

"Not since breakfast. Are you busy?"

She glances down at herself, and even in her stained server's uniform, I'd be happy to take her out. "I have to get home to take Genie out. She's been cooped up all day. She's probably crossing her legs by now."

I reach into my pocket and grab my keys. "Let me take you. You'll put her out of her misery faster."

"Damian."

The way she says my name makes me forget how to think.

"Are you trying to find out where I live? You already know where my sister lives and where I work. Yet I know nothing about you." Her tone is serious, but her lips form a smirk.

"Get in and I'll tell you whatever you want to know."

The hint of playfulness she displayed a moment ago disappears, leaving her with an expression I can't read. "One condition."

"I'm not agreeing until I hear your condition." I smile at her, trying to bring back playful Angel.

"You let me feed you."

"Feed me?"

She bites her bottom lip and glances at me from the corner of her eyes as she turns her head away. "You haven't eaten, and here you wasted however long waiting for me. It's the least I can do... unless you have something else to get to."

Her abrupt change in demeanour is surprising because she's never been anything but confident. I don't want her to shrink back.

"There's nowhere else I have or want to be." I open the passenger door of my SUV and gesture for her to get in. "Show me the way."

The smile she displays hearing my acceptance makes mine grow exponentially.

We pull up to her condo building and she directs me to a numbered parking spot she swears is hers, but she doesn't own a car. We enter the red brick building, which is well kept and clean with fake potted plants in three corners of the marble lobby with two elevators in the centre. She presses the button for the third floor and the doors on the left elevator open immediately.

"Are there no stairs?" I'm curious why she'd take the elevator up two stories, but maybe she's tired from her shift.

"Long story, but the stairwell is closed except for emergencies. There was an issue with people using the stairs to do drugs, leaving their paraphernalia behind. Management decided to shut them down."

I cringe, hearing her explanation. "Others who live here, or people who snuck in?" The lack of a doorman or security was something I noticed right away.

She shrugs like it's no big deal. "No idea. It's fine now. At first when it started happening I was"—the elevator dings and opens on the third floor—"worried I'd made a mistake moving here, but it all worked out. This is me." She gestures at unit 308. "Brace yourself for a wiggle butt."

I chuckle, but can't stop myself from glancing down. "Yours or Genie's?"

She flashes a playful grin back at me as she slides the key in her door. "Not me. I don't shake my tail for anyone."

Shame.

The door swings open and sure enough, Genie comes tearing toward us, her paws skittering across the smooth flooring. She jumps up at my legs and Angel scolds her, just as she did the first time.

"I'm so sorry. She never does this to anyone else."

How could anyone be upset with this face?

"Genie, I'm flattered." It might seem stupid, but I think dogs are excellent judges of character, so if she approves of me, that feels good.

"Let me take her for a short walk, then I'll come back to make you something." Angel's timid smile makes me want to reach in and pull her confidence back out.

"I'll come with you. We can even order something. My treat. You had a long day and don't need to cook."

"Are you afraid my cooking will taste like the restaurant's food?" She chuckles.

"Yes." I join in the laughter, noting how easy it is to say the truth with her. "That, and you must be tired."

"I'm fine, Damian. This is my everyday routine. Work, walk Genie, make dinner. I'll just be making extra."

For the first time since I stepped through her door, I lift my head up to take in her space. All I can see from my spot in the foyer is an open door to an office and a bathroom. Being in her home is surreal and I'm happy she invited me, but I still feel bad she's going to the trouble of cooking after a long day on her feet.

"Why don't I take Genie for her walk while you get started on dinner?"

She stares at me, not blinking for several seconds. "No offence, but I don't know you well enough to trust you with my baby."

"Offence taken." I snicker again, and don't overlook the fact I laugh and smile more in her presence than with anyone else. "Well, let's get a move on, then. I'm hungry."

A quick walk around the block has Genie satisfied and me starving. My stomach is grumbling with a ferocity I can't remember it ever having before.

When we return inside, I get to see most of her space, aside from her bedroom. Just like most condos in the downtown core, it's tiny, but has all the essentials. Her kitchen is a small U-shape with a stove at the bottom of the U, flanked by a fridge and sink on either of the long sides. The living space is open, and her patio doors look out at a defunct church, which I know now operates as a real estate office and a few other white-collar businesses. When I was a junior executive, I handled their advertising campaign.

Behind her dark grey sofa is an amazing piece of artwork and I stare at it, trying to take in all the layers. As far as abstract art goes, it's really captivating. It has a signature in the corner that looks like it says Angel, but it's hard to tell from the tiny, scrolling letters.

"Make yourself at home. What can I get you to drink?" Angel calls from the kitchen.

"Whatever you're having, thanks."

"You sure you want my eight-dollar bottle of wine I picked up from the grocery store?"

"Sounds perfect."

She tilts while standing at the counter. "Really?"

"Why not?" I ask, confused by her surprise.

"How do I say this?" Her eyes flick upwards, and she purses her lips. "You just don't strike me as the type to drink eight-dollar wine, is all. You seem more like a *Château Margaux* person."

"Ouch. Have I given you that impression?"

She blushes, and again I'm surprised by how fleeting her confidence has been tonight. "Kind of. Not that you come off snobby, but you've given me the impression you like to have things your way, and that way is usually expensive."

Her words cut to me like the knife she's wielding. That's the complete opposite of how I want people to perceive me. I don't know how to respond, so I do what I've been waiting close to two weeks to do. "I'm sorry about how I came across that day I dropped you by your sister's. My intentions were good, but I was out of line."

She continues chopping an onion silently for a moment. "I believe you had good intentions and I'm sorry for getting so angry."

With that issue settled, not feeling the need to dive into it any deeper, I stand beside a stool on the opposite side of the counter. "Can I do anything to help?"

"Do you want to handle the wine? It'll take me a few minutes to get to it."

I walk into her kitchen, and in the small space, I brush up against Angel's back as I reach for the wine. Her breath catches and I worry she cut herself. "Are you okay?" I ask, not moving from my position behind her.

She nods. "Corkscrew is in that drawer."

"Angel?"

"Mm?"

I inhale her floral scent, then whisper, "Thank you."

ANGEL

Like I Do

There's some serious tension developing between us, but I don't want him to think I invited him here to get lucky. "Damian."

"Sorry." He steps back, creating a draft across my back, making me miss his body heat.

"Dinner will be ready in twenty." The tension between us is practically creating an electrical current; I need to divert our conversation to something else. "Now, you promised me some insight into who Damian Taylor is. Please, tell me I haven't invited a serial killer into my home. Until I know for sure, I'll hold on to this knife." I laugh in an attempt to pass off my threat as a joke. It mostly is.

He holds the corkscrew, exhales, and starts turning the device to release the liquid courage within, seemingly unbothered by my knife comment. "What do you want to know?"

"We'll start easy. Tell me about your family. Siblings? Parents? Oh, and where you grew up."

With a half-full wineglass in each hand, he sets one on the counter beside me. "I grew up about an hour north of here. A potato farming community. One brother, Josh. He's ten years older than me, but a different dad. Mom was unlucky, marrying and divorcing twice before she gave up on the illusion of love entirely. Josh is married to his high school sweetheart, Lily, and they have two daughters, Dahlia and Daisy."

I take a moment to contemplate everything he's said as I sip my wine, but focus on his "illusion of love" comment. "So your brother didn't buy into the 'illusion of love' mentality, and married Lily. Where do you stand?"

He is seated on the stool at the counter and blinks several times before replying. "Jury is still out. I think that love can be a very real thing, but not everyone experiences it."

"Have you ever experienced it?" I smirk at him, curious about his answer.

"Familial love, sure. I'd give my last breath for my nieces, my brother, my mom, or Lily. But if you're asking about romantic love, no. I haven't been that lucky." He takes a sip of wine, holding it in his mouth before swallowing. If he thinks he's going to taste an oaky bouquet in this price range, he'll be disappointed. "What about you? Any great love stories?"

I release a ridiculous laugh that clearly relays my thoughts on the matter. "Not even close. I don't think you realize how off-putting it can be for men with fragile egos to have a woman who speaks nothing but the truth. I haven't gotten beyond a first date in the last eight years." That was an unnecessary addition to the conversation.

"Eight years? And you've never had a second date? So since you were—"

"Sixteen. And that was nothing spectacular either." I need to steer the conversation away from that topic, because I do not want to spill my guts to this man right now. "Tell me where you see yourself in ten years." In my experience, that question always prompts a few minutes of serious reflection and contemplation. Distraction from tales of my dating woes and tragic history.

"Honestly, I have no idea. Five years ago, I didn't see myself where I am now in terms of my career, so what ten years in the future holds is a mystery."

I send him a smile over my wineglass. "That sounds better anyway, doesn't it? The mystery? What would be the point of fighting for what we want if everything was predetermined?"

He beams at me, wrinkles forming around his eyes, obviously understanding it was a rhetorical question. He's gorgeous. Captivating. Dangerous.

I replace the lid on one pot, then stir the other before tilting the lid for air to vent and avoid having it boil over.

"What are you making? It smells great."

"Chicken Paprikash. It's a Hung—"

"Hungarian dish. With pasta?"

I nod. "Egg noodles, yeah."

His smile spreads wide across his face, his eyes practically sparkling. "Did you know I'm Hungarian?"

I choke on the wine I'm sipping, surprised by that tidbit of information. When my coughing stops, I reply, "No. I never would have guessed that based on your name."

"My mother is Hungarian. Father was... is French Canadian."

"Do you ever speak to your father?"

His smile falters, diminishing to a tense line. "No."

I shouldn't press that topic of conversation. He doesn't seem interested in sharing that part of his life with me; I sympathize.

"You ready to eat?" I ask, reaching into my way-too-high upper cabinet to grab a couple of pasta plates.

"Starving." His smile returns, and I'm glad we waded out of those treacherous waters.

When I turn back to look at Damian, there's a hunger in his eyes, and it's nothing to do with the food. Perhaps inviting him into my home was a colossal mistake. I am not someone who loses control, but his presence here is testing my limits.

I dish up our food and walk around to place it at the small dining table dividing my living room and kitchen. Genie is dancing around my feet as I walk, eager for her own dinner, which she usually gets at the same time I eat. So, before I settle down at the table, I serve Genie's pre-portioned raw food. Once she has her disgusting meal, I join Damian at the table. "Sorry, duty calls. She has expectations."

He chuckles, staring into my eyes.

I blink and look away. "Well, dig in. Hopefully it's edible."

As he glances down at his food, loading his fork and bringing it to his mouth, I focus on him taking his first bite, trying to block out the sound of Genie's greedy snort-slurping from ten feet away. When his lips close around his fork, his eyes widen in surprise.

"This is amazing," he mumbles around a mouthful of food.

I know I'm not inept in the kitchen, but his validation feels good.

He scoops up another bite. "Why aren't you cooking at the restaurant? You'd do a better job than the other cooks there."

"Oh, that place is definitely a candidate for *Kitchen Nightmares.* I would end up in prison if I had to work in there for more than five minutes. I don't know how Hannah does it."

"What's so bad about it?"

"Let's just say we don't have a human resources department, and it shows."

Damian sets his fork down on the circular placemat. "What does that mean?"

I take a bite of my food and nod in approval. "Not bad."

I'm not intending on avoiding his question, but I think he takes it that way if his facial expression is any indication.

"What does that mean, Angel?"

Another sip of my wine to delay this conversation another second does nothing but make him more impatient.

"It means that the men in the kitchen don't think women belong there except to gawk at or grope." Trying to downplay the perverts I work with, I continue, "Which is pretty stupid, considering their boss is a woman. She's in her early fifties though, so they leave her be, and she's oblivious to the attention the other girls and I get."

Damian is gaping at me. He closes his mouth, running his tongue along his upper teeth. "They grope you?"

"Not as much now since I threatened bodily harm, but a few of them still see it as a game."

"That's unacceptable. Your boss doesn't do anything?"

"My *boss* is the worst offender. He spends half of his day drinking his profits, and by the time the dinner rush clears out, he's inebriated."

Damian looks horrified, but I don't blame him, because it is appalling.

"Has he ever—"

"Can we change the subject? I'm sorry, but this isn't really relaxing after-work conversation. If it makes you feel better, the other girls and I have an unspoken rule to never leave each other alone. We have each other's backs." I take another bite of my food, hopeful Damian will let the subject drop. This isn't what I had in mind when I invited him here. "Tell me more about you."

12

DAMIAN

When You Put Your Hands On Me

When Angel confides in me about the behaviour she has to put up with at work, my appetite disappears. I was starving all day and briefly considered eating my suit jacket, but once she explains about her male co-workers, shame washes over me on behalf of all decent men around the world.

I want to press for answers, but she asks to drop the subject, so I do. Reluctantly.

"I'm not that exciting, if I'm being honest. My career was my focus because… uh… my brother made a lot of sacrifices to send me to university, and I became obsessed with making his sacrifice worth it. There was little time for anything else, but since I switched roles in the company, it doesn't feel as great as I had hoped it would."

"What's missing?"

I pick up my fork, pushing egg noodles around my plate, willing myself to continue eating so I don't offend Angel or make her think I'm not enjoying her cooking. "Life outside of work. Fulfilment that doesn't have anything to do with client accounts or company bonuses."

She nods but doesn't ask for clarification.

The rest of our meal passes with casual conversation, then we sit on her sofa, talking some more. We avoid reverting to serious topics, which I would have liked, but respect Angel enough to avoid a subject she doesn't want to address. When Genie is ready for her walk, I figure that's my cue to leave for the night, but it's hard to tell myself I've had enough of Angel's company.

We circle the same block we walked earlier with these two females who have tilted my world on its axis over the past few weeks, and for the first time since our misunderstanding eleven days ago, I feel content. Angel and I disagree over whether she'll walk me to my car or I'll walk her to her door, and in the end, the gentleman in me loses out because she is hard to argue with. She's obviously used to doing things on her own.

We say good night and I wait in the parking lot until she disappears inside her building. I drive home, which is only five kilometres away, but, after a long day, feels like it's on the other side of the province.

I roll my eyes at myself for not getting Angel's number, but hope she'll make use of mine.

The following day, I miss out on my lunch hour again, so Paxton orders a meal for me to eat at my desk. We're in the final stages of three different projects and my entire department is stressed out. I'm becoming more irritated by the day because my staff insist on sending me emails for simple things that could be solved by coming to my office, but it seems that's a last resort for everyone within my purview.

Michell Donnelly is the first person to darken my door for the past few days, and he does so when I'm tying up a phone call with the same man who wasted my lunch hour yesterday. When Mitchell makes eye contact with me and greets me with a meek wave, I roll my eyes, trying to express my frustration with Mr. Trans Fats. It must not come across that way because Mitchell's already nervous expression morphs into flat out fear, and he turns to leave.

"Mr. Tra… Mr. Warren, could you hold a moment, please?" I don't wait for a reply before pressing the red hold button and calling out to my fleeing staff member. "Mitchell, I'll just be a minute."

"It's fine, Mr. Taylor. I'll send you an email." He doesn't wait for a reply before vanishing past the wall of windows toward the employee area we refer to as "the pit".

I sigh into my hands, aggravated I'm failing to get through to people. The blinking red button is taunting me. I want nothing more than to "accidentally' disconnect the call, but that would only result in Mr. Warren calling back and having to waste time explaining how our call was cut off. Better to get it over with.

Forty more minutes of my life are wasted encouraging Mr. Warren to provide information from scientific journals backing up his claims on the health benefits of deep-fried or packaged foods. He doesn't think proof is necessary, and I should just take his word for it since he's been eating deep-fried food his entire life and is "the picture of health" at age forty-three. His arteries would claim otherwise. The one time I met him in person, my first impression was that he looked like he was in his late sixties and spent several decades as a heavy drinker. Maybe he has, but I'd be willing to guess his high-fat diet has done a number on his liver just the same.

I'm all for a little creative advertising, but an outright lie is a problem. Not only is it a moral issue, but it's also a legal one, and I'm not putting myself or our company on the line to appease a stubborn, ill-informed man.

Tension is building in my temples, so I massage the sides of my head in slow circles and blow out a breath. I try to think calming thoughts, and the first image to pop into my head is Angel. Not just Angel, but her and Genie, sitting on her couch, back-lit by the falling sun through her patio doors. Just like that, the pain in my head is gone. My heart rate has slowed.

I want to call her. I want to know if she's tired after a long day yesterday. Not even a lead-brick burger could deter me right now. Seeing her would be worth the digestive distress I'd suffer.

Unfortunately, work is waiting for me, and now that a large portion of my day was wasted on an unproductive argument with Mr. Warren, it's going to be another late night.

As much as I want to meet Angel after work again, I don't want to come on too strong, and there's no way I can get out of here in time to do so. I'll be lucky to leave the office by 10pm.

At 7:28, my phone chirps, and I glance down to see an unknown number.

416-555-2643: *Genie was looking forward to seeing you again.*

Immediately, I'm sporting a stupid smile, and of course, at this moment, no one else is around to see it. They only seem to walk in when I'm frustrated or annoyed.

Damian: *Tell Genie I'm sorry. Caught up at work.*

There's so much more I want to say, but I'm learning with Angel, less is more.

Angel: *Did you eat?*

Her concern is touching. It's been a long time since anyone asked me if I had taken care of myself. For years, anyone who isn't immediate family has only wanted me to take care of them.

Damian: *I did. Had a late lunch. Where are you now?*

Angel: *Walking home. Almost there.*

Damian: *...*

I start typing but delete my message three times because I don't know what to say without being too forward. Before I can think of something, she replies again.

Angel: *Get back to work. Maybe I'll see you around.*

I reread her message multiple times before I reply.

Damian: *I'd rather talk to you or walk with you, but I have to get this done. Message me tomorrow?*

She takes thirty minutes to reply and concentrating during that time is difficult. When my phone pings again, I reach for it fast enough I would be embarrassed if anyone saw.

Angel: *Sorry, walking Genie. Talk tomorrow.*

Those two final words set my mind at ease and allow me to power through as much work as I can with a smile on my face. When I return home with a bag of takeout at 10:40pm, I eat, shower, and crawl into bed feeling content and looking forward to tomorrow.

The following few days, Angel and I text back and forth, our conversations always light and carefree. She brings out a different side of me that I thought had long since disappeared. Her playful personality always makes me smile, and I'm eager to see her again.

My work schedule has been so demanding and the one day I had off, I went to visit my brother and his family. Aside from that, I've barely had time to sleep. Talking to Angel has been my only "down" time.

So when the bulk of our projects wrap up Friday morning, I breathe a sigh of relief, and the only thing I want to do is celebrate with her. I holler at Paxton that I'm going out for lunch and walk to my favourite-least-favourite restaurant. Abysmal food, stellar service. Right now, it's the only place I want to be.

13

DAMIAN

Say Something

After some negotiating with Alex, yet again, she places me at a table in Angel's section. She's not in the dining room when I take my seat, so I open the menu and start browsing, knowing that I'll have whatever she orders me, anyway. At least it gives me something to look at, so I'm not searching the room like a stalker.

I hear the kitchen door clang open and see a curly head of hair. Angel stutter-steps when her eyes catch mine, but she doesn't spare me a second glance before placing the tray down at a table with four men in cheap suits and bad haircuts. Okay, maybe their suits are mid-range, and their haircuts are fine. I'm just being petty because they have her attention at the moment.

Once she's served them, she comes to my table with the tray tucked under her arm, notepad at the ready. Her smile is timid, but her lips curving at me are irresistible in any degree. "Flat water, no ice?"

"Please." I reach out to touch her, but pull back. Seeing her now, I realize how much I've missed her. I'm already in over my head with this girl.

A moment later, she returns with my water, and when she places it on the table, I graze her fingers with mine, not able to resist that brief opportunity. She doesn't pull away, but before I can say anything, Cheap Suit Number One shouts, "Miss?"

I exhale loud enough I know it's obvious, and she winks at me, assuring me she'll place an order for my food. Never in my life have I thought the words "I hate to see you go, but love to watch you leave," but better believe I do when witnessing her walk away. Then I berate myself for eyeing her like a pervert. I just can't help but stare as she stands next to the table with the four cheap suits. Her silky curls brushing her shoulders. Her narrow waist. Her round… why is that guy's hand on her?

She swats the man's hand off her butt and I can't hear what she says because my heart is hammering so loud, it's drowning everything else out. I doubt it was an invitation for the man to do the same thing again, yet that's what he does. I want to rip his hand away from her and put him in his place but talk myself down because she didn't take too kindly to my attempts at rescuing her before when she didn't need to be saved.

My hearing is nearly restored as I take several deep breaths to calm myself without taking my eyes off of her. She removes the man's hand once more before she steps back out of his reach.

She says in a voice that is far kinder than he deserves, "I'd appreciate it if you kept your hands to yourself."

"That's too bad, honey. What if I pay extra?" Mr. Cheap Suit retorts, eliciting a laugh from the rest of his immature friends.

"Are you from a part of the world where women are possessions to be bought and traded? Because I'm not sure if you know this, but that's not how it works."

"Are you being racist?" The man shouts. His skin tone hardly qualifies him to claim racism from a woman whose skin is nearly the same golden shade.

But that doesn't stop the short, bald man I presume is the manager from appearing out of nowhere and questioning the scene playing out. He must have been in charge of the servers' ninja training because I didn't even see him coming. I may have been distracted trying to calm my outrage, though.

"What's going on here?" he asks.

"I'll tell you what's going on here. This chick is a racist."

The confidence I have that the manager will see through an irrational customer's words disappears the instant he turns and says, "Miss Blake, what do you have to say for yourself?"

My shoulders tense, but Angel replies without hesitation. "This young man thinks he can grope me in exchange for money while I serve his food. I told him women can't be bought and traded."

"That's not what she said. She called me a racist slur, and I won't stand for it."

I stand up from my seat, knocking my chair over, drawing attention to myself. Angel catches my eyes and gives a subtle shake of her head. I right my chair and continue to listen, but it takes every ounce of willpower I possess not to come to her aid.

"Mr. Harrington, I'd never say anything of the sort. The man is angry because I told him no." Angel's words are measured and matter-of-fact. She's not getting worked up and I admire her cool demeanour.

"She's a liar," the customer shouts, and all three of his friends nod.

If I weren't so furious over the situation, I'd laugh at them calling her a liar. Surely anyone who has been around her for more than five minutes knows that couldn't be further from the truth.

"Miss Blake, seeing as the man's friends are all in agreement, I'm afraid I have to ask you to leave."

I tighten my grip around my water glass and clench my teeth.

"For the day?" Her voice cracks, showing the first sign of emotion since the encounter started.

"No. You're done here. And don't bother asking for a reference. I won't endorse anyone saying racist things to anyone."

"Seriously? I've been here for two years without issue. You have always come to me when you needed an honest answer about something, and I've *always* given it. Now this guy's feelings are hurt because I wouldn't let him grab a handful, and you're firing me over it?" She scoffs, and I'm two seconds away from interfering.

Something tells me my intervention wouldn't help matters right now, but maybe I can speak to her manager to explain what happened when things cool down. She's already getting attention from the other customers here and doesn't need more.

"Pack up your things, Miss Blake. You're finished here."

She doesn't turn back to face me, instead walking calmly into the kitchen and out of my sight.

The manager turns to apologize for the scene and tells everyone the situation has been handled after he offers the liars a discounted meal. I flag him over to my table, wanting to clear the air.

"Lovely to see you again, sir. I'm sorry about the scene. I assure you, this is not typical for our establishment."

"You don't need to apologize to me. You owe Miss Blake an apology. I watched the entire scene over there, and that man kept pawing at her. She told him to stop, and he got angry. She handled it the best way she could, and you fired her over it. Is *that* typical for your establishment?"

The bald man's face reddens, and I think back to Angel's words about him imbibing a little too often, so I can't be sure if it's alcohol- or anger-induced redness. "I'm afraid you're mistaken, sir. Miss Blake has been on thin ice because we've had issues in the past. Please, enjoy your meal."

My appetite is gone. I'm furious. I want to punch all four of those guys in their smug faces and finish off the manager as a finale. Instead, I stand and make my voice as loud as possible without yelling. "No, sir. I won't enjoy any meal here ever again. In fact, I encourage every customer here to walk out in protest over the way this situation was handled. You can expect a call from the labour board."

I storm past the short man, bumping into his shoulder, and don't wait to see if any other customers leave in solidarity. Honestly, I don't expect them to, but it would have helped make a point.

What did he mean she's had issues before? Have customers done this to her on other occasions? I know he has allowed the problems with the kitchen staff to go unresolved. Maybe he's taken it personally because she hasn't accepted his advances in the past. The thought makes me sick. It has nothing to do with my feelings for her; nobody should have to tolerate that.

I wait outside of *Harvest* for Angel to emerge, but she doesn't by the time I have to return to work. I walk back with my head down, staring at my phone, hoping she'll send me a message, but I can't resist any longer.

Damian: *Are you okay? I waited for you but have to get back to work.*

I crash into a few pedestrians who grumble obscenities at me once I notice Angel left my message on read. She's got bigger matters to deal with right now than replying to me.

14

When I walk into the kitchen, Hannah is trying to keep up with the midday rush, so I don't want to bother her with my petty lunchtime drama. I mean, now I'm unemployed, so that's an issue, but still, the whole situation is stupid. That greasy creep thinking he can lay a hand on me and I won't say anything? Get real. I don't regret my reaction. It was only a matter of time before Harrington fired me for something. He was waiting for his opportunity.

I decide to shout at Hannah in passing as I head to the locker room. "Bye, Hannah. Call me sometime so we can get the pups together."

She's flipping a steak on the grill and turns my way with her eyebrows pulled together. "Why are you leaving in the middle of the lunch rush? What do you mean 'call me sometime'?"

"Harrington canned me. Apparently, I'm a racist for not letting a guy grab my butt."

Hannah sets down her tools and says something I can't make out to the cook next to her. Once she approaches me, she asks, "What happened out there?"

I give her the abbreviated version and her outrage is twenty times that of mine. She's not as good at bottling it up. Before I can wrap my head around what's happening, she unties her apron.

"What are you doing?"

"If you think for one second I'm going to work somewhere management thinks this is okay, you don't know me very well. We've already put up with enough, and this is the final straw." She throws the apron down on the ground and shouts, "I quit!" She turns back to me, not wasting time on anyone else's reaction, grabs my hand and walks toward the dining room. "Come on. We're going to get Vida too."

I try to dig in my feet, refusing to go back out there. I don't want to be met with pitying stares—especially not from Damian. "Hannah, no. You can't quit because of me. What are you going to do?"

"Don't worry. I've been putting out feelers at other restaurants. I'm so over this place."

Her words ease my worry. Even so, the thought of her being unemployed on my account bothers me.

She marches through the dining room with determination, and when Vida's head of distinguishable black coily hair comes into view, Hannah shouts, "Hey, Vida. Do you want to work for a place that fires their staff for telling customers to keep their hands to themselves?" Hannah shows no hesitation or doubt in my retelling of events—a perk of building a reputation for honesty, I guess.

If there were any patrons in the dining room who weren't privy to the drama of ten minutes ago, they are now. I see people around dropping their forks, glancing at each other with questioning looks and eyeing Hannah and me.

"Because Harrington thought Angel deserved to be fired for not offering her ass on a platter."

I can't help but giggle at Hannah's outrage. Note to self: don't get on Hannah Parker's bad side. I don't, however, want

Vida to feel obligated to leave too because I know she needs this job.

Before I can say as much, she replies, "No, I don't. Give me five minutes to cash out and I'll meet you outside."

Mr. Harrington charges into Vida's section, stammering to the remaining diners. "Please, enjoy your meal, folks. This will all be handled momentarily." He glares at me, making it clear he blames me for the situation.

I had no intention of leaving in a blaze of glory and taking his two best staff with me, but I'm not upset about it. Even though Alex isn't my biggest fan, I almost feel bad leaving her here to fend for herself. The rest of the female staff are in their late forties, at least, so they don't abide by our unspoken rule.

"Miss Ryan, you can't leave in the middle of your shift. You have customers depending on you."

"Mr. Harrington, Angel has been nothing but a hard worker her entire time here. If you were concerned about your clientele, you would have thought twice before firing her." Vida walks toward Hannah and me, embracing me in a tight hug, and whispers in my ear, "Wait for me outside. I'll be right there."

Before now, Vida has always been the type to keep her head down and get the job done. She's never been a victim, nor a participant in petty restaurant drama. I've respected her for that and appreciated her as a co-worker. But hearing the ferocity with which she spoke now, I'm honoured to call her a friend.

Mr. Harrington glares at me, so I shrug and reply, "Better put in a call for some chimpanzees."

Hannah leads me by the hand to the locker room, where we collect our belongings, then out of the side exit to wait for Vida. As promised, she walks out moments later, and squeals as she jumps toward us. I've never seen her so happy, and it's such an unusual scenario.

"He. Is. Furious! Ha! That'll teach him."

These girls; I don't even know where to start.

"You two are crazy, you know that? You didn't have to quit because of me."

Vida takes hold of my right hand, drawing my attention to her. "First and foremost, I quit because what just happened in there was wrong. If it had happened to Hannah or even Alex, I would have reacted the same way. Two, you didn't deserve that, and if it takes us dishing out a hard lesson for Harrington to figure it out, then so be it. Third, we've got the rest of the day free, and your girl here needs a drink."

I chuckle, but I feel the same way. If the roles were reversed, I would have proverbially set the place on fire as I walked out, too. "Come. We'll go to my place and get dressed up, then we'll get some drinks. I think we've earned a night on the town."

When we enter my condo, Genie seems startled to see me. Even she wasn't expecting me home so soon. She greets Vida and Hannah, who are both dog lovers, so she laps up the attention as they baby talk with her.

The four of us, Genie included, lounge around for a while, trying to come down from the events of today. We talk about everything from our dogs to our future career ambitions. We're all college or university graduates who got sucked into the life of a short commute and easy tips, but none of us ever intended to give *Harvest* as much of our lives as we did.

Maybe what happened today will be a fresh start for all of us, even if the situation is far from ideal.

Tonight, though? Tonight we let loose.

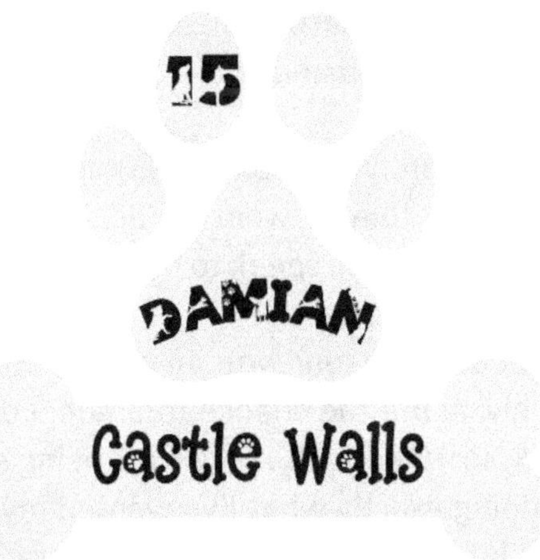

By the time I return to work, I'm so out of sorts over what just transpired at *Harvest,* I can barely think straight. How can one man be in charge of a staff and be so clueless? I hope Angel goes to the labour board to file a complaint for wrongful dismissal, because that's not acceptable. Beyond that, I'm worried that she's unemployed and will struggle without an income to rely on. Maybe that's presumptuous of me, but working as a waitress, I wouldn't imagine she has a massive savings account to fall back on. Living in the city is expensive; especially alone.

Then again, maybe she does have money put aside. Maybe she has a second job or a friend who she could move in as a roommate. I sigh into my hands with my elbows on my desk, accepting that there's so much I don't know about her, and little I can do to help.

Everything about her is still a mystery beyond her captivating dark eyes, soft hair, pert nose, and luscious curves. Beyond her firecracker personality that means she doesn't take any nonsense from anyone. I might not know her favourite colour or band, but I know enough that I want to keep learning more.

A knock at my door startles me, and I look up to see Elliot Hannon, one of my team managers.

"Are you okay, sir?"

"Fine, Mr. Hannon. What can I do for you?" My response is clipped and the last thing I want to do is give my staff the impression they can't come speak to me. "I'm sorry. You caught me in the middle of a thought."

"Sorry, sir. I can just send you an email." He turns to walk away without giving me the chance to argue. I drop a hammer fist on my desk, irritated with myself for being short with him when he was doing exactly what I've wanted my staff to do for months. Then I look up to realize two other staff members are standing on the other side of the glass wall surrounding my office. I throw my head back in defeat. Today is not my day, and I don't know how to get it back on track.

Rather than dive into work I won't be able to focus on, I decide to call Josh. Like a good big brother, he can always help me get my head on straight.

"Well, if it isn't my baby brother."

"Hey, Josh."

"Why do you sound so glum? Let me guess. Lady trouble?"

Josh and his wife Lily have been married for fifteen years. They have a great relationship and while I'd never say it out loud, I envy it. Considering the relationship examples we had growing up, the fact he and Lily have created a good life together is encouraging.

"I guess you could say that." I chuckle to mask my disappointment over the events of today.

"So what's the trouble? You want what you can't have? You're not eyeing your boss's wife, are you?" My brother laughs, making me do the same.

I confirm I'm not interested in my boss's seventy-year-old wife and continue to explain the situation, leaving nothing out, including the drool on the backseat of my $90,000 SUV. He lets me rattle out the entire sequence of events that took place over the last few weeks, only acknowledging bits and pieces with grunts or laughter.

By the time he has all the information, he says what I was afraid of all along. "I'm not sure what you want me to tell you, Damian. You have a hero complex, or whatever they call it, wanting to run around and save everyone from themselves, but you can't. It sounds like the girl has a good head on her shoulders, so just give her time to sort things out."

"She's unstoppable. I'm not worried she'll let this keep her down. I'm just angry it happened to her at all."

"Well, there's nothing you can do about it now. It's done. Keep your focus where it needs to be. I'm sure she'll reach out when she gets a chance and put your mind at ease."

She is good at doing that, even without trying. She also has the capacity to have me twisted in knots like no one else ever has, and she doesn't have to make an effort to do that, either.

"Why are there so many men in the world who can't think like rational adults? Doesn't it scare you for your daughters? It scares me."

"Sometimes. But we need to teach them to know their own worth, and like your Angel, how to handle themselves if the situation calls for it."

My Angel. I smile at that term, though I think "Her Damian" would be more appropriate.

"I'm going to sign the girls up for Krav Maga."

Josh chuckles. "They could use it after the crime spree here this year. It's not a bad idea."

I jot down on a scrap of paper to the right of me to look up self-defence training for my nieces to attend. I want them to be equipped to break a man's arm if he ever touches them without permission. As they should.

"Anyway, I gotta get back to work. Boss gets testy if I waste company time. I'll text you tomorrow to check in."

"Later, big bro. Love you."

I glance down at my phone and Angel still hasn't replied to my earlier message. An image of her sitting alone on her sofa, crying with Genie at her side, makes my heart clench. In yet another frustration-induced action, I slap the phone on my desk and growl like a deranged wildebeest. Whatever that sounds like. Pretty sure that's what I sounded like, though.

Sure enough, another employee is rushing past my wall of windows, and now in fifteen minutes, I've undone every bit of progress I've made with my staff since I started in this department. At this rate, it's not even one step forward, two steps back. It's moving forward like a Power Wheels with a drained battery, backward like a NASCAR... that makes sense to me.

I try my hardest to focus on my work for the afternoon, resigning myself to the fact that Angel can handle herself and doesn't need my interference. This time I'm not going to come in swinging my club like a neanderthal. That's not who I am, and I am kicking myself for ever making her think that.

Hopefully, I get the chance to show her more of the real me.

The girls and I are dressed, looking good, if I do say so myself, and ready to hit the town since none of us have work tomorrow—or any day soon. My condo is just over a kilometre away from one of the city's hottest clubs, so we're going there to wash away this disaster day with dancing-induced sweat and alcohol.

Since Hannah and Vida both still live at home with their parents, there are no concerns about them getting home to their dogs, so we're free to dance the night away and have a good old-fashioned slumber party. After they raided my closet, we helped each other get ready and now we're walking toward the club. It's been so long since I went dancing, I'm not sure I'll even remember how.

Hannah chose a black body-con dress, but because my feet are smaller than hers, she's wearing it with her red converse sneakers. Few people could rock that look, but Hannah is one of them. Her long, chocolate brown hair is flowing down to her waist, and despite the mass of hair she has, I've never seen one out of place. It's difficult for me to imagine having hair that behaves.

Vida is sporting a lime green mini skirt with a colourful neon top to match. It's one of those outfits I own but never wore because those colours look terrible on me. Vida's bronze skin glows in bright colours, though, so she looks stunning. Her hair is fierce, embracing her natural curls and swoon-worthy volume.

I opted for my most *fantabulous* pink and gold glitter miniskirt and a loose, flowing white camisole blouse. Since we have a bit of a walk and I don't want my feet to be killing me before I get to dance, I am wearing a pair of strappy sandals with a low heel. I'm short and need a little lift so I don't get trampled or turned away because a bouncer thinks my ID is fake.

We get in without issue and the crowd is filling in around us. I buy our first round, and we've agreed we'll have no more than three drinks, so we'll take turns buying. Not only are we unemployed, we have to walk home.

My sister and her bestie Hollis join us about an hour later, and after I tell Dina about the drama of the day, the girl cheers because we're both unemployed. She seems to think we can just spend the rest of our days having doggy play dates and eating ice cream. I don't have the heart to crush her lofty dreams, so I let it go for tonight. Starting Monday, I'm putting all my efforts into finding a new, long-term job where they will appreciate all the skills I bring to the table.

I'm out on the dance floor, surrounded by my girls, minus Vida, who is standing at the perimeter of the dance floor talking to a gorgeous blond with a five o'clock shadow begging to rough up Vida's cheeks... wow, girl. Alcohol lowers my inhibitions. But seriously, if they were talking any closer, she'd be in his shirt. I send her a wink when she looks my way, causing her to smirk.

When Christina Aguilera's *Dirrty* starts blasting through the speakers, I dance with my girls like no one is watching. Unfortunately for me, someone *is* watching. A body presses up behind me and I am not about that life, so I step forward before spinning around to put the creep in his place. Low and behold, it's the man and his three friends who got me fired earlier today. The four of them leer at me, no shame in their pathetic, cringey game.

"Funny how you were so offended by my racism earlier, and now you're grinding up against me." Not funny at all, really.

"What can I say? I forgive and forget."

Even with the amount of alcohol sloshing around in this place, I can smell the liquor on his breath.

"Well, I don't. Not that I was interested before you opened your mouth and got me fired, but there's no redeeming yourself now. Back off."

The colossal idiot with the poor-fitting jeans steps forward. "The offer is still on the table." He reaches a hand up to place it on my hip, but I swat him away. *Again.* "I'll pay for your time."

"There's a profession dedicated to what you're asking, and it's not mine. If you've got so much money to burn, why don't you put it toward a proper suit, a decent haircut, and cologne that doesn't smell like actual *eau de toilet*?"

The man has the audacity to look offended. "I see how it is. You're a gold digger."

"You're disgusting. I'll be digging my own gold, thank you." I burn my anger into him with my eyes, but I'm aware my stature creates limitations in that area. "I wasn't on offer earlier today, and I'm certainly not now, so back off."

"If you didn't want a man's attention, you shouldn't dress like that." This time, his hand grazes my arm and the touch makes my skin crawl.

Now, I pride myself on being a woman who can keep her cool. I don't think of myself as irrational or unhinged. But Heaven help me if that man did not set something off in me that I cannot reel in. Maybe the alcohol annihilated my inhibitions, or maybe I'm angrier than I realized over losing my job. Whatever the case, words are not getting through this man's thick skull. I swing my leg back and drive it forward, connecting my knee right between the scumbag's legs in a crushing blow. Not even the threat of an assault charge could make me feel bad for unleashing my pent-up fury on him. I set my face with an unapologetic glare to let his friends know I am an equal opportunist willing to give them the same treatment.

Two of his friends hook him under his arms and drag him off the dance floor, eyeing me like they're afraid to turn their backs. I keep my dagger-eyes focused on them, so they have no doubt I am not to be messed with.

Dina and Hollis stare at me like I'm a yeti, but Hannah is doubled over in laughter. Vida dismisses her suitor to join us and starts laughing alongside Hannah until I can't help but join in. Here we are, three girls having a laugh after a chaotic day.

It's a bummer when the bouncer comes over and asks us to leave. It took them a while, but apparently security cameras showed it was an "unprovoked attack." Whatever. Hopefully, that guy and his friends think twice before assuming that any woman dresses up because they want male attention, or that they deserve to be literally manhandled. My photo may end up taped to the wall behind the bouncer's lectern, or whatever it's called when it belongs to a bouncer... a pulpit? No. A podium? Anyway, sure, my photo may end up there, but it was worth it.

Hollis and Dina decide to end the evening and walk south toward Dina's condo. Hannah, Vida, and I laugh all the way back to my place, holding hands and acting like a trio of teenagers. After the day we had, letting loose feels good, and I'm so grateful for these women.

We're so amped up when we walk through my door, none of us can sleep, so we crack open a bottle of cheap wine and start gushing to each other. Vida tells us about the young gentleman named Cody she was speaking to tonight, but said she doubts he'll ever call. If he doesn't, that's his loss because

Vida is a rare combination of beauty, passion, drive, and kindness.

Hannah confesses she hasn't been on a date for more than two years after being in a long-term relationship for three years, but I trump that by telling them I've only been on a handful of dates since high school. That earns some gasps and a whole lot of questions. These girls know me and understand if they ask, they'll get a truthful answer, so I explain my short-lived dating history and why it has never proven fruitful.

Around that time, when I made the promise to myself that I would never tell a lie, I never considered the lies I could tell myself. That is, until I opened my mouth, and a truth came out that I hadn't yet processed. "I really like Damian, though."

17

DAMIAN

Obvious

Two weeks. It's been two weeks since Angel was fired and I haven't seen her since. We've talked on the phone a few times, texted back and forth daily, and made plans twice, which I had to cancel. She's unemployed, but she's managed to keep busy, even using her skills to volunteer at a soup kitchen. That's yet another thing that makes her endearing.

In all the times we've spoken, I've never asked about her career goals and aspirations. Not that there's anything wrong with being a server; I just never asked if she wanted something different someday. After she lost her job, I've avoided career talk at all costs, not wanting to upset her. She has said she's got a few interviews lined up, but none of them had her really excited. Her closing remarks on the matter were, "A job is a job."

Tonight, though, I'm going to see her one way or another.

I need to get my head on straight for now. My focus must be on my work and on getting these people to not only trust me, but interact with me. I swear, after my anger boiled over when Angel was fired, people around here gave me a wide berth. As far as they were concerned, I should have been happy because we wrapped up three major projects. Instead, a few of them witnessed me having a fit, word spread fast, and no one wanted to so much as take the same elevator as me. Sure, I behaved like a toddler, but everyone has those days. Do I need to bake them cookies? No, they'd probably throw them out.

That's a depressing reality to face, thinking people dislike me so much they wouldn't eat my cookies. I have no idea how to bake, though, so that's for the best. *Okay, no cookies, then.*

Do I host an office party? *No, that's an HR nightmare.*

Sleepaway camp? *What are you? Seven?*

That's the extent I'm able to focus on work before I give in and do what I really want.

Damian: *I need help.*

The three dots below my message bounce along the screen. One good thing about her lack of employment is that she almost always responds right away.

Angel: *The first step is asking. I'm proud of you.*

I laugh with an ease I haven't had all day. One quick message and I'm smiling.

Damian: *Any suggestions to make my co-workers not hate me?*

Angel: *Why do you think they hate you?*

Damian: *Long story. It's easier to call.*

Before I can call her, "Angel" lights up my screen.

"Dish," she says as soon as I answer.

"Hello to you too. What are you doing?"

"Currently, I'm sprawled out on my bed in my pyjamas. Such is the life of the unemployed."

I imagine her on her bed in pyjama shorts and a tank top—which I have no idea if that's what she wears, but it's my imagination, so accuracy isn't important—her hair splayed around her on a pillow and Genie curled up at her side. I've never been so jealous of a dog.

As envious as I may feel, her well-being is more important. "Have you given any thought to contacting the labour board?"

"Not really, no. I don't want to go backwards, and I don't want to waste my time on something that's not helping me move forward."

I hate that her boss will get away with how he treated her, but I can understand her thought process. "You'll find something. Any prospects?"

"I have a phone interview for a freelance gig in two hours. We'll see if anything comes of it. It's nearby, so if they like my work, maybe it could turn into more."

"A freelance… waitress?"

She bursts out laughing, telling me I'm way off the mark. "No, silly. As a graphic designer."

Interesting. Wait… "Graphic designer? Is that piece behind your sofa yours?"

She's silent for a beat. "It is."

"Angel! Why haven't you pursued that sooner? That piece is amazing. You should be using those skills."

"Chill, man. Waitressing was never meant to be permanent, but once I started, I couldn't argue with the tips and it was so close by. I just stuck it out. And you can't tell from one piece of crummy artwork what my skills are like."

"I can understand why you got sidetracked, but there's nothing crummy about that work. Anyone would be a fool not to hire you."

"Well, we'll see how it goes later. What did you need help with? Why do you think everyone hates you?"

I tilt my chair back and heave out a breath. It was easier talking about her. Especially since I don't enjoy broaching the work topic with her, given her current situation. Complaining about *having* a job makes me feel like a jerk. But I want her opinion. "From day one, it seemed everyone here was afraid of me. They never speak up or offer suggestions. They come to me for simple solutions, and it wouldn't matter what I said or how awful my ideas were, they'd run with it rather than argue."

"Maybe your ideas weren't awful."

"They were terrible. Trust me. I purposely pitched horrible ideas to see what they'd say." I pinch the bridge of my nose, trying to ease some tension in my head that appears every time I think about my work dilemma. "I'm not sure if they hate me or they're scared, but they made up their minds before I was able to even make a first impression."

"So change their minds. Or better yet, ask them why they're afraid of you." She makes it sound like a simple solution. Maybe it is.

"I've tried talking to a few of them, but no one ever wants to have a real conversation. It's that bad." I breathe out a long sigh. "You can't tell me if you were afraid of your boss and he asked why, you'd share the whole reason."

"Absolutely, I would, but I'm different. Most people are people-pleasers, afraid of confrontation or of losing their job."

"I'd never fire someone for being honest." I tilt my chair back further, throwing my feet up on my desk and relaxing into the conversation. The pressure in my head lessens the more I talk to her.

"Maybe they don't know that. You might be surprised how much you can accomplish with a little honesty."

Obviously, she isn't privy to the world of advertising. Honesty is not the best policy.

She exhales, and Genie is snorting in the background. "I'm sorry to cut this short, but I have to walk Genie and get myself ready for my interview. Are you in need of any more of my services, Mr. Taylor?"

What springs to my mind would not be appropriate to say. "Not at the moment, but can I keep you on retainer?"

"If this interview doesn't work out, that might be my only employment option. Good thing I'm so incredibly wise." She chuckles, and that simple sound puts everything back into perspective.

"Thank you, oh wise one."

"My pleasure. I'll deduct this session from your prepaid tab."

I release a childish sounding giggle. Never in my life have I made that sound before. "Text me to let me know how your interview goes, okay? I'll get in touch with some of my contacts to see if anyone is hiring."

"No, you will not." The ferocity of her voice startles me. "I'm not taking handouts or pity jobs. I appreciate the offer, but I need to find somewhere on my own. Okay?"

This girl continues to surprise me. Any other people I've encountered would have jumped at the chance for a handout. Even if it is stubborn pride, I can appreciate her motivation to find a job on her own.

"Okay," I concede.

With that, we end our call and I find myself counting down the hours until I can speak to her again. I got so caught up in whining, I forgot to ask to see her tonight. That makes the wait to hear from her again feel even longer.

Anticipation slows down the second hand.

18

ANGEL

Make the World Move

My interview is over the phone and there's no reason why I need to be in my office, but it feels more professional. Like I'll be taken more seriously. Genie has been walked, watered, and snuggled into contentment, so I'm ready for whatever comes my way.

Nervousness isn't a familiar feeling for me because I learned to go with the flow a long time ago and trust in what I offer. Nevertheless, I am on edge about this. It's been nearly two weeks since I sent out my resumes and applications and have gotten very few responses back, so part of me feels like my hiatus since graduating is a major turnoff for employers. The graphics I emailed to this company earlier will have to speak for themselves because of the eight advertising companies within walking distance, this was the only one to reply. I can't miss this chance.

My phone rings at 2pm on the dot, so I waste no time answering it. The man's raspy voice on the other end is difficult to hear, but after our greetings, he gets right to the hard-hitting questions. Typical things like school, what I'm strongest at, where my weaknesses are, and any potential events in my life that could derail my career—AKA the "politically correct" way of asking a woman if she's pregnant or plans to become pregnant in the near future. Hard eye roll.

The man on the other end gives nothing away in terms of emotion, so I have no idea where I stand with him by the time the interview ends, but I think it went well.

I text Hannah, Vida, and Dina to let them know how it went, because they were all waiting eagerly for me to report back. All three text back immediately, saying they're confident I'll get the job. Perks of having unemployed friends. Good news is, Vida has an interview at a sports bar near her house as a bartender, but Hannah is still having no luck. I feel terrible that they both left a stable—albeit horrible—job on my account. Dina, on the other hand, still doesn't seem to be putting that much effort into seeking meaningful employment... or any employment at all. She's content to be a stay-at-home dog-mom to Nacho while she finishes her degree.

Once my girls are informed, I ring Damian, hoping he's not too busy to pick up. How he became such an important person that I feel inclined to keep him up to date with the goings-on in my life, I'm not sure, but here we are.

"Hey. How'd it go?" he answers, out of breath.

"Did I... uh... catch you in the middle of something?"

"My staff are scared of me, remember? I took the stairs instead of torturing them with my presence in the elevator."

I chuckle because Damian is a likeable guy—very likeable. No one could genuinely hate him if they got to know him. "Have you ever thought maybe you're reading too much into people's reactions, and if you were just honest with them, they'd be more receptive?"

A door closes behind him and our reception improves. "I've told them time and time again that I have an open-door policy and that I want honest feedback."

"Yes, but saying it and implementing it are two different things. Give a little if you want to get in return."

He breathes out a sigh, and I take that to mean he's arrived to wherever he was headed. "I'll try. So, how did your interview go? I've got a video call in a few minutes, so I'm sorry if I have to cut you short."

"Not all of us can be gainfully unemployed, Mr. Taylor. I understand."

He chuckles into the phone, making me smile.

I lean down and rub genie's soft blockhead, soaking in a moment of contentment. "The interview was fine. I did what I could, but he didn't seem too excited. He said he'll let me know either way on Monday."

"I have a good feeling about this one. This is the start of a new career for you."

"Don't get your hopes up. It's a competitive industry." I glance out the window at the sun shining and hear the bustling on the street below. Suddenly I'm overcome with the need to get out of my house and soak in some vitamin D. "I should let you get back to work."

"Yeah, I have to go."

I'm disappointed hearing his words, even though I knew he was at work.

"Angel?"

"Yeah?"

"Let me take you out tonight. To celebrate your interview."

I'm not surprised he asked. I figured over the past several weeks of talking regularly that this was coming, and I really wanted it to. When I'm working again, I may not have the same opportunity or freedom to go out when I want. This time, the answer is obvious. "Yeah. I'd like that."

When he replies, I can hear the smile in his voice. "I'll pick you up at seven."

"It's a date."

What do I wear on a date? I don't have the slightest clue. The last time I went on a "date", it was to a beer festival, and I wore cut-off shorts and a *Rolling Stones* T-shirt. I've never been invested enough in another person to care if I looked nice. I'd gotten into the habit of assuming everyone wouldn't be interested in me once they realized I'm not the type to fake nice or go out of my way to please people. The past few years, I've wanted to date, but never found anyone worth investing in. Hence why there were plenty of firsts, but no seconds. Damian is different.

I rummage through my closet, tossing options on my bed, but when I return to them, holding each one up in front of me, none seem right. Back to the closet, I dig through the untouched items in the far corner and find a dress I bought three years ago to attend a wedding. The bride and groom went their separate ways three days before, and I never wore it. It was just a casual backyard affair, so the dress is pretty, but not extravagant. Now seems like a good time to dust it off and give it some sunlight.

My hair leaves me with few options in terms of styling, so I tame my natural curls, swipe on some mascara and a champagne-coloured eyeshadow, then slip into my dress twenty minutes before Damian is supposed to arrive.

I strap on a pair of heels I don't often wear because I walk everywhere, but tonight I'll take advantage of driving wherever we're going. The strappy gold stilettos help me reach average height for a woman my age, which is a nice change. Maybe now I'll be eye-level with Damian's chin instead of his chest.

When I glance at myself in the mirror, the girl staring back at me looks nervous. I twist and turn, trying to pose in ways that make me look less anxious, but it is obvious from every angle. What's wrong with me? This isn't the first time I've been around Damian. He's been in my house before. Being alone with him isn't a new concept, and besides, we'll be somewhere in public with tons of other people. What's the big deal?

Before I can stress about it any more, there's a knock at my door, sending Genie tearing across the living space, down the hallway.

"Genie, don't jump all over him this time, okay?" I look at my dog, waiting for her to nod and agree, but she's too busy wagging her entire body to acknowledge me. Something tells me she didn't listen to a word I said.

19

DAMIAN

Make Me Happy

When I arrive at Angel's building, another resident or guest is on their way out, so I sneak through the door and go up to her apartment. That seemed the gentlemanly thing to do, rather than ask her to come down or waste time with her buzzer.

The elevator doors open on the third floor, so I walk to unit 308 and knock. Maybe I should have let her know I was here, because me showing up might catch her by surprise. Too late now.

I hear her speaking from the other side of the door and realize she's talking to Genie. I chuckle because she's trying to discourage Genie from jumping on me. Little does she know, I love that her dog gets so excited to see me.

The door swings open and I'm paralyzed. Angel is bent over, trying to keep Genie from running out the door, one hand on the dog, the other on the door handle. Her hair is down in her signature curls, and her dress… What can I say about the dress? From her bent over position, I can see her exposed upper back and shoulders. Her skin is smooth, with tan lines from a tank top with wider straps than the spaghetti straps on her current outfit.

Finally, she speaks, "Come in for a minute?"

I step through the door, allowing her to close it behind me, and she stands straight, giving me the first full glimpse of her. Wow! Her dress is a satiny green floral number that hits below her knees but has a slit up her right thigh. The cowl-type neckline drapes over her breasts, and the rest of it hugs her curves in the most sinfully angelic way.

"You look stunning." The fact I asked her on this date only a few hours ago tells me she had this dress on hand, and a pang of jealousy strikes me when I think about anyone else taking her out looking this gorgeous.

Her cheeks have a hint of blush as she acknowledges my words. "Thank you. I figured you'd be coming from work and still in your suit, so I didn't want to wear jeans and a T-shirt."

Was that her only justification for dressing up? I reach out to place my hand on her arm and step closer to her so we're only a few inches apart. Her breathing picks up, and I can see her chest rising and falling under the thin silk. "Don't do that."

"Do what?" She tilts her head back to look into my eyes.

"Don't downplay how incredibly gorgeous you are. You'd be just as beautiful in jeans and a T-shirt."

The colour on her cheeks deepens, and I'm having to stop myself from kissing her—something I've been dreaming about for weeks. The timing has to be right, though. She deserves to be treated like a queen first.

Breaking my focus from her, I bend down and address Genie, who hasn't jumped up on me. I tell her she's a good girl, and her little spin-wobble dance is too cute not to laugh at. If there was ever a creature made of pure joy, it's Genie. She's the happiest dog I've ever met.

I stand, dragging my eyes up Angel's form along the way, and smile so wide my cheeks hurt. "Are you ready to go?"

She nods and even a simple gesture has me admiring the movement of her hair, the flutter of her lashes, and the way she chews her bottom lip.

Angel takes a moment to say goodbye to Genie before we walk out the door, and like it's the most natural thing to do, before we reach the elevator, Angel loops her arm around mine. I press the down button without looking at it because my eyes are drawn to the woman next to me. Her delicate touch on my arm is as soothing as a cool summer breeze. Like after the chaos of my day at the office, being with her is a breath of fresh air—something that can be scarce in the summer smog of Canada's most populous city.

"Where are we going?" she asks when the elevator arrives.

"Would you kill me if I said we were going to *Harvest*?"

Her facial expression makes me burst out laughing.

"Wow. If looks could kill. No, we're not going there. Have you ever heard of *Hibiscus*?"

She nods. "How do you expect to get in there, Mr. Fancy Pants? I couldn't even get in there to drop off a resume."

"I called earlier to make a reservation. I did some work for them, so they're happy to fit us in."

"Oh. You're one of those."

The elevator dings, the doors open, and she steps out, but I'm frozen in place for a few seconds. "One of what?"

She doesn't reach for my arm again when I step out, causing me to clench my teeth from the nerves pooling in my stomach.

"One of those guys who uses their connections to get what they want."

If she only knew how much I don't want to be that guy. Not even a little. I'm gripped by a wave of nausea, afraid I've given her the wrong impression. Yet again. "When I completed the work for them, the owner was grateful and told me he'd welcome me whenever I wanted. I've never taken him up on it. But today, I wanted to take you somewhere nice, so I called in a favour. If it bothers you, we can go somewhere else. I'm fine with *McDonald's*."

Angel's eyes glance down at her feet. "I'm sorry. Sometimes I make assumptions I shouldn't. I'd be honoured to go to *Hibiscus* with you." She smiles at me with one side of her lips tilted up and my bout of nausea disappears. She loops her arm back through mine, and before she takes another step, adds, "But *McDonald's* is fine too."

We walk toward my SUV, where I open the door for her and help her in. The slit up her thigh separates, exposing more of her smooth skin, and I force myself to avert my eyes before she catches me ogling her. I don't want her thinking I'm "one of those."

We weave through traffic on our way to *Hibiscus*, and if I smiled any harder, I'd resemble The Joker—minus the weird makeup. Unlike the other times she's been in my car, this time she makes herself comfortable. She fiddles with the radio, settling on a top forty station, and singing along to the lyrics of each song. Not well, I should add, but the way she is so genuinely herself is hard to ignore.

We pull into the underground parking for *Hibiscus*, just as *Genie in a Bottle* comes over the radio. Angel bounces in her seat, excitement oozing from her.

"Are you really hungry?" I ask, assuming she's excited we arrived at the waterfront restaurant.

"No. I mean, yes, but this is my song. This is why Genie is Genie!"

That answers a lingering question I've had since the first day I met the dog. "Really? This song?"

"This. Is. A. Classic."

I chuckle at her, which earns me a set of dagger eyes, only making me laugh harder. I find a suitable parking spot in the crowded lot, regretting my choice to come here on a Friday.

Angel makes me wait in the car until the song has finished, then flashes me a smirk that solidifies the thought I'd suffer through any number of pop-diva ballads for her.

We take the elevator up from the garage level to the twelfth-floor restaurant. Our server takes my name and ushers us to a table right away. We're seated by the window overlooking Lake Ontario, and I hope we'll be here long enough to watch the sunset.

Though, with Angel in this dress, it's hard to focus on anything else.

20

ANGEL

Light Up the Sky

Our server welcomes us and hands us each a menu, reciting the daily specials and taking our drink order. The prices on the drink menu blow my mind—fifteen dollars for a glass of carrot juice? No thanks. I order a flat water, no ice, and Damian asks for the same, to the obvious disappointment of our server, Maria.

"You don't want something different? Wine or anything?" he asks, while studying his own menu.

"Water is fine. Everything else is too expensive."

His breathy laugh makes his shoulders shake. "Don't worry about that. Have something if you want. This is supposed to be an experience." He waves his hand in front of him, gesturing to the space around us.

The décor is elaborate but not gaudy. Crystal chandeliers, a stunning floral mural running the length of the wall opposite the windows, gold tables with off-white upholstered chairs. It really is beautiful.

"I'm here for the company, not the overpriced alcohol."

He doesn't reply for a moment, appearing deep in thought. I don't want to interrupt his thought process, so I continue perusing the menu. The entrées are expensive too. This is not a feasible option for the unemployed.

"Has anyone ever told you you're amazing?" His random declaration catches me by surprise. His eyes bore into mine when I look up and it appears he surprised himself by saying that.

"I don't think anyone ever has." I laugh, fidgeting with my menu and pulling it open to block the blush creeping up my face. "Quite the opposite, actually."

Maria places our waters on the immaculately set table and I sympathize with the wait staff for having to deal with tablecloths. Such a hassle. Though chances are, in a place like this, they have the benefit of busboys to clean the tables after their patrons leave. Something we never had at *Harvest*. Different tax brackets. Maria asks if we're ready to order. Damian orders a charcuterie board for us to share, so I only order a wild mushroom soup in addition to that. The menu is too fancy for my taste. I don't need the lineage of my dinner traced back seven generations. Like their bison is some sort of wild game royalty.

Once Maria is several feet away, Damian stares at me with concern etched on his face. "What do you mean, the opposite?"

Not ideal to dive into poor-me stories on our first official date, but this is the price of honesty. "Most people don't like hearing the truth. It doesn't matter if it's my opinion or something I say for their benefit. It doesn't matter if it's a glaringly obvious indisputable truth. People want to hear what they want, and I disrupt that. As a result, not many people stick around for long." I take a sip of my water, hoping the refreshing liquid will lower my body temperature. "You'll see."

"That's their problem, not yours. My career has been based on spinning truth and telling people what they want to hear. In my industry, everything has to be calculated and analyzed. Perception is everything, so I find your truth refreshing."

"For now, maybe." I take a breath, wanting to change this conversation topic. "What is your industry? I just realized all the times we've spoken, we've talked about your job, but I never asked *what* it is."

He seems hesitant to answer, which makes me twist in my seat, bracing myself for something horrific, like a human trafficker or mobster. I can imagine they'd thrive by spinning the truth and being calculated in their efforts.

"I'm in advertising. I prefer more of the product ad campaign creation to the management side where I am now, but the company needed someone to fill the spot, so I stepped in."

Based on everything he's told me until now, that makes perfect sense—including his offer to ask his contacts if they had work available. "I can see what you mean about it being a tough industry—that's been part of my issue in pursuing graphic design."

Maria brings our charcuterie board and two plates, so Damian and I put our conversation on hold to dig in. There's a wide variety of options, from prosciutto to blackberries, leaving me conflicted over what to choose. I look up from the platter and see Damian watching me with a grin teasing at his lips.

"What?"

"I just find you fascinating."

"Watching me conflicted over deli meats is fascinating? Oh, honey. You need to find some excitement in your life." I chuckle, averting my eyes from his and popping a plump cherry tomato in my mouth.

"It's nothing to do with the deli meats." He smirks, grabbing a small slice of cheese and taking a bite. His eyes widen as he chews it, but not in delight. "That's a strong cheese." His expression morphs, as his nose scrunches and his forehead wrinkles.

As much as I try, I can't stop a giggle from bubbling out. I cover my mouth with my hand, not wanting to spray tomato guts across the fancy restaurant. My amusement causes Damian to laugh, and there we are, like a couple of fools, giggling over smelly cheese.

"Hopefully the rest of it is better," he says after taking a sip of water.

We pick at the food, commenting on each thing we try, sharing what we enjoy to get the other's opinion, and warning each other away from more offensive cheeses. Our entrees arrive, and I dive into my mushroom soup that has an obnoxious balsamic foam overtop, but I stir it in and hope for the best. Damian stares down at his meal, which is about the size of your average hamburger, all piled together to create edible "art". Looks like Genie would like it, but I don't say that out loud.

"I wasn't aware I'd need an engineering degree to dismantle my meal," he says, causing us both to laugh again, drawing attention our way. He takes his first bite, twisting his face as he chews, then leans forward to whisper, "Do you think the chef would be offended if I put ketchup on this?"

I snort, then clap my hand over my mouth and nose, trying not to upset the others enjoying their overpriced "gourmet" food. Apparently, I have the palette of a toddler, because I would have preferred chicken nuggets and a milkshake.

Our main course isn't any more appealing than the appetizer, but we choke down what we can. I mention Hannah and her dream to work in a restaurant like this, but claim she is far too talented to work somewhere else that turns out dog food. Conversation then lands back on the day I got fired, explaining why Hannah is now in the market for a new job.

"They walked out with you?"

"Sure did. Not just walked out. Practically set the place on fire as they did. Then we went out to a club later that night and

I ran into the same guy. For a big city, it feels really small sometimes."

Damian gapes at me, so I continue.

"He started to grind up against me—during a Christina song, nonetheless, tainting it for me for all of eternity, which is unforgivable—so I told him off. He said some things I hope he'll never even think again because I kneed him in the jewels and got kicked out of the club."

Silence.

Damian gawks at me a few seconds longer, then without another word, bursts into a fit of laughter. Other patrons are staring as I join in again, and soon we're struggling to catch our breaths. I can't stop picturing the look on the guy's face when I played nutcracker, and I'm sure Damian is imagining it too.

Finally, he composes himself to look at me. "You really are amazing." He grabs the napkin from his lap, tossing it over the remains of his food tower. "What do you say we take a walk along the waterfront? I can't take another bite of this."

My stomach is aching from the fits of giggles—and maybe a little from whatever I just ate that my digestive system is not accustomed to—but I smile and nod, not wanting to say good night yet.

As soon as I stand, I note my footwear. "Oh. I'm not really in walking shoes."

Damian levels me with a smile reaching his captivating eyes, and tosses some cash on the table before he takes my hand. "I can piggyback you. Come on."

"Oh, no. Let me pay for half. I insist."

He stops walking, which gives me a chance to free my hand and dig through my clutch, searching for some money.

"Let me get it. Please? Besides, you already took care of our first meal."

Heat rushes up my neck and face when I think back to that day at my house. I realize he's bound to argue with me if I insist on paying, so I let it go. "Fine, but whatever we do next is on me."

Again, he smirks, and my eyes widen as I understand the dual meaning of my words.

"Don't get any ideas, Mr. Taylor." I clarify and walk toward the elevator.

"Wouldn't dream of it, Miss Blake."

I am definitely dreaming of it. Things that shouldn't be thought of on a first official date with a woman I've searched my entire adult life for. I haven't even kissed her yet, and I'm already falling apart. She has me at her mercy.

We ride the elevator hand-in-hand, down to the street level where we walk out into the warm summer air. I survey the area to see what's around, not being familiar with this section of downtown. I didn't grow up in the city, and despite having lived here for over six years, I've spent much of that time working, not exploring.

Angel grabs my hand and drags me toward something she's spotted. "Oh, you have to try these."

I look to see a food truck parked near the pier named *Talko Loco*. Angel's excitement is contagious, as she trudges along in her stilettos—stilettos that make her calves look amazing. She could drag me to my death right now and I'd be too distracted to notice.

"Dina and I used to come here when she was doing her bachelor's degree. I haven't been for so long. You *have* to try the Carne Asada tacos. They are to die for."

Who am I to deny the woman her taco dream? We stand in line behind two other couples, and I reach my arm around Angel's waist, pulling her closer. I may have worked ten hours today, but the last thing I feel right now is tired.

Angel looks up at me, drawing my attention to her dark eyes sparkling under the fading sunlight and taco truck lights. Her eyes close and she turns away, but quickly turns back to me to ask, "Do you trust me?"

No hesitation. "Yes."

"Let me order for you. I've tried everything." She steps up to the window to order, barely able to see in the window, even wearing heels. Before she commits to an order, she turns back to me. "How do you feel about spicy?"

"The spicier, the better."

Five minutes later, we're sitting at a bench across the waterfront park, where Angel unwraps the food, which smells incredible. She tucks her curls behind her ears, staring at the flour tortillas as she licks her lips. Safe to say, this is the first time in my life I wished I was a taco.

She sets one in front of me. "Guarantee, you won't be needing ketchup for this."

I lift the taco with one hand, cupping the other beneath it so it won't drip on my suit, but as soon as I take a bite, I'm so focused on the flavour explosion happening, I don't care about the mess. I moan with delight as the different spices and aromas mingle together on my tongue. This is exquisite.

It's not lost on me that I took Angel to a ridiculously expensive restaurant, hoping for an enjoyable meal, and here we are, indulging in food truck fares that blow whatever that was I tried to eat earlier out of the water. Goes to show, I'm not cut out for the "high life".

I wipe my mouth with a paper napkin, praying I don't have taco sauce in my facial hair. "This is delicious. It… it's perfection."

"Told you. Amazing right?"

So amazing, but not only the food.

We polish off the four tacos Angel purchased, and she suggests finding somewhere to get a margarita to wash it down. If it means I can delay taking her home, I'm down.

She leads me into a decent-looking pub where we sit at the bar and Angel orders her margarita. I'm not a huge fan of sweet drinks, so I opt for whisky. The bartender places our beverages in front of us, and Angel takes a first sip through the straw. Her eyes close and she hums a short tune of admiration. I study her long lashes and the subtle swipe of eyeshadow she wears. Her eyes were always too distracting for me to notice before.

We enjoy the rest of our drink before we agree to head back in the direction of the parking garage. Angel stumbles on our way to the pub door, and I react quickly enough to stop her from falling. I wrap her in my arms, standing there for a moment, not wanting to let go.

"You good?"

She nods. "My feet hurt more than I realized."

"We can't have that." In this situation, my caveman tendencies in her presence come in handy. I scoop her into my arms, princess style, with one arm behind her back, the other under her knees. She instinctively wraps her arms around my neck, making me pause. Here we are, standing three feet away from the Pub's exit, and I'm too captivated by this woman to move.

Her giggle breaks my trance. "What are you doing?"

I step to the door, pushing it open with my back, exiting onto the sidewalk. "Carrying you. I loved these shoes already, but even more so now." I waggle my eyebrows, making her laugh again, and I feel the vibrations in my chest. That's not the only thing I'm feeling there.

"I shouldn't have worn these shoes. I knew they'd hurt after a while."

"Why did you?" Is it wrong if I want her to say she wore them for me? Because she thought I'd like them?

"Because I'm short, and I didn't want to spend the night staring at your chest."

That sounds like an awesome evening if the roles were reversed. "You're not that short. What are you, 5'2"?"

"For your information, I am 5 feet, one-and-a-half inches. I'm a small fry and I walk everywhere, so tonight I decided to wear heels I never get the chance to. Had I known you wanted to take a walk, I'd have worn something else, but this is fine with me." She winks, and I'm done for.

"I'm glad you didn't."

"Yeah?" Her playful expression pushes away the burning in my biceps.

"Angel."

Her eyes flutter closed, and she leans her head into my neck. My steps halt and I can't stop myself anymore. I lean down to capture her lips in a kiss. The instant we connect, I'm lost in the feel of her mouth on mine. It starts off tender, wanting to convey how much I like her, but before I know it, I set her down and have her backed up against the exterior wall of another restaurant halfway to our destination.

She doesn't hesitate to match my pace, and soon enough, her hands are raking through my hair. Mine are exploring the curve of her hip with one hand, and the soft skin on her neck with the other. She bites at my lower lip, making me groan into her mouth, which seems to spur her on more. Her lips part, allowing me to taste the margarita that I thought I hated, but mixed with the sweetness of Angel, nothing has ever tasted better.

I've been captivated by her since the moment I first saw her, but nothing has compared to this.

"Get a room!" a random pedestrian shouts.

I pull myself back, not wanting to, but also not wanting to embarrass her with an overtly public display of affection. Looking at her face, though, I don't think she's embarrassed at all. Her chest is heaving at the same rate as mine. Her lips are swollen and the perfect shade of pink under the streetlights.

"Damian," she replies with a wide smile. "Was that your plan all along?"

I chuckle. "Totally spontaneous, but I have no regrets." I lean my head down so my forehead rests on hers. "Have I told you how amazing you are?"

"You may have mentioned it." The playful expression she's worn all night disappears. "But you'll find out what I mean about people not wanting to hear the truth all the time."

"Maybe you'll find out that some people appreciate your honesty."

"We'll see." She swats at my chest and her curved lips reappear. "So, do you want me to carry you the rest of the way so we're even?"

I roar with laughter, picturing this woman trying to lift me at all. Let alone carry me anywhere. "Come here." I hook my arm under her knees, pulling them up to my chest and allowing her to wrap her arms around me again. With another quick kiss, we're on our way.

We garner a few strange looks as we giggle and chat all the way back to my car with Angel in my arms, but I couldn't care less what anyone else thinks of us. I'm too busy having one of the greatest nights of my life.

I open the car door for Angel to climb inside, and she backs in, leaving her legs out the door, surprising me by pulling my tie until I'm at her level. She snakes her hands around the back of my head and pulls me in for a quick kiss.

"Thank you for tonight."

Infatuation

Three days have passed since my date with Damian, and I've been replaying our interaction on a loop ever since. Saturday, I searched far and wide for remote job opportunities, not content to wait around for the other place to call me back. Yesterday, Genie and spent the day with Dina and Nacho—much to Genie's dismay. My sister immediately caught on that something was "off" about me, so I dished about my date and tried not to sound like one of "those girls" I spent my early twenties making fun of.

Our date may have just been dinner, and was hardly the type of night people write romance novels about, but it was so imperfectly perfect, I couldn't have asked for a better evening. This time I *want* there to be a second.

That was one night, though, and now it's time to get my life back on track. I'm getting to the point, if I don't find something in my field soon, I'll have to take up another waitressing job, and I'd rather not because I know I'd get complacent again and end up stuck. Getting fired from my job at *Harvest* needs to be the catalyst to get my life plan back in motion.

Another hour of job searching passes and I've reached the conclusion I've applied for every job within a fifty kilometre radius, and that will be a terrible commute on the bus. Moving wouldn't be ideal either. I suppose I could get a car but insur—

My *Beautiful* ringtone plays, interrupting my what-if scenarios.

"Hello."

"Hello, is this Miss Blake?" a man asks.

Be cool, Angel. Be cool. "It is. May I ask who's calling?"

"Garrett Nicholls. We spoke the other day regarding the freelance graphic designer position."

"Mr. Nicholls, of course. I'm sorry. You caught me by surprise."

"Not to worry, Miss Blake. I was calling because after speaking with you and reviewing your portfolio, I'd love to offer you the job."

Be cool! "I'm so honoured. Thank you, Mr. Nicholls."

"I'm happy to hear that. Now, of course, because it's freelance, it will be on a project-by-project basis. We have a designer on maternity leave and need someone to fill in that gap, but there's a possibility it could turn into a permanent position. However, I'm aware that people need to survive, so your contract will allow you to take on other freelance projects, so long as there is no conflict of interest or schedule."

This is perfect. "That sounds great. Do you need me to come into the office to sign the contract?"

"Yes. Since you're nearby, it's easier if you could come sign the forms to keep the tax man happy. While you're here, you can meet the project manager and other staff members so you'll know who you're communicating with via email."

"This means so much to me, Mr. Nicholls." Coolness has dissipated. "Sorry. I'm just excited, but you can expect nothing but professionalism from me."

He laughs, and it helps ease the embarrassment over fangirling a job. "I'm happy you're excited. We need that kind of enthusiasm infused into our project, so don't apologize." He mutters something to someone else in the room, but must have his hand over the phone. "My apologies, Miss Blake. I've got to tend to another matter, but I'll have my assistant email you the information and set up a time for you to come in at your earliest convenience. The sooner we get you started, the better."

"Perfect. I look forward to working under you… er… for you? With you. I look forward to working *with* you. And I promise by then, I'll have a better handle on English." Even Genie is flashing me a sympathetic look.

When we end the call, I pick up my massive mutt and prance around the living room like a Disney Prince. "This job is perfect, Genie! No more days of you stuck inside alone. Finally, I'll have a creative outlet again, and best of all, we'll be able to afford food next month." I set down my confused dog, who was none too appreciative of my impromptu dance, and she scurries off to the bedroom.

My instinct is to call someone to tell them. That person should be Dina, though she'll be disappointed we can't be unemployed together anymore. Even Hannah or Vida; but neither of them have found a job yet, so I don't want to sound like I'm rubbing it in. So I do what any illogical twenty-four-year-old woman would do. I text the guy I've been on one date with.

Angel: *I got a job!*

Well, that was anticlimactic, because he doesn't immediately open the message like I expected. I seem to have forgotten that he already has a job and is busy adulting.

After I get sick of waiting for a response, I call my sister to share my news, not wanting to listen to her whine about my new employment status, but wanting to celebrate with someone. We speak for a little over seven minutes before my phone buzzes in my hand, indicating a text message. I pull the phone from my ear while Dina is speaking and see it's from Damian, but I don't have a valid reason to hang up on my sister. Don't be that girl, Angel. The girl who neglects people already in her life in exchange for someone new. Who cares how searing his kisses were, or how beautiful he made me feel. Pish posh. She's your sister, and she deserves your attention.

"Angel? Are you there?"

"Oh, sorry. I was thinking."

"Gee thanks. Glad to know I'm interesting." She employs her usual sarcastic tone, but adds a laugh at the end, so I know she's not offended.

"Sorry, Dina. Damian sent me a text and—"

"Say no more. I get it. Go answer your lover and call me when you know your work details. We can do a shopping trip for new office clothes one day this week!"

"I'll be working from home most days. Pyjamas are fine."

"Nonsense. If you're going to join the corporate world, you need to look the part. Call me to let me know your schedule. Nacho and I will come by and help you prepare."

Genie quirks her head as if she heard Nacho's name through the phone. I give her a sympathetic pat, but I know how she feels.

"Thanks, Dina. I think I can handle it, but I'll let you know."

I hang up my second phone call in twenty minutes and click the text bubble to read Damian's reply.

Damian: *In mtng. So proud of u. Will cll aftr.*

I giggle at his message, and something about him trying to covertly text me during a meeting makes me smile. If I get any cheesier over this guy, someone could turn me into *con queso*.

Now that I have one job lined up, I feel more at ease. I still need to search for other freelance gigs to supplement my income, but at least it's something. One step forward is better than being stuck in an endless cycle of being undervalued and, at times, resented in a job I didn't like. This is exactly what I need.

Things are looking up.

23

DAMIAN

I Got Trouble

itchell drones on for way longer than he needs to about ideas for this hydrogenated oil campaign. None of them sit right with me, but I've put so much effort into encouraging my team to make decisions on their own, I'm battling between speaking up or not.

Finally, I remind myself that my duty is to our client, not my co-workers, so I have to put the paying customer first.

Before I can clear my throat—the international boss sound for 'let me speak now'—my phone buzzes. Normally I wouldn't check my messages during a meeting, but I can't shake my curiosity. After my date with Angel on Friday, she's been on my mind non-stop. I was even trying to find a way to get her a job here, which was motivated more by her obvious talent than anything else. Having her in the office every day would just be a bonus. Ultimately, I decided against it because I promised her I wouldn't interfere.

Her message reads that she got a job, and I'm hoping it's the one she interviewed for on Friday. If our celebration for an interview went that well, I can only imagine how incredible a getting-the-job celebration will go.

My mind has drifted so far from the meeting, as I text Angel back, I don't notice everyone staring at me until I lift my head up from my phone. I transform my deer-in-headlights look to one of authority as fast as I can.

"What do you think, Mr. Taylor?" Mitchell asks from his position by the projector screen.

I do not know what he's talking about. It wouldn't look good if I admit I just tuned him out for five minutes because I was thinking about a job-celebration evening with this woman I can't get out of my head. "Send me your notes on this and I'll go over them in my office. We have a lot to do on this campaign, so I'd like to know where everyone's at." I sound like such a jerk. That was not my intention, but as soon as I finish my sentence, everyone is packing up their files and pushing their chairs back to leave. You'd think I lit the room on fire.

I drag myself back to my office, once again feeling defeated for failing to inspire or motivate my staff. As a result, my own motivation wanes, and the only thing that's inspiring me is a curly-haired spitfire with a snorty dog.

With my office door closed behind me, I dial Angel's number.

"Hello?"

"Hello, working girl." Well, that came out wrong.

She laughs, at least, so that's good. "Not that kind of freelance job, Damian. I got the job I interviewed for on Friday, but I can still take on other stuff. The best part is, I can work from home most of the time!"

The excitement in her voice melts away the disappointment from my meeting. "That's great. I bet Genie will be happy."

"She'll be happy I can afford food."

My stomach twists in a pretzel-like knot. Was she not able to afford food? For how long? I let her pay for tacos. What if she can't afford her rent? "Why didn't you say something? I could have given you money."

She pauses for a second before she laughs again. "I'm just being dramatic. I promise, I'm totally fine. You are not giving me any more money."

If she says it, she must mean it, so that untwists my stomach. "Okay. So, where are we going to celebrate?" I have no doubt that I want to see her tonight. It's gravitating more toward needing to see her than wanting to.

"We can go to the taco truck. Or *McDonald's*."

The last of my post-meeting tension melts away when I realize she didn't resist at all or try to feign interest. She just came straight out with a reply.

"I think we can do better than that. Even though those tacos were epic."

"If you can top those, I'll be really impressed." She's practically singing everything she says, making her excitement both recognizable and contagious.

"What day do you start work?"

"Um... I'm not sure yet. I'm waiting for an email confirmation, but he said the sooner the better."

"Wow. So I should get as much time in as I can before you're too busy for me." After the words leave my mouth, I regret them, because I'm sounding desperate. She didn't take well to Caveman Damian, so I'd imagine Clingy Damian won't be a huge selling point, either. I blow out an exaggerated breath, trying to calm my nerves. This girl has me unhinged. "What time are you free?"

"I'm still free as a bird, so whatever works from you. Just let me know what to wear and what time so I can take Genie out."

I know she didn't mean it that way, but if I had a say in what she'd wear... focus, Damian. "Why don't we take Genie to the waterfront and try a different food truck, then?"

After a brief discussion where Angel argues on behalf of my backseat, trying to protect it from Genie's drool, we agree that

I'll pick her and Genie up at seven. So now begins the count-down.

By the time I get off the phone, my email inbox is flooded with project details from our earlier meeting and I'm conflicted over how to handle it. I'm not cut out for this job. People's approval never bothered me before. I never sought it, nor did I care when I got it. But in this position, I've found myself constantly at war with the idea everyone has of me and who I really am. I can't seem to get anything right.

I politely word my reply to each email, reading and re-reading each one multiple times before sending so I can be sure nothing will be taken out of context, and before I know it, Paxton is peeking his head through my door to tell me it's time to go. I asked him earlier to let me know when the clock struck six, which if I hurry, gives me enough time to go home to change and get to Angel's in time.

My journey to the parking garage is full of uncomfortable elevator silence and obligatory "Mr. Taylor" nods. I can't get out of here soon enough.

My condo is only a few kilometres away, yet it takes twenty minutes for the drive on account of traffic. That's part of the reason I stay late at work so often, because this small-town guy is not cut out for vehicle congestion and constant horn honking. Today, I have no issue braving the tension-filled drivers so I can get to Angel's on time.

It's a sad state of affairs in my closet when it comes to casual clothes. Most of my wardrobe contains suits, dress shirts, ties, and polished shoes in various colours. I settle on a pair of dark jeans, a grey long-sleeve tee, and casual sneakers.

When I get back to my car, I text Angel that I'll be there in twenty minutes, and she sends back a winking face. I have no idea why, but that winking yellow blob has me smiling all the way to her condo. I go to pull into her parking space, but there's already a car in it. A silver Toyota Camry. With no other choice, I park in the temporary guest parking and get out to meet Angel.

I'm no more than five steps from the car door when I see her exit the building wearing a baby pink cardigan, light-wash jeans, and gleaming white sneakers. If we stop anywhere for a drink, she'll get ID'd for sure. She looks sweet and innocent and… perfect.

"Hey." I smile at her, and bend down to pet Genie who is pawing at my leg. "Hi, girl. Are you ready for a car ride?"

The way her entire body wags instead of just her tail makes me chuckle every time. With my eyes on Genie's wiggle butt, I stand upright and Angel is within reaching distance. I pull her toward me and plant a kiss on her I've been dreaming about since Friday. She doesn't show an ounce of hesitation and each ticking second with her lips caressing mine makes me feel like she's been the missing part of my life all this time.

When we break apart, Angel is smiling with blush painted across her cheeks. She looks even more gorgeous than she did thirty seconds ago.

As if I'm seeing her for the first time again, I say, "Hi."

"Hi, yourself." She glances down at Genie, who has parked herself right between us. "I think someone is jealous."

I'd never admit that I was jealous of her too, because she got to wake up next to Angel this morning. "Your chariot awaits, Genie. Or your magic carpet…" I twist my face, recalling any Genie knowledge I have. "Your lamp?"

Angel gasps and my heart stops for a split second.

"Not a *lamp*, Damian. She cannot be contained. She's not calling anyone master; trust me."

I breathe a sigh of relief and laugh because I've only been around Genie a few times, but I know that to be true. I open the back door, and Genie jumps in, taking in her new gear.

When Angel opens her door and climbs in, she spots the new addition. "Did you buy that?" she asks, pointing at the 'dog hammock' on the back seat.

From my position at the back, driver's side door, I reply, "I didn't want you stressing over her slobbering on my seats. She has her own seatbelt now, too." I hold up the leash clip attached to a silver buckle.

Genie is less enthused about being restrained, but I want her to be safe. I think she has become my master.

24

ANGEL

Here to Stay

He bought dog gear for his car. Did he do this today? When did he have time? I want to ask, but... who am I kidding? I can't help myself. "Did you buy this stuff today?"

"Uh... no. I ordered it the other day, just in case. It wasn't a big deal. Cheaper than getting the car detailed again." He pulls out of the parking lot, onto the road heading south.

I'm lost for words because what should be considered a simple thing feels like a grand gesture to a girl who hasn't been on a second date in nearly a decade and the most romantic thing my last boyfriend did was push me on the swings or grope my boob. The bar is low.

"You look deep in thought. What are you thinking?" Damian glances at me from the corner of his eye. "Sorry, I shouldn't ask that."

I consider how to respond and opt for an attempt at rattling him. "I was thinking about having my boobs groped." I raise my eyebrows in a challenge to Damian and suppress the growing urge to laugh.

His eyes are wide as he stares straight ahead, and his mouth is gaping open and closing. After thirty seconds of him saying nothing, I burst out laughing and tell him the whole truth.

"That is a really low standard, but for future reference, I'm up for either of those things." We both chuckle, then Damian adds, "How am I doing by comparison?"

"On a pass/fail grading system, you're passing."

We spend a few hours enjoying the summer breeze off of Lake Ontario and strolling around the pier. Genie has Damian carry her on a few occasions, and I laugh at how easily she's trained him. She gives him a signature Genie smile and gets whatever she wants.

"So, did you get information about the new job?" Damian's strolling beside me, letting Genie lead him wherever she wants to go.

"I'm going into the office on Wednesday to meet my manager, and they'll get me started on my first job."

Damian's smile matches Genie's, and I can't help but return it.

"Are you excited?" He stops walking to focus on my face.

"Nervous, but yeah. I'm excited to create again, you know?"

His lips turn downward and I'm so confused by the change. "What's wrong?"

"No, nothing. I... I just miss creating. That was always my real passion when I got into advertising. There's a lot less of that in my role now."

I'm sad for him, but if my time waitressing taught me anything, it's that you can't get time back you've wasted on worthless pursuits. I could have spent the last few years building my portfolio and training to expand my skill set, but because I got comfortable, that time has passed. "If you don't love your job, find something you do. Paying the bills isn't always worth the grief."

Genie stops to sniff a wilting potted plant set beside an A-frame sign for a cafe. I take the brief pause to study Damian's expression. His carefree smile from moments ago is gone.

"I'm sorry. It's not as easy as getting fired and forced into a career change, and I get that. I just hate to see anyone I care about wasting away in a job they hate."

His eyebrows lift, forming perfect arches over his brown eyes. "Anyone you care about, huh?"

Those words slipped out without thinking, but I don't regret saying them. "Do you think I'd spend time with you if I didn't care?"

Damian's smile rivals Genie's again. The world feels brighter when they're happy in tandem. Less intimidating. Less dark. Like the curve of their mouths somehow chases away the nightmares that exist. The way Damian looks at me makes all the bad meals and mediocre tips from *Harvest* worth it. Because that's where I met *him*. That just makes the reality of him getting tired of me hanging around, being a rain cloud, dishing out truths no one wants to hear that much harder.

"Maybe your job is going to lead to something that will change your life someday, and everything will be worth it." I'm not normally one for hypotheticals and fluffy rainbow bits of positivity, but when I started slinging tables, I never would have guessed anything good would come from it. But I met Hannah and Vida, who I'm happy to call my friends. And standing here, it's hard to remember all the negatives.

We're on the move again, now that Genie has sniffed the area to her contentment.

"I can think of one good thing already," Damian adds a few steps later. "You."

"That's the way. The power of positive thinking." I slap him on the back like we're sorority brothers. "Not sure what I had to do with your job, though."

"The day we met, I was having a garbage day at the office and wanted to find somewhere none of my co-workers or clients would eat at."

"Gee thanks."

We both chuckle.

"Sorry, but you can't disagree. I wanted to go for a walk to clear my head, and I ended up at *Harvest*. Turned out to be one of my best decisions."

It's not easy to make me blush, but he does. A lot. "I don't disagree. With any of it."

Damian takes my hand and we walk along the waterfront, following Genie's nose.

For the first time in months—maybe years—my future looks exciting.

As much as I debated what to wear on dates with Damian, my first meeting with my new boss is ten times worse. How does one portray creative but serious? Fun but professional? Beats me. I even called Hannah for input because her aesthetic effortlessly says all of those things, but for some reason, everything I try on screams trying too hard.

I settle on black skinny ponte pants, a red blazer with a black and white floral print, and a white camisole underneath. I slip on a pair of nude heels, pray my hair doesn't grow exponentially between here and the office, kiss Genie goodbye—on her head, despite her eagerness to remove my makeup—and off I go.

Midway on my journey, I receive a text message.

Damian: *Good luck today. Call me later. xx*

That message puts a smile on my face for the rest of my journey. The fact he even remembered is kind of amazing.

I walk into *Harbour Campaigns*, my new employer, and make my way to the receptionist's desk, where I'm greeted by a grumpy blonde with alabaster skin and bright blue eyes. Her attitude is not the only intimidating thing about her. Her manicured nails, blown out hair, and obvious confidence make me feel like I don't belong here. I try to remind myself we are not in competition. *Be polite, and maybe one day you'll be friends with her.*

"Hi, I'm here to meet with Mitchell Donnelly. My name is Angel Blake."

While I wasn't expecting a hug and a warm cookie, I certainly wasn't anticipating the "Sit over there and wait" that I receive.

Okay. Perhaps friendship is not in the cards for us.

Like she says, I sit in the waiting area between reception and the security desk, which has one middle-aged, overweight guard on duty. One can only hope his role model is Paul Blart, and anyone with nefarious intentions will overlook him. Regardless, he smiles at me, so I return the gesture, grateful he's helped to ease my nerves. I don't even know why I'm so nervous. I've already got the job.

Five minutes later, a man, not much older than me, walks my way after getting directions from the abrasive blonde. She doesn't act any friendlier toward the tall brunette man, so I'm left wondering if she's sitting on a beehive or has some other explanation for her demeanour.

The man introduces himself as Mitchell, and he's friendly but professional. He gestures for me to follow him toward the elevator and makes small talk along the way. I explain my education and work history briefly, but he doesn't press for more details.

The building is dedicated to various public relations, marketing, and advertising divisions, as well as the standard accounting, legal, and human resources departments any large business requires. Mitchell gives me an abbreviated tour, which consists of telling me what's on each floor as the elevator ascends. The doors open to reveal the fifth floor, and I follow my new boss to the right as he continues to prattle on about the company's specialties and mission. Pretty sure their mission is to make big bucks, but they have to put something more profound on their website.

The department I'll be in for the time being focuses on food and beverage advertising. Not the most exciting stuff to design, but it's a job with potential for work in other areas.

Mitchell leads me to what's referred to as "the pit" and does a blanket introduction: "Guys, this is Angel. Angel, this is everyone." The obligatory *nice to meet you*s get passed around, whereas I just reply with hello. I don't know if it's nice to meet any of these people yet, so I won't say it.

Once that's out of the way, Mitchell pulls me into an office to the side of the cubicle area and leaves the door open a few inches, telling me to take a seat.

First order of business is signing a contract, tax documents, and a personnel form to include my profile in the company directory. I'm issued my own business email with expectations I will check it regularly during business hours. So far, so good.

When all is said and done, I have a clear direction for the first project I'm being pulled in on. Mitchell asks if I can return on Friday with any mockups I come up with between now and then. He'll give his input, along with his boss. I didn't realize there were so many bosses, because Mitchell's boss is not Mr. Nicholls.

"How many levels of management are there?" I sound like a total newb at this corporate world stuff.

Thankfully, Mitchell laughs. "I'm just the project manager. We have a team manager who oversees the projects on our team, then we have a department manager who oversees the entire food and beverage department, and then Mr. Nicholls who is a hands-on CEO, but you'll probably never see him or the department manager. Just myself and the team manager."

"Wow. That's a lot of… levels?" I cringe at my awkwardness.

Bless Mitchell for being polite and chuckling at my inexperience.

Before this job progresses any further, I figure it's best to get everything out in the open. "I'm not used to this corporate life. I mean, obviously. You're familiar with my work history. In a restaurant, we just had the owner and the head chef to contend with. There were no mystery heads pulling strings from behind the curtains."

Mitchell studies me for a moment. "From what I've seen, you're very talented. Why did you work at the restaurant for so long? Why not pursue this sooner?"

I hate answering that question. "It's silly, but the easiest explanation is that I got complacent. I was hesitant to look for a job, especially in advertising, because—"

Knock, knock. "Mitch, sorry to interrupt, but we're being summoned. You almost done here?" The man peeking his head in the door is short compared to Mitchell, but has a similar beard as if it's a company policy. He has short, dark hair and a friendly smile. He doesn't introduce himself, and I don't ask.

"Give me a minute to wrap up."

The newcomer's smile disappears. "Don't keep him waiting."

"I won't if you let me finish up here. If I'm late, I'll blame you."

That sends the man scurrying without another word.

What an unusual exchange. It, again, makes me curious. "Why does it sound like you're headed into the den of a hungry ogre?"

Mitchell grimaces instead of laughing. "That's an accurate description, actually. I'm sorry for ending this abruptly. Time got away from me. I'll have a security badge available for you when you come on Friday, so pick it up from the security desk on your way in, then come right up."

I nod, suddenly on edge over the change in Mitchell's demeanour. "Thank you, Mr. Donnelly. I'll see you on Friday." I stand to my full five-foot-three-and-a-half height, thanks to my two-inch heels, and shake Mitchell's hand before we both exit his office and I escape to the elevator.

As much as I'm disappointed I didn't get to explain to Mitchell my personal policy on honesty, my biggest concern is that I hope I never meet the ogre.

25

DAMIAN

Get Mine, Get Yours

No word from Angel before I have to go into my next meeting. I hope everything went okay with her intake interview. Her job was supposed to be a done deal, but that doesn't mean anything before a contract is signed.

Whatever the outcome, I'll have to find out later. I wait until I see the other team members file into the board room before I make my way over. The door is wide open, so I can hear their conversation from the corridor.

"She was pretty hot, but that's an HR nightmare. Steer clear, man. Trust me. You don't want to mess up your career for a fling or whatever you're looking for." Elliot's familiar voice sounds more stern than I've ever heard it.

"But she's a literal Angel. I've never met an Angel before."

The hair on the back of my neck stands like a defensive dog. I continue to wait at the doorway, out of sight—which is tough with the walls of windows in this place—listening to their conversation, reeling in my urge to exercise my managerial power. *Angel is a common name. Relax.* But this conversation, along with the email I just received from my boss informing me of a new freelance designer, is enough to have me grinding my teeth.

"I don't care what her name is, man. Focus on the job." Elliot gets bonus points for being a voice of reason.

"She's just freelance. I'll ask her out and see what she says."

I don't want to hear any more of this. I clear my throat, walk into the room, and drop my manila folder on the table with a loud *thwap*. Pretty sure my face is set in a furious scowl, but for the life of me, I can't relax it.

Once I have their attention, they both look startled. I haven't said a word and they look like scolded children. All these months I've been trying to endear myself to my staff, and right now, knowing Mitchell was ogling the woman who has occupied my dreams for the last seven weeks, I am finding it difficult not to go full alpha male. I know that's not me. I'm not this guy who views a woman as a possession, but I have a spark of jealousy. Mitchell and Elliot both got to see her today, and I haven't heard a word.

Through gritted teeth, I say, "Where are we at with this project, gentlemen? I need an update."

Mitchell raises his hand, and if there were more than three of us in the room, I might make him sweat by pretending I don't see him. I nod at him to proceed. My anger—no, I'll call a spade a spade; my jealousy—is making it hard to speak to him right now.

"We've hired a new freelancer who is going to work with some ideas and try to lock down some graphics for us to experiment with. She'll have some mock-ups on Friday."

"Who hired a freelancer?" I already know, but I don't know what else to say.

"Mr. Nicholls thought we needed some fresh eyes, and since Crystal is off on maternity leave, we were short a designer." Elliot rattles off his answer while digging through his own files. "Once this one is done, another project is hitting a wall and could use some new ideas, so this could be good to get us over this block."

"You can't expect one person to come in and save all the ongoing projects from your bad ideas. What's the point of paying you?" My voice hits an unnecessary volume, and my anger—ahem, jealousy—isn't directed at Elliot. *Pull yourself together, Damian.*

He fidgets with his tie before replying, "Of course not, but we've all been looking at the same images, the same tired slogans, the same computer programs for weeks and inspiration hasn't struck. She might be what we need to get things rolling in the right direction."

I stand in front of my two staff members with my eyes closed, trying to get my mind focused on the work at hand. More work for Angel is a good thing, and completing projects is a good thing. This should all be good. Excellent, even. Yet, I can't shake the feeling that it won't be good at all.

The role of a freelancer is to connect with the team or project managers directly. I've never spoken to a freelancer, so if that streak continues, Angel will never know I work here. *That's stupid, Damian. If you keep seeing her, one day she's going to know your company name.* That, of course, wouldn't bother me, but I don't want her thinking I pulled strings to get her a job after I promised I wouldn't. So I have a dilemma. Do I tell her I had no idea and hope she believes me? Or not say a word and hope we don't run into each other?

"Um, Sir?" Elliot clears his throat.

I give my head a shake and open my eyes to find him and Mitchell staring at me. "Sorry, I was running through ideas in my head." About my personal life, but I'll leave that bit out. "So, should we just reconvene Friday? I want to have something to tell Mr. Nicholls before the weekend."

"That would be a better use of our time—"

I cut Elliot off as I collect my things and leave the room. If I stay, I'll say something to Mitchell about interoffice fraternization, which isn't against any policies we have, so that would have raised more questions I don't have an answer to. Why don't I want you to ask out the new freelancer? Um… well… because she's… what is she? I don't even know. We've been on two dates.

My phone vibrates against my thigh from my pocket. My work emails send notifications to my phone, so I'm used to it going off, but I'm hopeful that's not what it is.

Angel: *Back home. Don't want to bug you at work. Everything was fine.*

I stare at her message for a moment, unable to shake the feeling that something is off. Does she know I work here? Did Mitchell say something about me? Her texts are usually funny and quirky. This is dismissive.

Damian: *Everything ok? You don't seem excited.*

Angel: *Lots of work to do by Friday.*

I've never been ditched before, but this must be what it feels like. Payback for stringing along women before.

Damian: *So that's a no to a Thursday date?*

Angel: *It's a probably not.*

Ouch. I'm typing out a reply when another message comes through.

Angel: *Unless you want to come here and give your input so I don't make a fool of myself.*

That message makes me smile and relief flush through my system. Maybe I was being a tad dramatic.

Damian: *Done. I'll bring dinner.*

Angel: *See you tomorrow.*

As smug as it is, the next thing to cross my mind is *take that, Mitchell.*

Since the moment I got home from my meeting with Mitchell, I've been staring at my computer, trying to figure out what kind of image makes hydrogenated oil appealing. Sure, the foods associated with trans fats are delicious, but it's pretty clear they're unhealthy, and making it appear like a sensible choice is part of my brief.

I'm already regretting my decision to pursue this field. I should have at least built up my freelance portfolio and worked on designing book covers and website graphics. Anything that gave me the freedom to accept or reject jobs as necessary.

The pay may be double what I made at the restaurant, even with tips, but I'm at a loss as to how to provide what my contract demands of me without being part of a bald-faced lie. And considering this campaign is mostly being sent to other food manufacturers, not the general public, I'm confused why the graphics are even that important.

I'm so out of my element, and now I've wasted thirty hours of my life stressing over it, with little to show for it. So stressed, for the first time in years, I cry. Why did I even think this was a good idea? I'm not cut out for this.

A knock at my door startles me. Genie goes bolting for the entryway, barking to let her displeasure known, until she sniffs the door and goes silent. I grab my phone, poised to call 911, when I notice a text from Damian fifteen minutes ago saying he was on his way. I completely forgot he was coming.

What choice do I have but to answer the door? I look down at my pyjama shorts and camisole, no bra, and I can't see my hair, but who knows what the condition of that is since I've been grabbing handfuls of it all day. I wipe away my lingering tears with the back of my arm and rush to the door, but not before Damian knocks again and calls my name.

I yank the door open, but I'm bent down to prevent Genie from jumping all over him. When I'm confident she'll behave, I stand, meet his eyes, and the smile he was wearing for a split second disappears.

He steps into my entryway, closing the door behind him and setting the paper bag full of whatever he brought on the floor. "Angel, what's wrong?" He places a hand on each of my arms, holding me at a distance before pulling me in for a hug. "What's wrong? Did something happen?"

I shake my head, trying to set his mind at ease. This is beyond stupid. "I'm so embarrassed right now. Our plans slipped my mind. I haven't even gotten dressed."

He looks hurt by my confession, but seems to get over it when he notices my outfit. "I think what you're wearing is perfect." He smirks, but his serious face returns. "Is everything okay?"

"Just being a baby. I'm not cut out for this whole grown-up job thing. It's harder than it looks."

"You're in tears over your new job?" His body tenses around me. "What's the problem?"

I nod for him to follow me into the kitchen. Beyond crying for two solid hours, I've only eaten a banana the entire day.

"Um, Angel?"

I spin around, covering myself with my arms, though it's a little late for modesty.

"Genie helped herself to our dinner."

I've become so immune to Genie's incessant snorting, I didn't even realize she was chowing down on our food. Any other day, I'd laugh, but today it sparks a new wave of tears. So here I am, standing in my foyer with a successful adult, while I have a meltdown over hydrogenated oil that I was hoping to eat, and that I can't design a graphic for. "Genie, that was bad!"

My dog shows no remorse for her actions. She sits at Damian's feet, sporting her self-satisfied smile.

"It's okay. I'll go grab something else. Do you want to go out instead?"

I wipe the tears from my cheeks again, which is getting annoying, and shake my head. "I can't. This is all overwhelming, and I still have so much to do. Plus, I'm on my period, so everything seems worse than it is." That was not a necessary point to share, but I was on a roll and it spilled out before I could stop it.

Rather than be repulsed, Damian chuckles. "I'll go get something else and grab some chocolate. Then you can tell me about the work issues."

If I were to craft the perfect response to the information I just blurted out, Damian's reply would be it. Food, chocolate, and a listening ear? Yes, please.

"That would be perfect. While you run out, I'm going to get dressed."

"That's a shame." He pulls me in toward him. "I didn't get a proper hello." The moment his lips land on mine, I'm stupefied. Everything else from the day melts away, and all I can feel is how his mouth teases mine. His left hand is wrapped around me, resting on the small of my back, while the other is trying and failing to rake through my hair.

The realization his hand is stuck in my curls breaks the magic of our kiss because I start laughing. "Rookie. You can't run your hand through curly hair when it's dry." I stand still as he untangles his fingers from my locks. "It's like a female praying mantis. You better be careful."

Damian chuckles at my lame joke. "That's better." He kisses the tip of my nose in a gesture that feels so affectionate, I can't do more than blush. "I like hearing your laugh. "He bends down to rustle Genie's head. "You keep her happy while I'm gone, okay?"

When Damian stands to leave, I ask him to wait a second. I rummage through my purse hanging inside my closet and hand him my keys and some cash.

"Angel, I can't take this."

"It's fine. I owe you now since my dog ate the dinner you already paid for. And you can let yourself back in."

He studies the key ring for a moment, paying particular attention to the faded Niagara Falls key chain. "You trust me with your keys?"

"Uh… I already let you in my apartment, so I'm not sure what more you can do with the keys. I trust you."

A subtle droop of his shoulders makes me wonder if there's something he's not telling me—some reason why I shouldn't trust him.

"Is there something you need to tell me?"

"No. Uh… no. I was just thinking if there's anything I can walk to. City traffic."

His awkward laugh creates even more tension in my body, but I'm emotional, exhausted, and hungry, so I let it go for now and plan to address it when he returns with sustenance.

He leaves, so I rush to my ensuite where I glimpse myself in the mirror for the first time, and it's not a pretty sight. My cheeks are blotchy, my eyes are bloodshot and puffy, and my hair looks like it's housing wildlife. I shake off my embarrassment and strip down to have a quick shower, but skip washing my hair because I don't have that kind of time to commit. Once I'm refreshed, I throw on a bra—not underwire, but still better than nothing—and a worn T-shirt from a concert I went to the weekend I turned nineteen. My last choice is between jeans or leggings, and in that scenario, leggings always win. Anyone who says they aren't pants can bite me.

"Angel? Can I come in?"

I rush toward the door to wrangle Genie and give Damian permission to enter, though I thought giving him my keys meant permission was implied. This time, I take the bags from his hands and walk them over to the kitchen counter while he removes his shoes and greets Genie again. She clearly suffers from short-term memory loss.

"I just grabbed Greek food from the place on the corner. I hope that's okay."

"Perfect. Their spanakopita is to die for." I watch as he saunters into the kitchen, but something seems off. "You look like you have a lot on your mind."

"Me? No, I'm just worried about you." He stands on the opposite side of the kitchen peninsula and begins removing takeaway boxes from the paper bags. "Wanna tell me what's going on?"

I'm not convinced that's the problem, but I forge ahead with my explanation. "The company I'm working for is called Harbour Campaigns, and my first gig with them is for a type of cooking oil. They want me to create a sort of press release with some twisted logic implying it's something it's not, and I just can't. But then the thought of telling them I can't is overwhelming, so I was regretting my decision to pursue this. I should just go back to waitressing."

His silence concerns me more than any words could.

27

DAMIAN

Anywhere But Here

When Angel explains to me that her new job—at my company—is bringing her to tears, I'm devastated. I want to step in and tell her she doesn't have to do something she isn't comfortable with, but the logical part of my brain tells me she wouldn't appreciate that kind of overreach or special treatment. The last thing I want is for her to think I pulled any strings to get her the job, because, even though I thought about it, I didn't, and she landed that job on her own merit. That's not an accomplishment I'll cheapen for her. She deserves to feel proud of herself for that, even if she's regretting it.

So, I'm at a crossroads. Which Damian does she need right now? Manager Damian who can make her work worries fade, or guy-she-kisses-sometimes Damian who can try to comfort her and help her through her first professional hurdle?

"Let's eat, then if you want, you can show me what you've got so far, and maybe I can help inspire the right idea. I've heard Greek food and a good make-out session can really get inspiration flowing." I grin at her and she laughs in response, some of the obvious tension leaving her shoulders.

She pulls two plates from the cupboard, along with two wine glasses, then pulls out a bottle of white. "Would the gentleman care for another bottle of grocery store wine?" She holds the bottle over her forearm like a sommelier, obviously trying to suppress her laughter.

"Don't mind if I do; thank you."

That's the end of her act because she passes me the bottle and the corkscrew as she sets the glasses in front of me. She takes the seat at the counter beside me and we dig into our food and wine in virtual silence, minus Genie's snorting.

"I'm such a jerk," she blurts around a mouthful of Greek salad.

"Why are you a jerk?" I study her face, looking for an answer.

"Because you've been here all this time and I haven't even asked how your work is going. I've just complained about mine."

I huff a laugh, a little surprised she drew that conclusion of herself. Then I recall having to refrain from firing Mitchell just because he wants to ask Angel out. "Work is work, I guess. Nothing of note."

"Really? No office gossip or Damian-hating pitchfork mobs?"

I wish that was what I wanted to tell her. I'd happily take on a gang of angry advertising executives over keeping something from Angel; especially knowing she's been nothing but honest with me. But panic takes over, and before I can stop it, my words are spilling out. "So what prompted your promise to never lie?"

She takes another bite of her dinner, chews slowly, then swallows it down with some wine before answering. "I'm surprised it's taken you so long to ask. Most people jump at the chance when they know I'll give an honest answer. But it's not easy to talk about." Her glassy eyes stare down at her plate.

"You don't have to tell me if you don't want to."

"No, you asked." She takes a deep breath before continuing. "My parents got pregnant with me in their last year of college. They weren't married yet, so they had a quick wedding before I was born. Having a kid before getting established wasn't easy, but they made it work. Mom stayed home with me for the first few years, and my dad worked hard to support us. Mom's family is all still in Guyana, and my dad had a tumultuous relationship with his parents, so they didn't really have anyone."

"I'm sure they did their best."

"They did… at least, as far as I can remember. Dina was born three years after me, and we were best friends."

"You still are, aren't you?"

"We are, I guess. She's one of the few people who tolerates me. But our relationship isn't the same as when we were kids. I think she still blames me, but I don't need her to because I blame myself."

I focus on her watery eyes, and it takes serious restraint to keep from pulling her into my chest to comfort her.

"When I was sixteen, my parents were celebrating their seventeenth anniversary. They asked me to watch my sister, but I told them I had plans to sleep at a friend's house. They didn't press me about it and made other arrangements for Dina. I left the house and went directly to my boyfriend's."

"So you snuck out to meet your boyfriend… like half of the teenagers in North America." I try to downplay her actions because nearly every teenager I know has done the same thing plenty of times.

"You don't understand. I was so caught up in my stupid boyfriend, who didn't even care about me. He wanted one thing, and I was too stupid to see it. I was blinded by immature infatuation, so I lied to my parents to see him."

"That's high school lust or love, whatever. I don't think any teenager sees themselves as immature, but most of them are. You can't blame yourself for wanting to experience things."

"Oh, I certainly can. I was obsessed with the guy who probably doesn't remember my name now, so when my phone kept ringing, I ignored it. I couldn't be bothered." Now a tear streams down her cheek, which she swipes away, but seeing it fall physically pains me. "After about fifteen missed calls, my friend, who I claimed I was staying with, started calling me and I knew something was wrong. She knew I was with my boyfriend, so she wouldn't have bothered me if it wasn't important."

I can't stop myself any longer. I reach out, placing my hand on top of hers on her knee. This is hard for her and I regret asking, but I want some insight into her and what makes her tick.

"When I answered, she was crying; I couldn't understand a word she said. I thought *her* boyfriend broke up with her or some other world-ending teen drama, but then she told me my parents were dead."

That's where I was afraid of this story heading. "I'm so sorry."

Her tears are flowing freely, and she's not making any attempt to stop them. She just stopped crying from work stress, and I've opened up old wounds.

"The last thing I said to my parents was a lie. They trusted me and I lied to them. And for what? A stupid boy who would have traded me in an instant, and in fact, *did* when I was busy grieving my parents." She squares her shoulders and wipes her face with the backs of her hands; all traces of vulnerable Angel have vanished. "So I figured my parents named me Angel and I better act like one. If I had been honest with them, maybe they would have made me stay home, or decided not to go out. They might have had the chance to live into old age together. I promised myself from that day I would never tell another lie, and I haven't since."

"You can't put that blame on yourself. You were a kid, doing things that teenagers do. I'm not saying your promise to yourself is a bad thing, but the blame doesn't belong to you." I clear my throat, hesitant to ask the next question, but we've come this far. "How did they die?"

It takes her a moment to tell me any more, and she's pushed her plate of food away. "They used to like taking long drives together. We didn't have a lot of money, so that was their thing to enjoy time with each other, driving through small towns outside of the city. A matter of wrong place, wrong time, landed them on a stretch of road where a group of people were street racing. A car plowed into them, killing my parents and the other driver."

My stomach twists again at hearing how she blames herself. "Don't you see? That's not your fault."

"Maybe not, but I can't stop carrying the blame. And I know Dina blames me."

"I don't know your sister, but I doubt that's true. It was an accident. You weren't the one street racing."

"I may not have been driving, but my stupidity drove them to that spot at that time. There will never be a time I don't blame myself, but being honest is the one thing I will never compromise on for that reason. Hence why this job is turning out to be so difficult."

Mention of her impending workload turns an already depressing mood more sour.

"Eat something, then you can show me what you've got." Even if keeping my involvement to myself feels all kinds of wrong.

We eat our meal, if you can call the little bits Angel picked at eating. She sits at the counter, sipping her wine, silent. I pick up her plate, stack it on mine, and walk around to the sink to wash them.

"Don't worry about those. I'll handle it," she says.

I know she *can* handle it, but it's one more thing I can do to ease my guilt over not telling her I'm technically her department manager. One more thing I can do to delay telling her something that could change our dynamic.

Is omitting the truth as bad as a lie?

28

Hurt

Damian finishes washing the dishes, so I lead him into my office to pull up the images I've been working on to fit the creative brief. Marketing to other businesses rather than consumers is unfamiliar territory and the points I need to hit don't leave a lot in terms of creative freedom. The words are written, and it's my job to make it look intriguing.

I have to be convincing enough with layouts and images that it looks like all of life's unanswered questions come in the form of fat that's solid at room temperature.

"This goes against everything I stand for." I click open the last three images I was fiddling with, showing Damian what I've got so far. The images that have drained thirty hours of my life and countless tears.

"These look great." He leans over my shoulder as I'm seated in my rolling desk chair, his face centimetres from mine.

If I wasn't so stressed about work, I'd kiss him. But beyond work, something feels off between us.

"It's not the images I'm having issues with. It's the words I have to include. How can any company market this as something it's not?"

He heaves a sigh that sounds an awful lot like the noises I've been making in here, then straightens and steps back a few paces. "There are laws in place for advertisements; whatever they've asked you to include, it can't be an outright lie. So if that's what you're worried about, don't."

"It might not be an outright lie, but it's deceitful. It's intentionally misleading, and that's just as bad as a lie."

"Sometimes omitting the full truth is done to protect people from things they don't need to know." He's staring at me with a different intensity and I can't help but feel there is a double meaning to his words. That's something a dishonest person would say to justify their behaviour.

"I disagree. I think people should always be told the truth and be able to decide for themselves."

He leans against the wall beside my small white bookshelf, crossing his ankles. "What would you put on the ad?"

I don't understand where he's going with this. "That's not my department. I'm not supposed to write the copy."

"Maybe they didn't ask you to, but say the client came directly to you and said he was really passionate about marketing this as a health food; what would you offer?"

Sure, this is hypothetical, but I've thought about rewriting this ad many times in the last two days. "I'd say 'It's okay to treat yourself.' Create an ad that doesn't flat out lie, but makes it okay for people to consume in moderation. It's not a matter of making it seem like something it's not. It's a matter of getting people to choose this product over its competitors."

"So do that. Give them a few options with the text they requested, but send them your vision too. Sometimes people get so hyper-focused on a project, it's hard for them to see another option. Give them another option. The worst they can say is no."

On one hand, he's right. They could just need another perspective because I'm not being pressured by the client and, therefore, blinded by their requests. But, the worst they could do is fire me and kill this opportunity before I have a chance to prove myself.

"I'm afraid to overstep. Apparently, the boss is a jerk, so I don't want to upset him. Not on my first project."

I look back at Damian and watch as he scrubs his face with his hands.

"Did someone tell you that? The boss is a jerk?"

I wish my chair could wheel me out of this conversation because it's getting more uncomfortable by the second. Whatever is going on with him, I don't have the energy to sort out today. Not with a deadline looming.

"They didn't say those words, but as soon as they mentioned the boss, everyone seemed terrified. I put two and two together. The one manager didn't disagree with my use of the word ogre."

He crosses his arms over his chest, making him appear really closed off, before meeting my eyes for a second and looking away. "Well, he might not be that bad. People judged Shrek, too. I think you should go for it because you'll never know if you don't try. Weren't you the one telling me to find a job I love? Make this the job you love."

That's easy to say when you have enough disposable income, you can leave thousand dollar tips.

"I can't lose this opportunity, Damian. Companies aren't knocking down my door for my skills. Nowhere else gave me a second look."

Something in him shifts. This entire night he's been weird, but now, he's not acting like the Damian I've enjoyed getting to know.

"I should probably just focus on this. I hate to say it, but..."

"Yeah, I'll get out of your hair."

If he wasn't being so standoffish, I'd laugh, considering he got caught in my hair earlier, but I don't feel like laughing.

"Oh, here." He reaches into his pocket and pulls out a milk chocolate bar, setting it on my desk. "I didn't forget." He leaves the room and walks straight for the front door.

"Damian, wait." I hop up from my chair and rush to where he's standing, slipping his foot into his shoe. "Are we okay? Did I do something wrong?" Deadline or not, if I don't get answers, it's going to eat away at me.

He exhales a long, exaggerated breath. "No, Angel. You're perfect." He leans down, kisses my forehead, then walks out the door.

When I hear the elevator chime, I slump back against the wall. "Well, Genie. I hope you have some inspiration because my last hope at finishing this just left."

Despite what my professional judgement was screaming at me all night, I took Damian's advice and loaded some alternatives onto my thumb drive to present to Mitchell. My stomach is churning as I pick up my badge from the security desk and ascend to the fifth floor.

When the doors open, no one is in the hallway, so I wonder if I'm in the right place. Once I walk toward "the pit", I hear the buzz of activity. I feel like I'm showing up to a party uninvited—if the party was sombre, dull, and intended to age people faster than gravity.

Mitchell greets me as we converge at his office door. "Angel, Hi. Glad you made it. We're going to meet the team manager in the conference room and you can show us what you've come up with." He doesn't wait for me to respond before ducking into his office. He emerges seconds later with a file folder and a laptop. "You ready for this?"

Confident Angel has left the building. "I hate to be cliché, but as ready as I'll ever be."

Mitchell's laugh is barely recognizable as he walks ahead of me. "You'll be fine. This isn't meant to be the final draft. Just sharing the ideas you've come up with. We'll go over what we do and don't like, then go from there. Don't take anything personally."

Why would anyone take criticism of creative work they spent hours pouring their heart into personally? I roll my eyes, grateful he can't see me as I plod along behind him.

I sit at the far side of the long table in the conference room.

A few seconds later, the other man who peeked his head in Mitchell's office two days earlier joins us. "Miss Blake, I'm Elliot Hannon, the team manager. Pleasure to meet you." He leans in to shake my hand, so I stand to greet him properly.

"Thank you for this opportunity, Mr. Hannon."

"Elliot is fine. Some of us try to keep the environment here casual."

Elliot and Mitchell pass a weird, knowing glance between each other, making Mitchell's shoulders shake in silent laughter.

I missed the joke.

Once Mitchell sets up his laptop, he turns it toward me, so I pop in my thumb drive, holding my breath.

"I... came up with a few ideas, so let me know which ones you prefer and I'll go from there." I pull up the mock-ups and turn the laptop to face the only other people in the room.

Their jaws simultaneously go slack, which doesn't ease my nerves one bit.

Mitchell speaks first. "Wow. We can hire you as a copywriter and a graphic designer." His smile widens. "What do you think?" he asks Elliot.

"I think having a fresh set of eyes was exactly what we needed on this. I'm impressed."

"Let's just hope boss-man agrees." Mitchell looks at Elliot again, with the same look as before.

Is this how underlings at all advertising companies view their superiors? Between these two and Damian's experience, I'm wondering if it's an industry standard. But then I lift my eyes to investigate the shadowed form walking past the wall of windows and my eyes lock on Damian. Now it's my turn for my jaw to go slack.

Mitchell clarifies what I'm afraid of. "I guess we can ask him now."

Whoever thought walls of windows were a suitable solution for a corporate building was wrong. Never once have I thought to myself, "Wow, I really love these windows," but I've cursed them several times. Never more so than now.

Angel and I lock eyes as I exit my office where I had drawn my blinds, having known she was coming today. Mitchell told me the meeting was after lunch, so I assumed I'd have time to run to document storage and back before she arrived. Standing here, looking at her with my arms full of manilla folders, I'd say that was a wrong assumption.

My mouth gapes as I try and fail to find the right words to explain my presence. I mentally curse Elliot when he flags me into the room with an obnoxious, flailing arm. No sense in pretending I didn't see him.

I enter the room, sweating under my charcoal suit. Angel is standing next to a laptop, wearing a navy floral pencil skirt, light pink blouse and strappy heels that remind me of our first kiss. The main difference between then and now, aside from the lower heels, is that she's glaring at me with hatred in her eyes.

"Elliot, Mitchell." I nod at them, delaying acknowledging Angel as long as possible. "Angel." I send her a pleading look, hoping she can see the regret in my eyes for not disclosing my role before now.

"You have got to be kidding me," Angel mutters loud enough for all three of us to hear. "If you'll excuse me, gentlemen." She doesn't break eye contact with me as she walks toward the door.

She can't lose this job on my account.

"Angel, wait." I try to grab her arm as she walks past, but she rips it from my hand.

"Don't touch me. You lied to me," she seethes.

I watched her keep her composure when a man groped her and got her fired. The fact she's losing her cool right now tells me I've really screwed up.

"I didn't lie. Please, come to my office and let me explain." I look at Elliot and Mitchell, who are both staring at this office drama I've always tried to avoid.

"No. I trusted you. I confided in you. And it never once occurred to you to tell me you were the boss at my new job? You didn't think I deserved to know? Did you make them hire me?" She raises her arm to point back at Mitchell and Elliot, never taking her eyes off of me.

"This is exactly why I didn't say anything when you told me where you were working. I had no idea you'd been hired, and I had nothing to do with it."

She drops her gaze to look at her feet and it feels like a brick wall assembles between us. "I might have believed that if you'd told me before. I'm not sure I can now." She exhales, causing her shoulders to droop as she turns to address the two silent observers in the room. "Thanks again for the opportunity. I'll leave my badge with security when I leave."

Both Elliot and Mitchell jolt to stand, but I'm already trying to talk Angel out of quitting. I stammer and struggle to find the right thing to say, and my anger with myself is reflected in my words. "You can't leave, Angel. Don't give up on this."

She had stepped past me on her way out the door, so she spins back around, jabbing a blush pink fingernail in my chest. "What 'this' are you talking about, Damian? Oh, sorry, Mr. Taylor. The job or us?"

"I mean—"

"You know what? It doesn't matter. I'm done with both. The one thing I can't handle is dishonesty. You knew..." Tears pool in her eyes and I've never felt like a bigger idiot. "You knew it was important to me. You may not have lied, but you deceived me and withheld the truth. I don't care what you tell yourself to justify that."

There's nothing left for me to say. Not here, anyway. Not in front of an audience of people I'm supposed to maintain an image of professionalism in front of. I can't grovel, begging her to see my reasoning. If I thought getting on my knees and asking for her forgiveness would help right now, I would.

So instead of begging, I stay silent. Hang my head. Absorb her well-deserved anger. Soak in the pitying stares of men who are supposed to respect me. All because I made the wrong call.

I should have just been honest.

When she walks away, it hurts more than anything has since the day my dad left. The man I've spent my life trying to prove to that no job is worth the people you care about.

What a miserable failure I am.

"Make sure she gets paid for the work she did," I say to Elliot before exiting the room to retreat to the safety of my office.

When I knock on the door of my brother's house Saturday afternoon, his wife Lily answers and her facial expression tells me she's as surprised as I am that I ended up here. I couldn't stay in my condo another minute, and when that wasn't enough, I didn't want to be in the city either.

"Damian, hi!" She pulls me in for a hug.

"Hey, Lil. Is he home?"

Lily nods as my nieces, Daisy and Dahlia, come running from the family room, nearly bowling me over with their excited hugs. This is what I need today. To feel loved. To not feel like an utter failure. These little girls never fail to bring a smile to my face, just by existing.

"Girls, let Uncle Damian come in. You have good timing, D. Mom's here, too."

"Seriously? I'm not interrupting anything, am I? I just…"

"Get in here. We're happy to have you." Lily leans in, squeezing me again as a woman who is like a second mother would.

I'm not even out of the foyer, and already the tension I brought with me is melting away. When I enter the family room and see my mom and brother, I feel even lighter. "Surprise."

Josh stands to greet me with a wide smile. "Little brother. What brings you here?"

"I wanted to get out of the city for a bit, so I figured what better place to come than here?"

My mom remains seated, so after a literal bro-hug from Josh, I lean down to embrace my mother and plant a kiss on her cheek.

"What a pleasant surprise. I didn't know you were coming today."

My mom and I sit next to each other on a deep red sectional sofa, leaving room for Lily to sit beside Josh.

"I didn't know I was coming either. It felt like a good family day, I guess."

Daisy climbs on my lap, which she's almost getting too big for, and I take a moment to soak in the pure joy from an eight-year-old child who exudes optimism like a ray of sunshine. I kiss my niece on the top of her head and make conversation with her for a while about school, dance, and her friends. I got suckered into buying three chocolate bars for a fundraiser for new playground equipment. The chocolate reminds me of Angel.

Daisy and Dahlia skip off to do something more exciting than listening to adults talk, and Lily pops up to tend to something in the kitchen.

"Okay, what's going on with you?" My brother, who is the closest thing to a father figure I have, knows me better than anyone.

"Nothing. Why do I need a reason to stop by?" Why am I lying to my brother?

"You don't, but it looks like there is a reason. Don't make me tell mom." Josh has always been a jokester and always made me laugh, but even as I hear Mom giggle beside me, I can't force one out.

"I'm fine. Really."

"Mom, Damian's being difficult!" Josh whines in a childish voice, which does make me laugh. "You show up at my house unannounced, which, believe me, I'm not complaining about, looking like someone kicked your puppy, then deny anything is wrong. I don't buy it."

What did I get from hiding the truth from Angel? I'm an idiot. *Live and learn, Damian.* I glance at my mother, who's sitting as a silent observer with her forehead creased and her hands crossed in her lap. She's ready to listen, so I decide to talk. "Fine. Girl trouble." I shrug, trying to downplay how much this "trouble" is really bothering me.

It takes ten minutes to explain the situation to Mom and Josh, not sparing a detail. They listen to me whine and complain, defend my choices, and question everything I am before Josh responds.

"Your pride is going to keep you from getting everything you want. You're so stuck on proving you're different from your dad, you're missing what's right in front of you. Run your own race. Live your own life. Don't be him."

I look at my mom who hasn't said a thing, but she's one of those people who says things with her face, so words aren't needed. She's thinking about my dad, and I hate that the mere mention of his name still makes her grimace.

"He needs someone to talk some sense into him, Mom."

Mom smirks at Josh. When her eyes settle on me, the look that was there disappears. "You really like this girl." It's a statement. Not a question.

"I do. She's… different."

She reaches over to grab my hand. "Then it seems like a simple solution, don't you think?"

"You didn't see her. I screwed up." I rub my thumb over the back of Mom's hand.

"No. You screwed up from her perspective, but from yours, you made the best decision you could. What she's afraid of, you didn't do. Make sure she knows that."

"You think it's easy to forgive because you're my mom. I doubt she'll even talk to me. At least, not for a while."

"Then send her a letter, Damian! Hire a carrier pigeon, for all I care. A skywriter. A billboard. Do what you have to do to tell *her* she's different. That she's worth it." A single tear trails down Mom's cheek, but she swipes it away with the hand I'm not holding.

I'm not sure if it's my situation or the reminder of hers that's making her so emotional.

"Okay. I will."

Lily lightens the mood by calling everyone for dinner, which I wasn't expecting, but I'm going to enjoy with my family, anyway. While we eat and conversation floats around the table,

I start formulating a plan to prove to Angel that I can be trusted. That honesty will be my only policy from now on.

A night out with Hannah and Vida is exactly what I need. I was employed for less than seventy-two hours, most of which was spent crying over said work, so I'm chalking it off to a lesson learned. I'm not cut out for advertising. Or dating.

As much as I tried to see things from Damian's perspective, I couldn't rationalize how he listened to me mention his company name, stood over my shoulder looking at my work, knowing he would be the one who had to approve it, and he never said a word. I can't even be sure he didn't pull strings to get me that job, and I don't want a job because of preferential treatment. He might not see it, but finding success on my own is one thing that eases the guilt surrounding the deaths of my parents.

I want them to be proud of what I've accomplished by being honest and hardworking. They can't be proud of me for using someone else to get me a job. Whether or not it was intentional.

Hannah's name lights up my phone, so I read her text that they're minutes away in a taxi. We're going to a restaurant and bar near the distillery district with no definitive plans afterward. Anything to get my mind off of Damian. Off of being unemployed. Again.

"Ooooh, Damian who?" Vida squeals as I slide into the open seat in the back of the orange and turquoise Town Car.

The temperature has dropped a little, now that it's late summer, but the girls are still dressed to kill. Hannah is in black shiny leggings and a backless champagne shirt. Vida is wearing an emerald-green bandage skirt with a black long-sleeve blouse. I opted for a black bodycon dress that reaches my knees and an olive army jacket. It was hard to find an outfit that says "approach with caution" but still cute. I'm not in the mood for anyone's nonsense today. I won't hesitate to get banned from another fine establishment in this city.

"Please, let's not say that name again tonight. How are my ladies? How's the job hunt going?"

Hannah shoots me a sour look from the corner of her eye. "I won't say what's-his-name if you don't mention job hunting. Deal?"

"Deal. How are your doggies?"

There's a topic we can all talk about for hours. Vida's Maltese, Cosmo, recently had a spa day, getting his seasonal haircut and bath. I can't imagine having a pure white dog, but that little guy's fur looks better than my hair ninety percent of the time. Maybe I should ask for her groomer's number. Hannah's pug, Akili, is sassy, snorty, and spoiled, much like Genie. We share random dog tales for the fifteen minute cab ride to our location. It's refreshing and starts our night off on a pleasant note.

By the time we arrive, we're all giggling, gushing over our fur babies, and we stumble into someone familiar.

"Alex," Hannah greets. "Since when do you work here?"

Our former hostess looks past Hannah at me, still with an alarming amount of hatred in her eyes. Clearly Alex can hold a grudge.

"About a week. Not that it's any of your business."

What concerns me in this scenario is that she was still working at *Harvest* when we all left, so she was either fired or quit after that, and got another job before the rest of us. How's that for a blow to the ego? She spent ninety percent of her time at *Harvest* picking dirt from under her nails or flirting with customers.

Whatever, I'm not letting it ruin our night.

"Table for three, please." I'm not interested in small talk with one of the many people in the 'hate Angel for telling the truth' club.

She looks down at her restaurant map, probably trying to decide who the worst server is to saddle us with. That doesn't matter either, though. Nothing is going to ruin this night out. After deciding on a spot for us, Alex grabs three menus, leads us through the dimly lit dining room, and places us at a booth right next to the bathrooms. Convenient.

"Thanks, Alex," Vida adds without a hint of sarcasm.

Our conversation picks up where it left off until a server named Brayden comes to take our orders. He's handsome in an obvious way. Like the kind of guy who's working as a server until he makes it as an actor. His wheat blond hair is slicked back and the sides are neatly trimmed. His tanned skin is flawless, making me wonder if he has concealer on because a complexion that even seems impossible.

He walks away after assuring us our drinks will be right over, and Vida fans herself with the dessert menu. She flips it open and studies the pages. "Damn. He's not on the menu."

Hannah and I both crack up laughing because Vida is not the thirsty type—or at least, she never has been before Braydon, the waiter/maybe actor.

"I know we promised not to talk about it, but I'm dying here, Angel," Hannah blurts after our laughter subsides.

Please ask about my job search. *Please* ask about my job search. I stare back at Hannah, doing my best to replicate Akili's effective puppy dog eyes.

"What happened with Damian?"

I close my failed puppy dog eyes, trying to figure out where to start. Hannah knows as well as anyone that once the question is asked, I'll answer.

"That job I got"—I look to my friends for visual confirmation they know what I'm talking about—"it was his company."

Braydon sets our drinks in front of each of us, which gives me something to distract my hands. He takes our food orders and removes the oversized laminated menus.

"Anyway, I was stressed out over a *stupid* ad campaign that I didn't want to be a part of. He came over to my place, basically lied straight to my face, and didn't tell me he was overseeing the *stupid* campaign. Not as the guy I first met with, obviously, who was the project manager, but as the manager's manager's manager. Not a word until he walked past while I was presenting the *stupid* graphics and I ended up standing there like a *stupid* idiot in front of the manager and the manager's manager."

We all sip our drinks in silence for a moment before Hannah chimes in. "So what exactly did he lie about?"

I will my gin and tonic to give me a buzz already, but it's useless. All the eight-dollar wine has increased my tolerance. "He didn't lie, per se."

"Ohhh-kay." Hannah's eyebrows pinch together over the bridge of her nose. "So what *did* he say?"

"It's what he didn't say that's the problem. He knew I needed a job. He said he'd talk to his contacts and put my name out there. I flat out told him not to because I needed to find something on my own. Then when he came over on Thursday, I told him the name of the company, but he didn't even seem surprised, now that I think about it. He had to have known, and he didn't say a word. Then he asked me to show him what I was working on and gave me some advice, knowing he was going to be the one to have the final say." I suck back more of my drink, upset with myself for being so bothered by this.

Vida runs her finger around the rim of her glass. "Do you think he got you the job? Or was it just a coincidence?"

"All the jobs I applied to, no one has called me back. Ever. Does it seem like a coincidence that the one time someone does, it just happens to be the company where the guy I made out with is a department manager? The department they hired me into?"

"So, what's bothering you the most is feeling like you didn't get the job on your own?"

I stare down at the mint leaf floating around my glass. "Yeah, I guess."

Hannah slouches back on the bench seat, wiping sweat from the side of her cocktail glass. "But have you asked Damian if he did get you the job?"

"Why would he keep it a secret if he didn't? That's what doesn't make sense to me. If that was the case and he told me right away, it may have been weird, but I would have believed him. It's the fact he hid it from me, knowing how I felt about it."

Hannah and Vida exchange a knowing look—a scenario I'm really tired of being an outsider on—before Hannah clears her throat. "Angel, I adore you, but for someone who makes a point of being truthful in all she says, you sure shy away from having honest conversations with other people."

Braydon arrives with our meals and offers a refill on my drink. I didn't realize I had finished it on account of my nervous sipping. I oblige.

Once he's out of earshot, I respond to Hannah's claim. "What do you mean? Is it too much to expect people to tell me the truth about things?"

She takes a bite of her food, looking across to Vida, who remains silent. "It's not too much, no. The problem is, you give people an honest answer when *they* ask, but you don't ask." She leans forward, positioning her elbows on either side of her plate. "Take Dina, for example. All these years, you've been assuming she blames you for your parents' death, but have you ever asked her?"

I stare down at my chicken piccata, no longer interested in eating it. "Is there a need to ask when you know the answer? I wouldn't ask you what three plus three is, because it's easy to figure out."

"Three plus three is an absolute. It doesn't change. Even if, once upon a time, Dina did feel angry toward you, emotions aren't absolute. There's such a thing as forgiveness." She takes a dainty bite of her steamed fish and scrunches her nose; must not be up to the chef's standards. "All I'm saying is, don't let your fear of knowing the truth stop you from actually getting it. You might be surprised. And even if you're not, at least you have a definitive answer."

I muddle my remaining mint leaf against the side of my glass with the skewered lime peel.

Has my commitment to the truth made me afraid of it?

Visits with my family are always a mix of conflicting emotions. I'm always happy to see them, but then sad when I have to pull myself away to return to my empty condo. The space always feels lonelier after being around the people I love. The people who have always been there for me and said what I needed to hear, even if they knew I wouldn't want to hear it.

But now, I have a clarity I didn't have before.

I lie in bed, unable to sleep, running through ways I can reach out to Angel and make her understand I wasn't trying to lie to her. I didn't mean to hide the truth, either. A carefully crafted text message is the best option. Assuming she hasn't blocked my number.

Before I can reach my phone on the bedside table, it buzzes against the glass top. It's nearly 2am, so my immediate reaction is panic. People don't call at 2am with good news.

I'm relieved when I look at the screen and see Angel's number, but that sparks a fresh wave of worry.

"Angel?"

"Why didn't you tell me?" she slurs. There's commotion in the background—traffic and muffled voices. She's not at home, and by the sounds of it, she's drunk.

"Where are you? I can come get you."

"I don't need you to come get me. I just need answers."

"Angel—"

"Don't say my name like that." She sniffles. I'm hoping it's from allergies and not because my stupidity reduced her to tears. Maybe she's an emotional drunk.

"Like what?"

"Like *that. Angel.*" She impersonates my voice, which makes me laugh. "It's not funny. I... I like when you say it, and I don't wanna like you right now." No, she's an angry drunk.

"Angel." I can't help myself.

She exhales and the sounds behind her get quieter. "Damian. I need the truth."

"I'll tell you everything you want to know, but not while you're drunk. Tomorrow."

"Okay."

I'm afraid she's going to hang up and I'm not ready for that. "Wait. Where are you?"

"Walking into my condo." Her keys jingle for a second in the background, then I hear a door open and the sound of Genie scurrying across the floor.

I breathe a sigh of relief. "Okay. Do you have to take Genie out? Want me to stay on the phone with you?"

She groans. "I forgot about that. No, it's fine. I'm a big girl."

No, she's a woman who turned my world upside down and I can't turn it back. Nor do I want to. "I'll be here if you need me." Those words are loaded with hidden context.

"Good night, Damian."

She ends the call, and instead of sleeping, like I should, I decide how I'll prove to her she's different. That she's important to me. And that she's earned her place at *Harbour Campaigns*, every step of the way.

By 11am, I still haven't heard from Angel, and I start to worry she was drunk enough that she doesn't remember our conversation. I'll give her another hour because she's probably hungover and sleeping in. That's what I keep repeating to myself as I pace my kitchen, drinking an inhuman amount of coffee, anyway.

At 11:29, my phone rings. I dash for it like an Olympic sprinter, reaching the kitchen counter in under two seconds. Just shy of a world record pace.

"Hello."

"Hey." She doesn't sound excited, but she's not slurring. Though it's hard to slur one syllable.

"How are you feeling?"

Silence.

"Angel?"

"Stupid. I'm feeling stupid."

I'll take that as a sign she remembers our conversation from last night. "Can I pick you up so we can talk?"

She's silent again, but I can hear her breathing. "I haven't gotten out of bed yet. It will take me a bit to make myself presentable."

I picture her lying in bed in the pyjamas she was wearing on Thursday. Even hungover, I can't imagine her being anything other than perfect. "One o'clock?"

"Yeah. Okay. I'll be ready."

I got myself ready with a stealth and efficiency I never have before. My conversation with Angel requires privacy and vulnerability, so I'm going to bring her to my place, hoping she'll see it as me opening up to her and not think I have ulterior motives. I pick up some Chinese food on the way, but when I pull into her parking lot, I find her spot occupied again with a different car.

A sick feeling grows in my stomach, laced with confusion. If she had company, or she brought someone else home last night, why would she have called me? That doesn't make sense.

I pull over in a guest parking spot and dial Angel's number. "Hey."

"Uh... I'm here. Your parking spot is occupied."

"Oh, yeah. Sorry. I'll be right down."

Before she hangs up, I add, "Bring Genie."

Angel chuckles, and it might mean nothing, but it's a small step toward her not hating me.

She exits the building a few minutes later, Genie leading the way. The little bulldozer wags her entire body when she sees me. I missed her smiling face. Both of them... but one out of two doesn't look as happy.

As much as I want to kiss Angel, I don't. I'll respect her space until she gets the answers she's looking for. Genie hops in the back when I open the door and makes herself comfortable in her seat hammock.

I explain my plan, giving Angel a chance to protest. She doesn't, so we travel fifteen minutes to my building. We're getting close when she laughs out of nowhere.

"What's funny?"

"The bar I went to last night is right around the corner."

"*Dizzy Dragon*?"

She turns her head to look at me, leaning against the door. "How would you know that?"

"That's the only decent one around. I go there for dinner sometimes." I want to approach the mystery car situation, but don't want to offend her before we have a chance to clear the air. I go for it anyway. "Did you get a car?" I press the button to open the garage door for my underground parking.

"No. Ever since I bought that place, I listed the parking spot for rent for extra income. One of the other units had a visitor for the weekend, so they asked to rent it."

That's actually genius.

"You're an entrepreneur."

"Yeah, well, at this point, it's my only income."

"Angel—"

She holds up a hand and closes her eyes. "Let's just talk inside. I hate trying to have a serious conversation when someone is focused on something else at the same time."

I nod, park the car, then lead her and Genie to the elevator door. We arrive on the forty-fourth floor, and the U-shaped hallway has only five doors. Four corner units and a garbage chute. I unlock my door, and Angel walks inside, spinning in circles as she takes everything in. It's not a huge condo, but the large windows and outdoor spaces make it feel open.

"Wow. This is beautiful."

I never know how to reply to that. I didn't build it or decorate it. My money paid for it, but that seems like a stupid thing to take credit for. I settle on, "Thanks."

Genie welcomes herself, walking from one piece of furniture to the next, sniffing things as she goes. Having her here makes it feel more like a home and not just somewhere I sleep and sometimes eat.

I set the paper bag of takeout on the table, but notice Angel staring out at the largest balcony off of the living room. "Do you want to eat out there?"

She glances over her shoulder with a stunning smile. "Please."

Easy decision. There's nothing she could ask for that I wouldn't give her right now. The only things she wants are to eat outside and the truth. No brainer.

I grab plates, utensils, and the food, then Angel slides the door open to the balcony since my hands are full. I place everything on the patio table, but instead of sitting at the chair to eat, she walks to the plexi-glass railing and gazes out over the panoramic view of the CN Tower and Lake Ontario. The view is one reason I bought on this level and not higher up. This was the only unit on the southwest corner available. I don't regret my choice, but over time, the view has lost its wow factor. That is, until I see it for the first time with Angel in the foreground. I couldn't dream up a more beautiful image.

I watch her peering out at the water. The people. The birds flying below. The rat race that's so easy to get caught up in, it can be hard to slow down and appreciate these moments. She shivers and I realize the breeze up here is a lot harsher than at street level. She's so distracted by the view, I don't think she notices me going back inside.

"Here." I hand her the rumpled fabric when I return a minute later.

She holds it out in front of her. My worn university hoodie is the smallest article of clothing I have. It's also my favourite.

"Thanks." She slides it on over her navy knit sweater and I stifle a laugh, watching as she tries to force her hair through the neck hole.

I step forward to help. When her head finally emerges, her cheeks are flush, and she looks flustered. She looks... kissable. But there's something I owe her first.

I really thought he was going to kiss me, and I didn't hate the idea. As much as I try to stay upset with him, I can't. I've always been the type of person who doesn't give second chances. Never forgive easily. Certainly don't forget. With my own mistakes more than anyone. But with Damian, I want to hear his side of the story. I may have told myself that the matter is black and white, and his answer will determine whether I offer a second chance or leave to lick my wounds, but I'm not sure it's going to be that simple.

He may have heard me say I didn't want his help in getting a job, but he doesn't understand why that was so important to me. If he tried to help, is that really a bad thing? It all seems so foolish now.

"We should talk." Damian gestures toward a chair at the end of the table.

I scan the massive balcony to see where Genie is, and she's off sniffing empty plant pots in the interior corner. "Yeah. Can we eat? I'm starving."

He laughs and walks over to pull out a chair for me. I sit, but before he does, he asks, "Want a mimosa or something? Hair of the Dog?"

I roll my eyes. "No, thank you. I'm never touching alcohol again."

"That bad, huh?"

"I've heard far worse drunk dialling stories, so I guess not the worst-case scenario, but I'm still embarrassed. Not to mention, my time here today is basically sponsored by *Tylenol*."

He slides into his chair, twirling a fork in his left hand. "I'm glad you drunk dialled me."

"Who said you're the only one I called?" I try to get a rise from him, but I can't stop the smirk from spreading on my face.

"Angel." He says my name the same gentle way he did last night. The way that makes it sound like everything is right in the world. Like he'll do anything to undo what happened. "I'm sorry."

That's a good start. "I know. Me too, if that matters." I half-stand to pull the containers of food from the bag.

"You have nothing to be sorry for. You've always been honest with me and I should have extended you the same courtesy. But please believe me when I say I had nothing to do with hiring you. I didn't know anything about it until after your first meeting with Mitchell, and even then, I only found out because I heard him talking about you."

I watch his eyes and facial expression as he explains his side of the story, and I don't detect anything deceitful. "He was talking about me?"

He looks straight up as he jerks his head back a few inches. "Mitchell thinks you're hot. He wants to ask you out."

That makes me laugh. A full cackle. I'm surprised birds don't scatter, thinking I'm a predator—a vulture or something. That may have been my opportunity to get a rise out of him after all, but I decide to set the record straight. "Mitchell's not my type."

"Is that so? What's your type?" The left side of his lips lift in an irresistible smirk.

Maybe I will toy with him. "Dark skin, short, baby face, long hair. Maybe a Middle-Eastern prince or something. Or a nepotistic son of an oil tycoon. Someone with no ambition beyond spending money they did nothing to earn." That was tough to get out. It's been a long time since I said an outright lie and it feels weird, even dripping with sarcasm.

"That's too bad for Mitchell, then." Damian's smirk turns into an irresistible smile. "Anyway, I heard them talking about you, so I asked about the new freelancer. It didn't take a genius to figure it out. I've never interacted with a freelancer before. Normally they connect over video conference or email, so I thought it would be safe to stay out of it and let you focus on the work, not on me being the boss. I didn't want that to come between us."

There's so much remorse in his face, I feel bad for overreacting. I should have listened to him.

Hannah is right. I do shy away from the truth. Has my relationship with Dina suffered because I was too stubborn to see her perspective? All this time, I felt like my honesty was driving people away, but maybe it was my refusal to ask for their truths.

"I'm sorry for how I acted. It was really unprofessional, but beyond that, it was just a crappy way to treat you. I just... Not to make excuses, because it's totally on me, but I'm determined to make my parents proud of me. Even if they can't see me, believing that they'd be proud has been a driving force in my life. Accepting a job because someone else used their position to get it for me... that didn't sit right with me. I was afraid they wouldn't be proud."

He finishes chewing a bit of fried rice, then wipes his mouth with a napkin. "Angel... I wouldn't go behind your back like that. I know it was stupid of me to not say anything, but it won't happen again." He sets the napkin on the table, not breaking eye contact. "If you'll let me prove it to you."

I nod, giving him a closed-mouth smile because I'm chewing an egg roll. That's all that needs to be said about the situation.

The rest of our meal passes with laughter, light conversation, and Damian sneaking Genie pieces of food, thinking I didn't notice. I'll let that slide because I love seeing them bond.

Damian takes the dishes inside while I stay on the balcony, soaking in the magnificent view. For all the chaos and stress that happens within these city limits, from up this high, it seems like a well-choreographed dance, timed in sync with the rhythm of street lights and honking horns. The waves crash against the harbour front at a steady pace, and if you listen hard enough, you can hear the water over the unrelenting wind.

When enough time has passed, I head back inside, hoping Damian is finished with cleanup, and find Genie washing a plate, chasing it around the floor. Damian looks at me with a grimace. I can't help but laugh.

"She has you figured out."

He dries his hand on a dish towel hanging from the stove, then walks toward me. "I can't say no to her smile. So, what now?"

With Damian standing inches away, all I want to do is say the things that can't be said. I stand on my tippy toes, grab two handfuls of his shirt, and pull his face to my level. The second I feel his lips on mine, all rational thought flees my mind. My self-control vanishes. Part of me expected him to hesitate or pull away, but it only takes him a split second to seize control.

He walks me backwards until my calves hit the edge of the couch and he eases me down without breaking his lips' contact with mine. I don't let go of his shirt. He's smooth and gentle, but at the same time, our kiss feels raw and passionate, as if it's saying everything we should have said so much sooner. I'm sorry. He's sorry. I can trust him.

Can I trust him enough to have my heart? Time will tell, but I don't think my heart is giving me a choice.

His body is hovering over mine and this could get out of hand quickly. Before it does, Damian pulls his head back, panting. Even though his body is pressing against me, the absence of his kiss makes me miss him with every cell of my body.

"They would be proud of you." He holds his face over mine, giving me a chance to absorb his words.

My hands release the fabric they were clenching and fall to my sides. My chest is heaving, but now, all I can think about is my parents. About how the last time I got this absorbed in a guy, the worst day of my life happened. Then, as I picked up the pieces, he tossed me aside and moved on. I know sixteen-year-old boys and Damian aren't in the same category, but it still gives me reason to slow things down. I shimmy myself out from underneath Damian, so he lifts himself to allow me up.

"Sorry if I killed the mood. I just realized I hadn't said that earlier." He sits on the off-white sofa, leaving a few inches between us.

"No, it's fine. I just got a little freaked out."

He reaches his hand over to hold mine. "What are you freaked out about?"

"All of this. Us. Giving my heart to someone else after it's been locked up for so long. I'm afraid you'll get tired of me because, trust me, everyone does eventually. Before this goes anywhere, I need you to understand, I'll never compromise who I am, so if that's going to bother you someday, it's better for both of us if you tell me now." Wow, sometimes the things I spew out even catch me off guard.

"Can I tell you a secret?" He leans over, bumping my shoulder with his. He's smiling, but there's something more in his expression.

"Please don't tell me you're a convicted felon."

His smile morphs into a laugh, deepening the lines around his eyes. He's beautiful when he laughs. "No. I mean, if I was caught for some stuff I did as a teenager, I guess I could be, but no." He tilts his head so his lips are near my ear and whispers, "I really like you, Angel, and I can't imagine that ever changing."

It's hard for me to imagine his feelings toward me *not* changing. Some couples grow closer over time, whereas others drift apart. Resent each other. Regret giving someone else time they can never get back. There's no guarantee that this is going to end well.

Yet, I'm still willing to try because there's also no guarantee it will end at all.

Then Damian lobs more surprising words at me. "Will you come back to work on Tuesday?"

33

DAMIAN

Masochist

I cannot explain why I thought interrupting whatever she was thinking about with mention of work was a solid plan. Her reaction confirms it was a stupid idea, but I promised to be honest going forward, so I rush to explain. "Now that you know you were hired on your own, there's no reason for you not to take the job. I can be objective and keep work separate."

"Damian. The way I left the other day… people will talk." Her shoulders slump as she exhales a long breath. "I don't think it's possible to redeem myself."

"They already hate me. You can tell them whatever you want."

She turns her head to stare into my eyes. "I wouldn't tell them anything but the—"

"Truth."

The weak smile she flashes gives me some hope that she's considering it.

"You deserve this job. But if Mitchell hits on you, I'm firing him."

Her smile turns into a snort-laugh, which is apparently Genie's signal to join in. She jumps up between us, snorting and licking faces.

For the first time in the three years I've lived in this space, it feels like home.

Tuesday at work doesn't feel as daunting. That could have something to do with having a long weekend and spending yesterday with Angel and Genie, but I'm more inclined to think it's because she's coming into the office today.

I've tried to avoid the angry glares of some employees, but a few were intense enough I felt them without needing to see. I'm not sure what they think I did to Angel—obviously something worse than what actually happened. Or maybe I'm imagining it and their glares are the same as they've always been. The same looks that told me I was public enemy number one from the first day I moved into the corner office.

I haven't done much to change that perception of me.

Paxton buzzes through the intercom to tell me Angel is here. She's supposed to meet Mitchell and Elliot in fifteen minutes, so I wasn't expecting to see her until after.

"Send her in, thanks."

Angel walks through the door wearing that same pink sweater she wore when we walked along the waterfront. She looks innocent and sweet, but I know she has a hidden fire behind her dark eyes. "Am I interrupting?"

I stand and walk around my desk, wanting nothing more than to hold her in my arms. I promised we'd separate work life from our relationship, though. "No, not at all. What can I help you with, Miss Blake?" I lean back against the desk with my arms crossed so I can stop them from wrapping around her.

She tucks a rogue curl behind her ear from her position just inside the wide-open door. "Is this okay? Me being here? It's weird, isn't it?"

The temptation is intensifying, but I have to keep these work boundaries intact. Otherwise, she'll feel even more weird.

"We talked about this. It's fine with me."

"Yeah, you said that. But do you mean *fine* fine, or does this really not bother you?"

I push myself from the desk and walk toward Angel, stopping two feet away. Just within arms' reach. "You're really *fine* fine, and I'm happy you're back."

The trepidation she was wearing disappears as a smile spreads across her lips. "Okay. I'm trusting you to tell me if things get weird, okay? I can find another job."

"We'll keep work at work. But after work…"

A throat clears from behind Angel, making her jump. I look up to see Mitchell leaning against the doorframe.

"Sorry to interrupt. Are you joining us today, boss?"

I shake my head. "Just tying up some loose ends before Miss Blake comes in to save your project." Why do I sound so petty? This isn't me. I keep saying it's not me, but then it keeps *being* me. I'm not this guy. "Let me know if you have any issues you need my input on, but otherwise, I'll trust you all to get the project completed by the deadline."

"Will do." Mitchell waves his hand to have Angel follow him.

Before she leaves, she shoots me a wink, and it's pathetic, but that blinking brown eye is going to replay in my head for the rest of the day.

※

Angel's time at the office is short and without issue. I'm not sure what she said to everyone else, but it appears she's won them over. The earlier tension and angry stares have diminished somewhat. I'll take it. At least I haven't gone further in the opposite direction again.

My email pings, notifying me of another message, which feels like one more thing to add to my to-do list. This one, however, isn't business related.

It's from Jacob Taylor. The man formerly known as my father. The man who married my mother, insisted on creating a family, then disappeared without a word for twenty-one years. I stare at my computer screen for long enough, my eyeballs feel dry by the time I blink. My mind is reeling as my mouse hovers over his name, begging to be clicked.

No.

Whatever he has to say now, I'm not interested. I drag the email to my trash folder, irritated by the "Please read" subject line. If he found my email address, he could have found my phone number or work address just the same. Emailing is a coward's way of saying whatever he wants to, but that's what I'd expect from the coward I share half of my DNA with.

A knock at my open door draws my attention. "What?" My shoulders slump as soon as the word comes out. I look up to find Mrs. Brady from the accounting department. "I'm sorry, Tara. What can I help you with?"

"Have I caught you at a bad time? I didn't mean to intrude."

"Not at all. You just caught me wrapping up a… personal matter."

"Ugh. You know what helps with those?"

I raise an eyebrow, surprised by her forwardness. A stark contrast from other employees here. "What's that?"

She responds as she walks toward my desk. "Whisky. A good top shelf bourbon and some peace and quiet. There's nothing you can't sort out with that combination."

I resist the urge to smirk as she drops into the seat opposite me. "I'll take that under advisement. What can I do for you?"

She slaps a manilla folder on the desk. "There are a lot of miscellaneous expenses in this report from one of your teams. I can justify a few, but when half the budget is marked as miscellaneous, I feel more like a mafia bookkeeper than a reputable ad agency. If you catch my drift."

"Caught it." I open the folder to look at the expenses, immediately spotting the error. "We had a freelancer do work on multiple projects. Somehow the entire cost was added into this account under miscellaneous rather than being split. I'll sort it and get this back to you by the end of the day."

"Don't rush. I'm leaving early today. I've had it up to my eyeballs with dollars and cents. If I don't get out soon, I'm liable to burn this place to the ground just for a day off."

My instinct is to laugh, but Tara's face is determined and resolute. I can't tell if she's kidding.

"Right. Well, I'll speak to the team managers and get it sorted ASAP. Anything else?"

Tara releases a grumbling sigh as she stands, using both armrests to push herself up. "No, that's it for now. I'll let you know if anyone else makes any major screw-ups." She turns to walk to the door, stopping just short. "You know, you're not as bad as everyone says."

I'm not sure how to respond to that. Can I ask her what people are saying about me? No. No one wants to be the rat. "Uh. Thanks, I guess."

She exits my office right as my phone chimes. A sickening feeling makes my stomach tighten. If it's another email from Jacob, the man I've spent my life trying to prove wrong, I'm going to need some of that whisky Tara mentioned.

My nausea disappears as soon as I look at my phone and see Angel's name lit up with a photo of her and Genie I snapped yesterday.

Angel: *How awkward was it when I left?*

I chuckle at her message because my encounter with Tara was a little awkward—and concerning—but there's been no awkwardness surrounding Angel's return. Still, I decide to play with her.

Damian: *It's torture. Had to listen to Mitchell talk about how hot you are for twenty minutes. So I fired him. Report to me tomorrow.*

My phone rings no more than twenty seconds later.

"Hello."

"Damian Taylor, you better be joking with me."

So much for my attempt at a prank. I laugh, unable to control it after hearing the indignation in Angel's voice.

"Yes, I'm joking. I haven't even seen anyone from your team since before you left. How did it go?"

"Fine. Well… yeah. Fine. They're using some of my copy suggestions, which was surprising, but the rest has to be truthful enough to comply with industry standards, right? So I'm trying to focus on what they asked me to do." She exhales, which makes me think her words and her feelings are not in alignment. It makes me worry she's already compromising her promise to herself after a few days in this industry.

"Do you want me to—"

"Don't even think about it. I'm serious, Damian. I was just answering your question. You don't have to swoop in and save me. Got it?"

"Yes, Ma'am." My mood shifts as the infuriating memory of an email from my estranged father resurfaces. Angel has been so open with me, but I haven't explained to her about my past. About the things that have shaped me. Maybe before I can tell her about the broken parts of my past, I should share the whole parts of my present. "Are you free this weekend?"

Damian pulls into my parking lot, stopping a few feet away from where I'm standing. He was cryptic about where we're going, only telling me to dress in comfortable clothing.

I slide into the leather seat, leaning over to greet him with a kiss. Tuesday was the last day I went into the office, and since then, we've both been so busy, we've barely seen each other. Our nighttime phone calls aren't as enjoyable as his physical presence.

He pulls my head toward him, taking full advantage of the proximity a phone call can never offer. "Hey."

"Where are you taking me?"

The corners of his mouth drop, which tells me he's not taking me to *Wonderland.* "It's about an hour-long drive. Just... trust me, okay?"

I squeeze his hand and lean back to buckle my seatbelt. "Okay."

He pulls onto Euclid Avenue with a smile, and we fall into casual conversation as we travel north out of the city. I stopped trying to guess where we were headed as soon as we got on the highway, because I haven't been outside of city limits for years. A downfall of not having a car at my disposal. Or a license.

Forty minutes later, we take an exit off of Highway 400 that looks like it leads to an outlet mall in one direction and nowhere in the other. He turns left toward nowhere. I soon discover there are a couple of little towns along this road, so instead of questioning Damian for answers, I soak in the scenery and study each adorable storefront we pass.

It's another twenty minutes before we pull onto a residential street, and Damian slows in front of an orange brick house. It's a cute suburban neighbourhood. There's a short man being pulled down the sidewalk at a forty-five-degree angle by his Dogue de Bordeaux, making me giggle. Kids are playing in the front yard of another house, while an old lady with curly white hair glares at them from the end of her driveway. I've lived in the city my entire life, but this is almost exactly how I would have pictured suburbia.

"Why are we here?"

Damian blows out a breath as he shuts off his car. "I want you to meet my family."

"What? Damian! A little warning would have been nice. I would have tried to look presentable. I thought we were going mini-golfing or something."

"Your outfit doesn't make a difference, Angel. This is a casual visit; you being comfortable is important." He reaches his hand out to squeeze mine on top of the centre console. "They're going to love you."

It's too late to turn back now. I'm assuming he told them we were coming and if we don't go inside, it's not going to take a genius to figure out it was because of me. That doesn't bode well for future meetings. "I wish you had told me. I realize that your family is important to you, but it's been so long since I was part of a family dynamic, I'm not sure how to navigate it anymore."

Damian's lips turn downward and the bit of excitement he was showing disappears from his eyes. "I'm sorry. Just come with me. You'll see it's nothing to be nervous about." He squeezes my hand again. "Come on." He exits the car and walks around to my side to meet me along the curb. "Ready?"

"No."

He chuckles. "Let's go."

We walk up a few stairs onto a porch and knock on a white door. I hear young kids and a man's voice from inside the home.

It swings wide open and we're greeted by a brunette man who is several inches shorter than Damian, with two blonde girls standing behind him. "You must be Angel. Come in."

Damian steps in first, holding my hand to pull me inside behind him. "Angel, this is my brother, Josh. These munchkins are Dahlia and Daisy." He rustles the hair of the taller girl, making her shriek and giggle.

"Thank you for having me." I peek around Damian, already feeling blush intensifying on my cheeks.

Two women come strolling toward us, each wearing a wide smile.

The older woman with auburn hair speaks first. "Angel, it's lovely to meet you." She stops inches in front of me, pulling me in for a tight hug. It takes a few seconds for me to relax enough to accept it. It's been a long time since I felt motherly affection. Eight years long.

"I'm Laura, Damian's mom."

Once everyone has been welcomed and hugged, Josh leads us through their modest, but clean and well-decorated home toward a family room with a big red sectional sofa. Laura pats the cushion beside her for me to sit down. In all the years since my parents died, I missed out on having a maternal figure show any concern for me. This is foreign and makes me nervous.

"Don't grill her, Ma," Damian says as he sits on the opposite end of the L-shaped sofa from his mother.

I park myself beside Laura as Josh plops down between Damian and I. The girls seat themselves on the floor, and Lily has taken a detour, so I'm not sure where she is.

"I do not grill, Damian. The only thing I'm concerned about is getting to know this young lady who has made my son happy."

Heat creeps up my cheeks, and when I look at Damian, he is suffering the same affliction. He has the added camouflage of facial hair, but it's still noticeable.

"So, tell me about yourself. Damian has been pretty tight-lipped with details." Laura gives Damian a look, but it doesn't flash disappointment or upset. It's more of an understanding, supportive glance.

"There aren't many exciting details to share. I spend most of my time working or with my dog. Actually, most of my time is spent doing both things at once because I work from home." I let out a nervous laugh when I notice the two young girls staring at me with rapt attention.

"You're pretty." Daisy gets up from her spot on a floor cushion and climbs onto my lap.

I haven't been around kids since sixteen-year-old me babysat a few times. This is another reason I'm out of my element here, but I try my best to be friendly. "Not as pretty as you or your sister."

"I like your hair. I wish my hair was curly. It looks like a lion's mane."

Um. That could be taken as an insult, but I'll choose to focus on how regal and powerful lions are. "Thank you. I like your straight hair." I run my hand over her smooth blonde ponytail as she sways it back and forth.

The adults in the room take charge of the discussion again and we fall into comfortable conversation, where I explain little bits about myself. I wasn't kidding when I said there aren't many exciting details, but everyone else contributes random factoids about themselves, so it doesn't feel like I'm under a spotlight.

That is, until Laura asks, "Where did you and your sister go after your parents passed?"

I had hoped with the pace of our conversation, the brief mention of my parents dying when I was a teenager was enough to disclose for one day. Damian hasn't even approached this topic with me. When I make eye contact with Laura, she looks apologetic, but I don't want her harbouring any guilt over asking her son's *whatever I am* a simple question.

The answer isn't always simple, but I try to keep it that way. "My dad's sister took us in. We were able to stay in our house until Dina turned seventeen. Then we agreed to sell our family home and moved into the condo where I am now."

"Oh, darling, I'm so sorry. That's nice your aunt was able to take you in, though."

"Not really." Another nervous laugh escapes my lips before I can rein it in. "Sorry. That was rude, but it wasn't nice." This is an instance of my honesty being off-putting to people who aren't familiar with the random truth blurting. Normal people would have said it *was* nice and moved on.

"I... well, I'm sorry for... we know all about uncomfortable family dynamics."

"Why don't we go see if dinner is ready?" Josh pops up from the couch and interrupts what was surely to become an even more uncomfortable conversation.

I lock eyes with Damian and note his troubled expression.

"Excuse me. I'm going to see if I can help bring food to the table or something. Might as well flex my waitressing muscles." I slide off the sofa and follow the direction Josh went, off to the left.

Lily is buzzing around the galley kitchen in a fury that would make Hannah proud. She's got an entire station set up with different items, and I like what I see. Josh has taken up position at the sink, washing a large pot. Neither of them notice me.

"Can I help you guys with anything?"

"Oh, no. That's so nice of you, but we've got it under control. We're doing a DIY taco station, so I'm just finishing up everything." She stops what she's doing and sweeps her fine blonde hair off of her face with the back of her hand. When it doesn't cooperate, she blows it back with a twisted lower lip. "I'm sorry. Can I get you anything? I've been a terrible hostess trying to get everything ready."

"No, no. Not at all. I've been well taken care of. I'd just like to help if you have any jobs for me to do. Many hands make light work." I offer a meek smile. "Plus, I'm kind of running away from a conversation I'd rather not have, so you'd be doing me a solid."

Lily chuckles and passes me a large serving tray with cooked chicken breasts. "Say no more. Can you shred chicken?"

"Better than any guitar I've ever touched." My lame joke earns me another laugh from Josh and Lily. I breathe a relieved sigh and shred chicken like I've never shredded before.

As I stand next to people who are clearly comfortable in their family dynamic, I realize it doesn't feel as distant as I thought. I remember these simple moments with my family, and it's nice to be around one again—even if it's only for a day.

Ten seconds after Angel leaves the family room, I am inclined to go after her, but my mom stops me.

"I'm so sorry if I overstepped. Do you think she's okay? I'll apologize, but I want to give her a moment."

When Angel answered my mother's innocent question, her entire body tensed. I could tell she didn't want to dive into it, but in true Angel fashion, she did. Her response left me with more questions, though, and I can't ask her about them here because she'll feel obligated to answer. I don't want her to think I resent her for her honesty, but I don't want her thinking I take advantage of it either, probing for answers she isn't ready to share.

I spend a few minutes explaining the abbreviated version of Angel's promise to herself and why the death of her parents impacted her so much. My mom's reaction was much the same as mine, concluding that it wasn't Angel's fault.

After our hushed conversation, I enter the kitchen to find Lily and Angel giggling together at the counter while Josh stands against the opposite counter with his arms and ankles crossed and a wild grin on his face.

"Our girls have bonded over tacos, little brother." Josh waves me into the kitchen.

As soon as he says tacos, I think back to Angel's expression as she devoured the food truck fares we ate on the night of our first date. A memory that will be imprinted in my mind forever. Her eating tacos surrounded by the people I love seems like a fantasy. A weird one, but still.

Lily and Angel become fast friends, and after a sincere apology from my mother, Angel brushes off the earlier discomfort, telling Mom she has nothing to be sorry for. After hearing about Angel's pact with herself, my mom beams over Angel's willingness to overlook her detour down an unfortunate line of questioning.

Over dinner, everyone buzzes around in a flurry of activity, filling their plates, then rushing back to the kitchen to refill with a new combination someone else gushed over. Angel seems to be the resident expert, but Lily could give her a run for her money.

When it's time for us to leave, everyone looks gutted that I'm tearing Angel away from them. They never get this upset when I leave, but I won't take offence. She is pretty incredible to be around. With strict instructions to bring her back for another visit soon, we say our goodbyes and walk back to my car.

It's hard to gauge Angel's reaction to meeting my family. From my perspective, everything went well. The only reason I don't want to know is because she's sitting in the passenger seat, not saying a word, and it's making me question every one of the 240 minutes we spent in the Miller house.

As I pull onto Highway 400, headed toward home, Angel breaks the silence after twenty painful minutes. "Will you tell me about what happened with your dad?"

I blow out a long breath and focus on the road ahead. Literally and figuratively. "Yeah. I've wanted to explain for a long time, but it never felt like the right time." I pause for a second. "Will you tell me about your aunt?"

I can't see her expression, but I can almost sense the tension in the vehicle.

"There is never a right time to bring up things that hurt. You just have to get it out, so I'll explain what I can."

"Okay, I'll go first. Rip off the Band-Aid." With the radio playing an unrecognizable top-forty pop ballad in the background, I dive into the time of my life that shaped not only me, but my mom and brother as well. "Have you ever heard the saying 'it was fine until it wasn't'?"

"Not that I recall, but I get the gist."

"That was my childhood. Everything was fine until one day it wasn't. From my perspective, my parents got along well; they were happy. My father wasn't home a lot—he was a venture capitalist, travelling the world to invest in start-up businesses or takeover failing ones. But when he *was* home, he was present. Taught me how to play catch, ride a bike, that kind of stuff." I grind my teeth after saying that because it almost sounds like I'm defending him. Like he had a single lapse in judgement that changed the course of all our lives. "Anyway, one day he came home from a work trip and told my mom he wanted a divorce. No questions of clarification. No chance to try counselling or effort to make things work. He just left."

"Wow. I gathered they had a messy divorce or something."

"No. There was no mess. He didn't want our family. He wanted his job and said he was leaving to pursue his career goals." Saying those words out loud makes me feel even more pathetic than they did when I was a kid. All the nights I cried in my room because I wasn't enough for my dad to love me. Instead of healing over time, I grew more resentful. "He emailed me the other day."

"Really? Out of the blue? What did he say?"

The image of his name popping up in my inbox renews my irritation. "I have no idea. I deleted it before I read it. He's had two decades to try. There's nothing he could say now to fix it."

"I'm sorry. If it's any consolation, it's his loss. You turned out pretty great without him."

Her words bring a smile to my face. "That is a consolation. I care about what you think. What he thinks doesn't matter anymore, but that's what prompted this visit." I pause a second before continuing. "When he first left, I got into so much trouble. For years I acted out, lashed out, misbehaved... Really, I was lucky mom didn't ship me off to military school."

Angel chuckles, but that was a genuine concern for a while. It still didn't make me smarten up.

"After a few years, when Josh was about to graduate high school, he made me make him a promise. He said he'd pay for my university so I could get a job and prove to my dad that I didn't need him. Prove that it was possible to have a successful career without throwing away the people you claim to love."

"He paid for your schooling?"

I nod. "He did. Him and Lily were high school sweethearts, but school was never his thing, so rather than go off to college for something he didn't care about, he started working in construction. I can't even fathom the amount of physical labour he had to do to pay my tuition. But it was his willingness to sacrifice for me that set me straight. I saw how hard he worked and how dedicated he was to improving my life. Even though Josh's sacrifice was a huge motivator for me, proving to my dad that I didn't need him kind of took over by the time I graduated. I wanted to be just like him and nothing like him at the same time. I wanted the success he had, but refused to become one of those people whose bank account becomes their greatest accomplishment."

"And what do you want now?"

"Now?" I glance at her for a split second, trying to keep my eyes on the road. "I just want to be happy. Instead of being motivated by anger, I want to do things for the right reasons."

"I can relate, you know? The things that shaped me were different, but I can understand how defining moments in your past shaped who you became."

From the corner of my eye, I see her turn to face out the window as we pass the King City rest stop, indicating we're about halfway home.

"My aunt was what you'd call a rolling stone. She was never the type to settle down in a job or a relationship. She'd be out partying at all hours and burned through a lot of the life insurance money my parents left Dina and me. I already felt awful over my parents' deaths, and she made it clear on a daily basis how much she hated me for ruining her life, which piled on more guilt.

"By the time Dina turned seventeen, I had full control over the house, so I decided to sell it and buy my condo. Dina lived there with me until she turned nineteen, then we used the rest of the money to buy her place. My aunt was furious, but she'd already blown everything else, so I was afraid if I didn't take control, Dina and I would have nothing."

"Wow. That was really selfish of her. Do you ever speak to her now?"

"Never. Not since the day we sold the house. It's just been me and Dina."

I glance over when there's an opening in traffic, but Angel is still staring out the window. "Have you ever talked to Dina about her feelings on everything? I know you blame yourself, but has she ever said she blames you? You were just a kid, too."

"Not yet. It's something I need to do. Either way, at least I'll know and give her an opportunity to heal, you know?"

"Yeah. Sometimes hashing it out is the best remedy." Those words are meant to apply to Angel's situation, but they strike a chord with me just as much.

"Maybe it's time for both of us to be happy. To stop trying to prove something to people we can't prove things to."

My hand moves of its own accord, wanting to touch her. To be connected to her. I grab her hand over the centre console, rubbing my thumb along the soft skin of hers. "That sounds like a good plan."

She smiles as I glance at her again. "Easier said than done, but it's something we can both work on."

"Does that mean you'll give up on your promise?"

She shows no hesitation before answering. "No. For all the times it has landed me in hot water, it was always situations when the other person just didn't want to hear the truth. That's not on me. But, in truth"—she laughs—"being honest is just the right thing to do. I'm not going to change that."

Her straightforwardness was one of the many things that attracted me to her. It certainly lit the spark that has grown into a fiery inferno over the past few months. Her insistence on being frank and blunt may send some people running, but she's right; that's not the truth's fault. I find it refreshing and it simplifies things when I know I can turn to her with a question and get a straight answer.

"Good. You should ever have to compromise what's important to you for other people."

She weaves her fingers in between mine and gives my hand a gentle squeeze. "Sounds like we both have complicated pasts. But here, with you, the future doesn't seem so unknown." She tries to pull her hand away, but I latch onto her before she can. "Is that crazy?"

The reality that Angel sees me in her future does something to me. Call it butterflies or a stampeding heart rate; I don't know how to describe it. What I do know is that this woman has made a permanent imprint on my brain—my heart—and no job opportunity in the world could make me give that up. "If it is, then I'm crazy too."

Our visit to Damian's brother's house was unexpected, but despite not being around a whole family for a long time, it didn't hurt as much as I thought it would. The opposite, really. They welcomed me into their home and I felt as though they cared for me without question just because Damian does. At least, I assume he does.

This guy has my heart now, and admitting that is terrifying.

Genie's taking me for a walk around the neighbourhood to help me clear my head, but the bustling city streets and chilly wind don't provide a tranquil escape to think. By think, I mean over-analyze what I've gotten myself into with this man who seems to have it all. I can't stop questioning what he even sees in me. At no time over the past four days have I come to a peaceful resolution to set my mind at ease. I guess answers will require an honest conversation. Something I also owe Dina.

Unfortunately, I have too much work to get done today, so once Genie and I are back home, work is my priority. There's no time for over-analyzing my relationship with Damian, and I will hold off on opening old wounds with Dina until a day I can dedicate my attention to her.

Four hours later, I'm immersed in another freelance gig designing some logos and graphics for a website when my ringtone plays. A call from Hannah.

"Hey, girl!"

"Hey, stranger. I take it that things got sorted out with Damian?" Her sing-song voice makes me giggle.

"Yeah, you could say that. Thanks for setting me straight."

"That's what friends are for. So, are you two official now? Do I get to meet him yet? Akili is a superb judge of character. I can bring her to give him the once over."

Again, I laugh, imagining Damian trying to win over Akili, who would never hurt a fly. Unlike Nacho. "Genie's put him through his paces. So far he's passed with flying colours. But no, we're not official. I don't know what we are, actually. We're just kind of... us." I get up from my office chair to go search for Genie. Since I'm not working at the moment, I might as well give her attention. "What about you? How are things going?"

"Ugh. Being unemployed is the worst. I'm so bored, I've been begging my mother to host a dinner party so I can cook something for other people."

Hannah's words hit me a punch to the gut. I still feel that it's my fault she is unemployed.

"I'm so sorry. You'd still have a job if it weren't for me."

"Don't you dare start that!" Hannah shouts into the phone. "I quit because I *wanted* to. You didn't make me. The situation that Harrington allowed made the choice for me, not you. Beyond that, this is pushing me out of my comfort zone. I've applied for jobs from Vancouver to Halifax, though I skipped Quebec because *ma francais est tres mal.*"

Her terrible French makes me laugh. At least she hasn't lost her quirky sense of humour.

I find Genie in my bedroom, sprawled across the bed in a slant of sunlight peeking through the curtains. "You really want to move out of Toronto? Out of Ontario?"

"Not if I have a choice, but I thought a fresh start could be good. So don't worry about me. We're tough. You picked yourself up and dusted yourself off. I'm still dusting, but I'll get there."

Genie snorts as I snuggle in beside her and she flops her big brick head toward me, wiggling onto her back.

"Let me know if I can help somehow. I know I wasn't your boss, but if I can be a reference for you or something, I'm happy to. We worked together, so that has to count for something."

"Thanks. I might take you up on that. Lord knows Harrington won't give me a reference. I spent years keeping that place afloat, dealing with the perverts in that kitchen, but I stand up for one injustice and I get blacklisted."

No matter what Hannah says about this not being my fault, I still hold all the blame. She's so talented, but she's being held back because of a situation I handled poorly. If I had done something different, maybe she could have moved from one job to another without issue. She could have cashed in on the references she spent years building by proving herself as a capable chef.

"I just wish there was something more I could do. Maybe I can talk to Harrington about giving you a reference. Or Norene." The thought of going to speak to the manager or head chef at *Harvest* isn't a pleasant one, but if that's what I have to do, so be it.

"Don't sweat it, Angel. I'll be fine. I've made it through harder times than this."

That doesn't ease my guilt at all. She's dealt with enough adversity in the past few years; she didn't need this. I'm not sure what to say.

"So, you talked to Damian and sorted things out. Have you spoken to Dina?"

Everyone else is making this sound like it's such an easy conversation to have. It's not. Patching things up with Damian was a lot easier. I haven't known him long, and that issue only festered for two days before we sorted it out. But talking to Dina, it's busting open a severe emotional wound that has just started to scab over. I know it needs to be done, though. "Not yet, but I will. I was going to talk to her today, but I'm swamped with a project I need to get done, so I decided to wait until I can give her the attention she deserves."

"Say no more. I forgot you're a working woman with a flourishing career in front of her. I'll let you go so you can kick butt and take over the world." Hannah mutters something to Akili before continuing, "I have to take her royal highness for a walk, anyway. You know, my busy schedule and all."

I know she's joking, so I try not to let that pile on more guilt. "Put my number down on any new applications, okay? I'll sing your praises so loud, everyone will want to hire you."

"Thanks, Ang. And for what it's worth, I'm proud of you for planning to talk to Dina. You'll feel better. Promise."

"Maybe. Thank you for calling me out."

"I wasn't trying to call you out, but I can always count on you to show me tough love, so I wanted to do the same for you." I hear Hannah clicking on Aliki's leash in the background and the familiar sound of excited tippety-taps on the tile floor from dancing dog paws. "Go kick butt now and call me when you're not being occupied by your boss." Her giggle makes me laugh in response.

"He's not technically my boss." I give Genie one last pat on her belly before I hoist myself up off the bed. "I better get back to work, though. Hopefully your dream job is around the corner."

We say our goodbyes as Hannah rushes out the door with Akili and I return to my office to face off against image editing software.

Three hours later, my creativity is flowing like dried cement. I've stared at the same image for far too long, so I decide to take a dinner break, then I'll walk Genie. Maybe by the time I'm done, I'll have renewed inspiration.

I whip up a box of mac and cheese, not wanting anything elaborate today. Damian has become a regular feature in my evenings, so not having heard from him since this morning, it feels weird cooking for one person. I'm uninspired. It's just sustenance to stay alive, rather than a carefully curated meal to enjoy along with comfortable conversation after a long day of work.

Mac and cheese gets the job done, though. I eat as much as I can before the salt content leaves me feeling fuller than I probably am. Genie has slurped up her meal and is busy lapping up water, so I take the opportunity to grab a glass myself. She doesn't waste time indicating she's ready to go for her post-dinner walk.

The late summer weather has made way for early fall temperatures, so I grab a thin jacket, leash Genie, and we're on our way. Her excited snorts as we wait for the elevator are more exaggerated than normal. When a girl's gotta go…

But the elevator doors open, and I discover it was not voiding her bladder that she was excited about. Standing in the mirrored elevator, looking down at his phone as he leans against the handrail, is the one man who has made me feel like committing to someone might not end in heartbreak. The man who has made me believe he isn't afraid of the truth, no matter how hard it is.

He glances up from his phone after Genie lets out an exuberant yelp.

"Hey. What are you doing here?" I step into the elevator car behind Genie, who has already jumped up on Damian's legs.

"Hi, girl." He leans down to rustle her head, then stands to meet my eyes. "I missed you all day." He hooks his arm around my waist and pulls me in for a searing kiss. "And I have to ask you something."

The elevator dings for the lobby and the doors open wide, revealing an empty space. We step out and walk to the door. Damian takes a few long strides to get there before me and opens the first door for Genie and me. I push open the second and we exit into the chilly evening air. During the entire sixty-second period, I'm trying my best to guess what Damian could need to ask.

"Okay, out with it."

Damian falls into stride beside me, reaching down to grab my free hand as Genie roams the right side of the sidewalk. "Do you own a formal gown?"

37

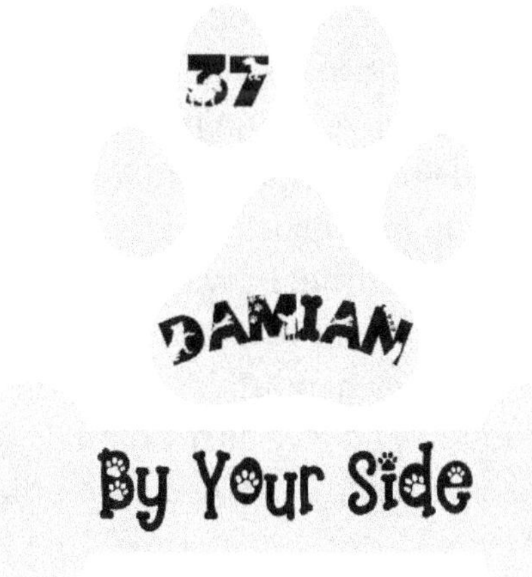

By Your Side

Never once have I looked forward to a stuffy fundraiser. For hours, I'm forced to listen to rehearsed conversations with complete strangers who want to tell people how amazing they are, or about all the 'good' they've done by donating money from their surplus accounts to worthy causes. The situation always turns me into a Scrooge. I don't doubt that your twenty-seven million dollars helped the children's hospital, Glen, but they already named an entire wing after you. Do people really need to kiss your feet too?

Anyway, when Mr. Nicholls informed me I'd have to represent Harbour Campaigns at a fundraiser for an international medical charity, I wasn't happy about it. Until I realized I got to bring a plus one.

So now I'm ascending to the third floor in Angel's elevator, ready to take her out for a night of uncomfortable conversations and not-so-humble bragging.

I knock on the door once, but before I can tap on it again, it swings open. Angel stands in her entryway wearing a bold red gown with a high neckline, displaying the silky skin of her arms and her legs beneath a ruffled asymmetrical hemline. It's shorter in the front and has a tantalizing slit over her left leg that exposes her thigh. Her hair is styled in perfectly formed curls, reaching her shoulders. She looks like a ruby goddess.

"Wow. You. Look… wow. Stunning." I lean forward to kiss her, noting her muted lipstick shade and neutral makeup.

"No, you'll mess up my lipstick and it took me forever. This all feels too much, yet too little. How is that possible?"

I smirk, hovering my lips over hers. "I'd say it's the perfect amount of everything." My hand slides along the smooth fabric over her hip and suddenly I'd give all my money just to stay here with her. I've been so distracted, I didn't notice Genie was jumping up at my legs. "Sorry, Genie. How's my good girl?"

"Now she's got fur on your tux. I told you I should have met you downstairs."

"And miss walking out with you on my arm? Not a chance."

She laughs, making her dark eyes sparkle. "I think you mean you'll be on my arm."

That's fine by me. We say goodbye to Genie, exit the building, and climb into my SUV. I'm guessing to myself how long she expects to keep her makeup mess-free. Hopefully not all night.

We arrive at the venue, which is decorated to an extent that a member of the Royal Family could get married here. I tamp down my Scrooge-ness to focus on enjoying the evening with Angel, rather than creating a mental tally of the dollars and cents or analyzing people's motivations for being here. At the end of the night, all that matters is the charity's ability to continue their work.

The valet opens the door when we reach the front of the vehicle lineup, hands me a ticket, and we exchange pleasantries. Another person who bombards me with "yes, sir; thank you, sir."

I loop around the car to open the door for Angel, but she's already on her way to me. She looks even more stunning under the bright lights of the venue than she did inside her front door.

I can't help but smile when she grabs onto my arm and we walk through the doors side by side.

We tour the room, shaking hands with a few people I recognize from the Toronto fundraising circuit, but I don't remember anyone's name. Angel slides in effortlessly, introducing herself to people I can't remember, so they give up their names. I never asked; she just knew. She's winning over everyone she speaks to, but there's nothing pretentious or fake about her. She couldn't be more opposite to most other people here.

"Damian, so nice to see you here."

That voice is familiar. As soothing as tinnitus.

"Serena, hi." I take in the black designer gown the brunette socialite is wearing. I couldn't guess how much she paid for it, but I promised myself I wouldn't go there. Focus. "Serena, this is my girlfriend, Angel."

Serena and Angel both raise their eyebrows at me. Technically, Angel and I never had the girlfriend/boyfriend chat, but I assumed that was an accurate description of our status.

"Girlfriend, wow." Serena looks surprised, though her fake excitement is obvious. "Must be recent, considering we went out not long ago."

I look at Angel, whose facial expression is neutral. She's not even going to lie with a fake smile. She needs to know I'm just as honest with her.

"What's it been? Eight, nine months? I remember it was snowing." My words are matter-of-fact and leave no room for Serena to question them. The truth doesn't leave room for interpretation.

Angel's shoulders relax.

"So what do you do, Angel? Let me guess. A kindergarten teacher. Or a waitress." Serena's words are laced with contempt, which is not going to fly.

Before I can say anything, Angel handles the situation. "Good guess. I was a waitress until recently. It's a great character builder, you know? Having to work for a living."

I've never heard Angel respond to anyone with that level of snark. It makes me feel better after all the times I've reacted out of character.

Serena doesn't take it as amusing. "Not all of us need to waste time waitressing when we're busy working in a law firm."

That almost makes me laugh. "Well, Serena, it was nice seeing you. All the best." Without waiting for a response, I lead Angel away, farther into the crowd of middle-aged people in overpriced clothing.

"Well, that was fun," she states while trailing behind me, clinging to my right hand.

"I thought you always told the truth." I chuckle and stop walking so I can look at her.

"My sarcastic tone didn't give that away? She seems nice." Angel flutters her eyelashes at me and flashes a delectable smile.

"I like sarcastic Angel." I swing her around so she's standing in front of me and I no longer care about her makeup. Or the eyes on us. All I care about is feeling her against me and making a statement to her and everyone else here. The room around us fades away as I get lost in Angel Blake.

She pulls back after a moment, allowing me to look into her sparkling eyes. "So sarcastic Angel is good girlfriend material?"

I huff a laugh as a smile spreads across my tingling lips. "Sorry. That wasn't the romantic moment I was planning for, but I'm still hoping you won't tell me I'm wrong."

"Damian—"

"Angel, if it's not obvious by now, I really like you. I think the best thing we can do is see where things go between us. Don't say no. Please."

The corners of her mouth upturn as she levels me with her gaze. "I was trying to say, if I didn't think it was true, I wouldn't have gone along with it. But don't forget what I said. I'll never compromise who I am, so if it's going to bother you, get out now. I have no intentions of getting wrapped up in someone just to have my world come caving in again."

"Never."

She kisses me again, but this time, it's a quick, seal-the-deal kiss. "So, what's the story with Serena?"

I lead Angel toward our table where we'll be eating a stupid-expensive meal on stupid-expensive china. All so people here can celebrate themselves for collecting money for doctors who are travelling the world, actually providing life-saving procedures in mud huts—no, Damian. Focus.

Our name cards are side by side at a ten-person table. I glance at the card on the opposite side of me and find Serena Horvath. Of course. Her mother is often involved in these fundraisers, so it doesn't surprise me that she wormed her way into the seat next to me. As if the three-quarters of a year without seeing each other wasn't enough of a hint.

"Speaking of Serena." I gesture my hand toward the name card, earning an eye roll from Angel. "So, long story short, before she shows up. We met at one of these events last year. While we were standing in a crowd of well-to-do business people I was sent to impress, she suggested we should go out one night. I didn't want to embarrass her, so, like an idiot, I agreed. We went out one time, during which I hoped she'd realize we have nothing in common and she'd move on. But she didn't. She called me a few times after, but I avoided her as much as possible. Tried to let her down gently, but was afraid of business blowback. Oh, and, by the way, she works as a mail clerk in her father's law firm because she failed classes to become a paralegal."

"That's the short story? So basically, she's got a thing for you and you don't have a thing back?" It sounds so simple when she says it that way.

"Yes. That sums it up."

She slides her chair out and drops into her seat, setting her small champagne clutch on the table. "Have you tried... I don't know... being honest with her?"

I pull my own chair out, avoiding her questioning gaze. "No. I just kept hoping she'd give up and there would be no hard feelings."

Angel pours herself a glass of white wine from the open bottle on our table. "I didn't realize my boyfriend was a coward. I'm going to have to rethink this arrangement." She takes a sip, leaving a trace of nude lipstick on the rim of her glass. "Switch places with me."

"What?" I knock my empty wine glass with my elbow and scramble to right it.

"Hurry, before she gets here. Switch spots with me." She takes another sip of wine and stands. She's not kidding, but then again, I should expect nothing less. "Move it, boyfriend. Let your woman work."

38

ANGEL

Ain't No Other Man

Serena Horvath. Sounds Hungarian. I remember Damian telling me his mother's family was Hungarian, so maybe Miss Horvath is looking for someone with a cultural link. Whatever she's looking for, she'll need to find it elsewhere.

The beautiful brunette strolls toward our table and stops at Damian's left with intention. The look on her face is comical when she realizes her name isn't there. She glares at me, and I'm struggling to keep a straight face.

A normal person might fake nice and say something like, "Oh, Serena, so nice to have you sitting with us." I'm not a 'normal' person.

"Your seat's over here, Serena. Next to me." I don't flash a fake smile, but I do flash a victorious one. I almost feel bad for her because Damian wasn't exactly forthcoming, but she was snarky with me for no justifiable reason. Other than jealousy. Which is what makes me *not* feel bad.

She glares at me from her hazel eyes. "I think there's been a mix up."

"No mix up. I asked Damian to switch seats with me."

Damian's eyes widen as he looks at me with an amused smirk. I shrug in response. Something tells me Serena isn't used to other people being straightforward.

"Well, thanks for ruining my evening." Serena strolls over to her seat, looking every bit the socialite I get the impression she dreams of being.

It's harder to suppress my giggles with each opening of her mouth.

"Now, that's not fair. You haven't taken a moment to get to know me. Why would you assume I ruined your evening?" This is a question I'm genuinely curious about. Because of my former job? My income level? Or just because I'm here with the man she's interested in?

"You're a waitress," she spits. As if she's not sitting here tonight *waiting* for servers to bring her food. Somehow they're allowed to breathe the same air as her to cater to her, but not sit beside her.

"Correction, I was a waitress, but even if I still was, what would be wrong with that?" I've never understood people who look down their noses at others on account of their job. Though, I've been guilty of making assumptions about people before, too.

"Just don't speak to me for the rest of the evening, *waitress*."

I roll my eyes and turn to face Damian. "Gladly."

He chuckles and leans in to whisper, "See why I was afraid of being honest with her?"

She doesn't seem like a rational person. Maybe it's wrong of me to judge her based on our limited interaction, but she's shown herself to be a spoiled little rich girl thus far. She judged me before I said a single word.

I commit to ignoring Serena as the rest of the guests fill our table, each greeting us with a terse smile or a nod. I don't belong here. Damian places his hand on my bouncing knee under the table, which reminds me that he asked me here. He's the only person at this table whose opinion I care about.

Damian strikes up a conversation with the balding gentleman beside him, Mr. Klein, introducing me as his girlfriend again. This is going to take some getting used to. It turns out Mr. Klein was one of Damian's first bosses and took him under his wing when he was fresh out of university. My decision to switch seats makes me even happier now.

Mr. Klein speaks past Damian to me. "So what do you do, Miss Blake?"

"Graphic design pays my bills, but mostly I'm a dedicated dog servant." I had noticed dog hair on the man's wrinkled suit jacket and took a wild guess that he'd be content to discuss topics other than work. Even his facial expressions and demeanour appear far more relaxed than other people here.

I'm rewarded by his deep belly laugh.

"My wife and I have two dalmatians. Both of them think they're lap dogs, so I can relate. They each have their own personalities that make it hard not to love them." He looks at his wife with a glimmer in his eye that would make me "aww" if it didn't remind me so much of my parents.

Now is not the time for a trip down my traumatic memory lane.

"How sweet. They must be a lot of fun. Mine is an American bully, and she puts the 'bull' in bull-headed. It didn't take her long to learn how to manipulate Damian to do anything she wanted."

Mr. Klein claps Damian on the back. "She's a keeper, son. I'm happy for you. It's nice to see you finally settling down."

I choke on the wine I'm attempting to swallow at the mention of "settling down". Damian and I have been in an official relationship for thirty minutes. Long-term plans haven't come up quite yet. He doesn't seem fazed by the comment, though.

"Thank you, Bill. I have no intention of letting this one go."

That surprises me almost as much. Not that I got the impression Damian wasn't serious, but him saying it out loud is different from an assumption. I'm staring at him with one eyebrow raised, which earns me a smirk and a wink. Suddenly, a sharp elbow digs in my back. It was too hard and for too long to be accidental.

"Ow!" I turn to face the offender. "Was that necessary? You don't like me, fine. I'm not your biggest fan either. But this event is for doctors doing life-saving work, not for airing your petty grievances. Grow up."

Once again, Serena seems surprised by my words. I gather she's used to people shrinking back and catering to her every whim. Sorry, not sorry, Miss Horvath. The only living thing that makes me bend to her whims is Genie, and I'm pretty sure she'd have been better behaved. I'd be more forgiving if Serena stuck her face in my plate to steal my dinner or drooled on my dress.

"Little girl, you have some nerve talking to me like that."

Fair assessment. Serena towers over me, probably measuring in around five-nine, but I'm not the one acting like a little girl.

"Like what? How you deserve after elbowing me in the back? I have no interest in arguing with you, but I'm not interested in being abused at the dinner table, either. I respected your wishes not to speak to you, so respect mine and rein in your tantrum."

Damian places a hand on my shoulder before leaning around me to address Serena. "Don't do this, Serena. You're embarrassing yourself."

"Myself? I'm embarrassing myself?" She scoffs, then raises her voice so others at the table can hear her. "You're the one who showed up at this event with a *waitress*. You should be embarrassed."

Why is there always some petty girl who wants a guy she can't have and has to try to get in the way? Is dignity a thing of the past? Or is it not common in higher tax brackets? Why on Earth would anyone want to waste their time pursuing someone who isn't interested in them? A complete waste of life, if you ask me.

Damian responds before I can. "Serena, I was trying to spare your feelings, so I wasn't honest with you, and that's on me. But after you treated my *girlfriend* how you have, I'm not concerned about your feelings anymore. I wasn't interested in you romantically. Ever. Nor will I ever be. I knew from the first day we met that you were the epitome of everything I dislike that comes along with social status and money. You perpetuate a stereotype that I want no part of." Damian slides his chair back to stand and reaches a hand toward me. "So, if you'll excuse us, I think I'll take my *girlfriend* somewhere we can enjoy the evening. Alone." Once I take his hand and grab my clutch from the table, he pulls me to his side. "Mr. Klein, Mrs. Klein, enjoy your evening. I apologize for the drama."

With just enough time for me to examine Serena's expression—which is a combination of a gaping mouth and narrowed eyes—Damian leads me toward the exit, stopping for a brief second to drop a cheque in the box for donations.

The second the fresh air hits us as we exit the building, I feel guilty. "I'm sorry. I should have kept my mouth shut."

Damian hands his ticket to the valet with his eyes focused on me. "Don't be sorry. You were right. I should have been honest with her. I'm the one who needs to be sorry for putting you in that situation." He scans our surroundings before leaning in to whisper, "But it was so hot seeing you tell her off."

I swat his chest. "Damian, stop. I don't know what came over me. She turned me into a savage and it was hard to keep from clawing her eyes out."

He grabs my hips, pulling me flush against him. "You were perfect. You're always perfect."

When our lips meet, the irritation I carried outside with me disappears. The faint sounds of conversation inside the open doors, the damp autumn air, the elaborate lights draped underneath the carriage porch, all fade away. My senses become consumed by Damian's scent, his taste, the sounds of his soft moans as his hands run over my body.

A voice clearing behind me startles us apart. Damian smiles and now my sense of sight is lost in him, too.

"The valet is waiting. Let's go."

Damian drives from the venue, back to my place, and I invite him in since we weren't gone as long as I had expected.

First order of business when we get inside is to get comfortable. Damian undoes his bowtie and the top buttons on his shirt. He throws his suit jacket over the arm of my sofa and rolls up his sleeves. He's still half dressed in a tux, but he looks casual. Natural. Like he belongs here. Genie climbs up on the sofa once he sits down, so with her to keep him company, I duck into my bedroom to swap out my dress for pyjamas.

The rest of the night is just as I could have hoped. Comfortable in Damian's presence, with no one but Genie to interfere.

Ever since Angel and I went to the fundraiser three weeks ago, things have shifted between us. In a good way. Our transition from two people dating and enjoying each other's company to boyfriend and girlfriend has been seamless. At least, I think so.

Angel doesn't come into the office much at all, so there's been no issues from mixing our business and personal lives. As far as I know, everyone has been treating her well, which tells me their fear of me doesn't extend to her. Though I'm sure they censor their true feelings about me when she's around.

Mr. Nicholls has called me into his office for a one-on-one, which hasn't happened for months. He's a hands-on CEO, but aside from the frequent check-ins via phone call or email, and monthly department manager meetings, he doesn't often require me to come to his office. Sitting in the reception area, waiting for the big boss who built this company on his back, makes me feel the same way I did all the times I sat outside the principal's office as a kid.

"Mr. Taylor? He'll see you now." Nicholls' receptionist, Whitney, gestures for me to enter his office. He got one with solid walls, so I'm unsure what I'm walking into.

I knock twice and swing the door open to enter. The septuagenarian is seated in his cognac leather office chair, which seems to grow each time I'm here. He reminds me of my father, in a way, because he's given everything to this company, and now he has no life outside of it aside from a wife he never mentions. He's in his early seventies, but he's made no indication he's planning to retire.

"Damian, have a seat." He closes a file folder and slides off his thick gold-framed glasses, placing them on the desk beside his computer mouse.

I drop into the seat across from him. "It's good to see you, sir. Hard to believe we work in the same building and go so long without a face-to-face meeting."

"Well, as long as each department manager does their job, it makes mine easier."

This is so much worse than being chastised by the principal. My stomach sinks at his implication that I'm not doing my job.

"First thing's first. You and your lady friend made quite an impression at the fundraiser a few weeks back. I spoke with Mr. Horvath earlier and he informed me you insulted his daughter."

I jolt in my chair, wanting to jump up and shout over the outrageousness of that claim, but I gather my thoughts before replying. "That's not even remotely true, sir."

"Yeah, yeah. I figured as much. I've known that girl since she was small and she never did take well to being told no."

Do I laugh at that? I want to laugh, because it sounds a lot like Serena, but Mr. Nicholls isn't so much as smirking. This is awkward, but sometimes the truth is. If the situation with Serena taught me anything, it's that sidestepping the cold, hard facts is only prolonging the inevitable. Better to get it over with.

"I'm sorry if we reflected poorly on you or on Harbour Campaigns, sir, but Miss Horvath was angry with me and behaved... well, she was really childish and I told her as much. I wasn't going to subject my girlfriend to that, so we left." As strange as it feels discussing personal matters with my boss, it's a relief to explain my reasoning.

"Nor should anyone have to put up with that. Bill Klein and I met for a drink a few nights ago and he told me what actually happened. It sounds like you did a fine job of representing us, son. That's not why I called you in, though."

The tension that had dissipated for a moment is back with a vengeance. I'm clenching the leather chair cushion at my sides to keep my hands from shaking. I'd take my public school principal, Mr. Peever, over the man holding my livelihood in his hands any day.

"There's been some mumblings around the office that your department is descending into chaos. Now, the reason we fired Mr. Woodward from your position in the first place, was because his teams had become ineffective. I won't let history repeat itself."

I'd hardly call it chaos. We've still met all of our deadlines and put out good work. The biggest issue is that my team has a distinct lack of confidence and wastes time running things by me or running away from me. But the blame doesn't belong to them. I'm the one who was pushed into this role and I'm the one who has to figure out how to make it work.

After some deep thought, I respond, "There's been a breakdown in communication somewhere along the way. It's an issue I'm aware of. I'm trying to rectify it, but it's a diagnostic issue. The symptoms can have many causes, so I've yet to figure it out. I promise you, sir, I'm doing everything in my power to lead a successful team." I almost say, "nothing is more important to me than the success of this company," but that would be a flat-out lie. Sure, I want the business to do well, and I'll do my part to make that happen, but it's not at the top of my list of important things. Never will be.

"Let me know what you need from me to make that happen. Our food and beverage division is our bread and butter,

Damian. I entrusted it to you because I saw your promise. Don't make me regret my choice."

"I won't let you down."

"Very well. I just wanted to discuss that with you man to man. I'll leave you to get back to work." Mr. Nicholls has a reputation for saying what needs to be said without saying it. That's why he's built a successful marketing and public relations company. What he's saying now is "get out."

"Thank you for speaking with me. If you have any concerns or suggestions in the future, I'm all ears." I stand from my chair, re-button my suit jacket, and turn to leave.

As I'm a few feet from the door, Mr. Nicholls calls, "How's that new freelancer working out? I was wondering why you never asked why I hired someone for your department without consulting you. Most managers take issue when I go over their heads."

I spin back around to face Mr. Nicholls. "To be honest, sir, it didn't occur to me you went over my head because you are over my head. If you think a decision is right, I'll support that."

He gives me a stoic nod in reply.

"And for what it's worth, you were one hundred percent right about her. She's been an incredible addition." Personally and professionally, but I don't add that. Even though that's a very clear truth, not everything needs to be said.

I return to my office a few minutes later and find a meeting happening in the boardroom across the hall. I'm not sure how to feel about what Mr. Nicholls said, but I am sure who I want to talk to about it. With a quick tap of my touchscreen, my phone is ringing in my ear.

"Hey. I was just thinking about you."

That makes my smile grow twice as wide because I know she isn't just saying that.

"Hmm. What were you thinking?"

"Wouldn't you like to know. I'm just taking a break to tend to Genie's incessant need for belly rubs. It's a mystery how she ever survived when I was working full days at Harvest."

"Maybe I'll have to implement a pet-friendly policy in the office. She wants you there; I want you here. One of us is missing out."

Angel stays silent for a count of ten. "I think it's best how things are. Too much of a good thing, you know? Like how microwave radiation isn't harmful once or twice, but after prolonged exposure…"

Did she just…? "Are you relating yourself or me to radiation?" I furrow my eyebrows, even though she can't see me. "Never mind. Neither of us are harming the other with our microwaves or gamma rays or… neutron rays."

She snorts a laugh. "Are neutron rays a thing?"

"Angel." I say her name how she told me not to say it when she was mad at me. "Point is, I wish I could see you more." I got so distracted being jealous of Genie's belly rubs, I forgot why I called, so I revert to my planned conversation and away from Clingy Damian. "Mr. Nicholls called me into his office today."

She doesn't seem put off by the abrupt subject change. "Oh, really? What did he have to say?"

I relay the pertinent information, leaving out the nonsense regarding Serena because that situation is over, as far as I'm concerned.

"Descending into chaos? That's a bit much."

Her matching reaction to mine makes me chuckle. "That's what I thought. Don't get me wrong; a lot of work needs to be done, but it's hardly chaos."

"I'd offer to play double agent and find out who the rat is, but nobody really talks to me and I wouldn't be good at being deceitful."

That bothers me. Probably more than it should. I was under the assumption her relationship with me didn't affect her position with colleagues. That was naïve of me. Maybe my department is in chaos.

Before I can say anything else, I glance up to see Elliot waving me into the boardroom from the other side of my wall of windows. "I'm sorry. Duty calls. Can I see you tonight?"

"Same time, same place."

We say our rushed goodbyes, then I walk out into the hallway.

Elliot looks tentative and afraid. "Sorry for interrupting. We were hoping we could get your input on something."

Of course they were.

40

ANGEL

The Real Thing

Even though my freelance capacity at *Harbour Campaigns* is limited, I've still been keeping busy between the work they give me and a few other gigs I've had roll in. My portfolio is shaping up nicely, and Genie is pretty thrilled we won't have to go hungry. Damian and I have been spending as much time together as our schedules will allow. My work may be freelance, but I've been too busy to carve out time for my sister because whenever I'm free, she has other things going on.

Today, however, I'm going into the office for a brief on a new job. I'm still under Elliot's purview, but with a different project manager; much to Damian's relief. He's warmed up to Mitchell, who has stopped making passes at me. Plus, he submitted the finalized campaign to our oil-loving client, and the man was happy with everything after a few minor tweaks.

The next project is for a vodka distillery, so as I walk to work, I rack my brain, trying to come up with a new concept. I spent last night searching for other campaigns, running numbers based on their production and revenue, trying to find a common link amongst what works. I'm not going to leave things to chance by just creating something that looks pretty.

By the time I reach the office, I'm freezing because the threat of winter is looming—far too soon, if you ask me. It's only been fall for a month. The lobby is warm, but still not inviting on account of the crotchety blonde at reception. At least the security guard flashes a smile.

I arrive on the fifth floor, and as much as I want to go say hi to Damian, I resist. It's far too easy to blur personal and professional lines; I don't want that to happen to us. Things have been going well between us for the past few weeks, and I don't want to disrupt that. So instead of stopping, I continue into "the pit", where I find Elliot and my new project manager, Meghan. She takes a minute to introduce herself, which quickly spirals into a history of her entire life, from where she grew up to her four children at home. I'm confident there won't be any tension between her and Damian on account of her hitting on me. She seems pretty smitten with her husband, Jorge.

Elliot, Meghan, three other team members tasked with working on this project, and myself all enter the boardroom to discuss the project brief. From my position at the table, I can see across to Damian's office, but his blinds are drawn, which is unusual. I must be staring and missing something important, because Elliot clears his throat and calls my name.

I apologize for drifting off and attempt to focus for the rest of the meeting, listening to the ideas shared by the other staff members to present this vodka as superior. None of which seems very appealing to me, but I'm just a graphic designer. And an eight-dollar wine drinker.

When everyone gathers their things to leave, I'm eager to get back home to my fur baby, but Elliot stops me before I exit the room. "Angel, a minute, please?"

I nod at everyone else as they walk out, mainly because aside from Meghan, I don't remember anyone's name, and I don't want to admit that.

Once we're all clear of other ears, Elliot says, "I know you have… something"—he waves his hands around in some misguided interpretive dance—"going on with the boss, and it might not be my place, but I just wanted to say, you seem like a nice girl, so you should be careful."

Part of me wishes *Dirrty* was playing in the background because that's my fight song now, but alas, I'm going to need to draw my own inspiration here. "Mr. Hannon, that's a gross overstep on your part. You may think you know Dam… Mr. Taylor, but you know him in a minimal, professional capacity. I knew him personally before I started working here and I'm capable of making my own decisions. I also consider myself a good judge of character, though I was wrong about you."

Elliot looks at his feet for a moment, but I harbour no guilt for calling him out for overstepping.

"Actually, besides that, how *dare* you claim to know anything about Damian as anyone other than your boss. What gives you the right to interfere in someone's personal life because you don't like something about them at work? Have you ever taken the time to get to know him? Have you tried to forge a friendship outside of work and learn who the man is behind those office doors? No, you haven't. For months, Damian has been devastated over how much his staff seem to fear him or refuse to speak up because that's not what he wants. He wants to be questioned. He wants push back so everyone can bounce ideas off of each other and grow as a team. But no one here has been willing to do that. So don't come to me, acting like you're trying to save me from him just because you don't understand him."

I don't wait for Elliot to reply before I storm out of the room. I was lucky I still had a job after my initial blow up with Damian weeks ago. Now, they'll probably see me as a loose cannon and fear me more than Damian. Maybe they should.

"Angel."

I turn around to see Elliot speed-walking down the hallway behind me as I beeline to the elevator.

"Look… uh…" He scrunches his face and uses his right hand to rub the back of his neck. "You're right. I'm sorry."

"For…?"

"Everything. Making assumptions. Overstepping. It wasn't my place to say anything."

"I'm less concerned about you bringing it up with me than I am about you writing Damian off as some villain without getting to know him. He's your boss. Last I checked, most people don't like their bosses, but yours is actually pretty great. And I don't say that as someone with a personal connection to him. I say it because it's true. If I can return your caution, Mr. Hannon, it would be not to base opinions of someone off of office gossip or assumptions."

As I finish my rant, I look up to see Damian's assistant, Paxton, peering over his desk at us. He works closely with Damian, so I call him over, knowing if he's fallen victim to company gossip, this could backfire.

"Yes, Miss Blake?"

"Angel is fine." Like I've said fifty times already. "You've worked for Damian for how long now?"

"About ten months."

"And has he ever mistreated you or been what you'd describe as a jerk?"

The kid looks like he's going to pass out. He's sweating, running a finger between his shirt collar and his neck, as if it's closing around his throat. "No, ma'am."

Oh, good grief. That's even worse than Miss Blake.

"Have you ever seen him mistreat another employee?"

"No, ma'am."

I turn back to Elliot, resisting the urge to roll my eyes at Paxton's ma'aming, and level him with a sharp gaze. "See. For whatever reason, people made up their minds about him without collecting facts. Now, I know advertising is largely about the perception of something and not the reality, but maybe this time you should do some independent research, hmm?"

"Yes, ma'am," Elliot replies with a smirk. "Again, I'm sorry."

"So make it up to me. Put the work in and you'll see. Don't be afraid to speak up to him or eat lunch in his proximity. He'll respect you for it, and he won't bite."

With everything that needed to be said out in the open, I step into the elevator after our goodbyes, and descend to the lobby, then out onto the cold sidewalk. I pull out my phone before I get outside and discover a text from Damian.

Damian: *Want to grab lunch?*

Angel: *Sorry, I'm already headed home. Come over for dinner?*

Seconds later, **Damian:** *It's a date.*

I spend four hours working on my new assignment when I return home. I wrapped up the other freelance gigs I had over the weekend, so this one can have my sole focus. So far, so good.

With my conversation with Elliot still replaying in my head, I start preparing dinner for Damian and me. I can't explain why, but knowing he can go to any of the city's most expensive restaurants, yet chooses to come into my little condo and eat home-cooked meals means a lot to me. It feels more intimate, and we're able to focus on each other, not on the atmosphere around us or the inflated five-star restaurant prices.

My phone rings, so I answer and buzz Damian up. I guess he couldn't sneak in today.

"Damian's here, Genie. Remember what I told you. Be a good girl."

She stares at me with her big bright bully smile, but I know she's just giving me false hope. Sure enough, as soon as he knocks, she takes off to the door like a woman possessed.

I open the door to find a smiling, roguishly handsome man waiting to enter. A man with a bouquet of roses, carnations, and gerbera daisies.

"These are for Genie." He beams at me with his mischievous eyes as he steps into the foyer, wraps his free arm around me, and pulls me in for a kiss.

As captivated as I am by his lips on mine, I can't help but giggle against his mouth. That puts an end to the romantic moment. "For Genie, huh?"

"What can I say? She's wormed her way into my heart and I wanted to get her something special."

I swallow the lump forming in my throat, eager to break the sudden tension. "You know heartworm is deadly, right?"

"You have no idea."

41

DAMIAN

Keeps Gettin' Better

When I enter Angel's condo and find her in a casual T-shirt and leggings, something just clicks. It feels like coming home, and her being the one to greet me feels right. Her and Genie. Even though this isn't my address, I get more of a sense of home here than in my forty-fourth floor condo.

Watching her put flowers in a vase shouldn't be fascinating, but it is. How she arranges and smells each one, closing her eyes and inhaling the fragrance. She appreciates the little things, and it makes me want to bring her flowers every day.

Meanwhile, all I can smell is the intoxicating aroma of Indian spices from whatever she's got on the stove. "What are you making? It smells amazing."

"Mm. So do these. Genie says thank you, by the way." She stands on her tiptoes to give me a peck on the cheek, then walks over to the stove, removing the pot lid. "I'm making butter chicken and garlic naan. Just packaged naan because I'm not talented enough to make it from scratch."

I can't stop myself from standing behind her and wrapping my arms around her waist. Her hair interferes with my plan to trail kisses down her neck, so instead, I end up laughing. "This hair is out to get me."

She chuckles while stirring the steaming creation on the stove. "It's a better guard dog than Genie sometimes. This is almost done. Go have a seat."

A few short minutes later, Angel is bringing two wide bowls of butter chicken and a small plate of naan to the table. The ease with which she carries everything makes it clear her waitressing skills haven't gotten the least bit rusty.

We settle in and start enjoying our delicious meal, all while Genie snort-gobbles her food a few feet away. Most people would prefer soothing 80s music and dim lighting for a romantic dinner. Not me. This is perfect.

"How was your time at the office this morning? Anything interesting?"

The second Angel started explaining her conversation with Elliot yesterday, I wanted to fire him. But the more she explained, the lower my level of rage became. By firing him, I'd prove him right—that I am some kind of hot-headed monster. I can't be that guy. Nor do I want to be. Angel handled it well, and sounds like she put him in his place.

Needless to say, when I hear a knock at my office door and look up to see Elliot, I'm a bit surprised.

"Can I come in, boss?"

I click save on the document I'm drafting and close my laptop. "Sure. Have a seat." Now that I know what Angel said to him yesterday, I'm curious about why he's here.

I study him as he walks through the room. From his personnel file, and what I've learned from my time here, Elliot is married and welcomed his first child about a year ago. He's always been a reliable employee and turns in quality work. I doubt he knows that I'm aware of any of that. Or that I care.

Elliot slides his lithe frame into the chair on the opposite side of my desk. "I came to apologize."

Not what I expected, but I don't want to let on that Angel told me about their conversation. I don't need to give her a reputation as someone who runs to me with everything, because that's not what happened. "Okay. I'm all ears."

"Since you started working here, I... we, all of us in your department, haven't given you a fair chance."

"I'm a little lost here, Mr. Hannon."

Elliot takes a deep breath and I notice both hands have white knuckles, clenching the arms of the chair he's seated in. "Our last boss, Mr. Woodward, was a dictator. If he said jump, he expected us to ask how high, then reach heights twice that in half the time. He wanted everything run by him, but didn't allow anyone to question him. If they did, they'd be shamed in front of the rest of the employees or fired without notice."

That is the exact opposite of everything I stand for. "So, he was a jerk."

Elliot chuckles, but reins it in quickly to study my face. "You could say so, I guess. Though I could think of a few more colourful words. Anyway, you came into this department essentially out of nowhere. None of us knew you, and we assumed you'd run things the same way."

"I'm sorry he treated you that way, though that's not how I want to operate." I blow out a long breath, feeling like an idiot for not learning this sooner. Any one of the staff members in my department could have spoken to co-workers in my last department and learned that's not me.

"Yeah, I'm starting to realize that."

"It sounds like I owe you and everyone else an apology, Elliot."

He furrows his brows and finally releases his grip on the armchair. "I don't follow."

"There's somewhere I'm failing as a leader, and I need to figure it out. I never set out for this job. I just wanted to create and do what I was passionate about, but I was thrust into this position with no management experience. It's harder than I realized." Now I want to slap myself because here I am complaining about the incredible job opportunity gifted to me. The last thing I want is sympathy. "I'm not trying to complain, and don't mean for it to sound that way. But I need to figure out a way to make everyone more comfortable around me. I assumed I'd come in here as a complete stranger and people would warm up to me, but never questioned how things used to be done. I thought I'd learn your methods, rather than employing my own, and it appears we've gotten our wires crossed because you are all maintaining the status quo."

"If I may, sir?"

I lean forward, placing my elbows on my desk. "Please, I'll take any advice you have."

"Let everyone see your human side. I... um, I'm ashamed to admit, I approached Angel yesterday and cautioned her about you."

He raises his hands up to protect himself from my reply, but I don't budge. I'm impressed he's fessing up.

"Now, before you get angry with me, I realize how wrong that was. Angel was none too impressed either, and she laid a verbal assault on me that lingered on my mind until I walked in here just now. She was right. We all made assumptions rather than taking the time to get to know you. So, more than anything, I'm sorry for perpetuating that mentality on my team."

I suppress a smile as I imagine Angel, standing all of five-foot-one-and-a-half, berating Elliot for speaking against me. But the reality is, it's not her job to make people comfortable around me. "I have no one to blame but myself here. Frankly, I thought everyone hated me and it was hopeless to try, but that was irresponsible. And while I don't condone sticking your nose in personal relationships, I appreciate you looking out for Angel with good intentions… Unless you were trying to make an opening for Mitchell."

We both laugh, and for the first time since Elliot walked in here, he looks relaxed.

"No, sir. She'd eat him alive."

I'm pleased to look up and see other employees walking by, taking in the scene of Elliot and me laughing and smiling. This is the most at ease I've felt at work in months. It's as if the veil has been lifted, and we're seeing each other as more than boss and employee.

"I won't take up any more of your time. Thanks for seeing me, and again, I'm sorry for everything."

"No apologies necessary. This is on me. I appreciate you opening up to me and giving me some ideas on how to proceed." I stand and reach my hand across the desk to shake Elliot's. There's no time like the present to employ new methods to prove to everyone I'm not the jerk my predecessor was. "How are your wife and daughter?"

Elliot's face splits into a wide grin, indicative of a man who is in love with his family. "They're great, thank you. We're expecting again in March."

"Wow. Congratulations. Let me know when the time gets closer so we can make sure you have some time off."

"Oh, no, that's fine. Don't go to any trouble." The speed at which he jumped to decline my offer is concerning.

"One thing that's going to be a clear difference between me and most other bosses is that work will never take precedence over family. Don't let this job take over your life, okay? Promise me that."

Elliot stares at me again, looking as though he isn't sure how to reply. I'm not about to dive into my complicated history of my father abandoning me, but now that Elliot and I have opened the lines of communication, I want to make it clear where my priorities are. Never will I allow another child to feel as if they were less worthy than a job.

"Thanks, boss. I really appreciate that."

After Elliot leaves, I sit at my desk feeling a sense of calm I have yet to experience in the last ten months. For the better part of a year, I allowed a cycle to perpetuate and did nothing to interrupt it or change its course. I could give up on management altogether and ask to be transferred back to my old job, but I'm not a quitter. The employees working under me don't know the real Damian Taylor, so I'm going to make it my mission to create a department where people work hard because they're treated like humans and feel valued. One where employees feel confident voicing their opinions and don't slink back in fear of losing their livelihood.

I may have landed this job out of desperation on Mr. Nicholls' part to fill a void Mr. Woodward's departure created, but it won't be a mistake. This job can't have my "all" because there's so much more to life that deserves attention, but I will give it my best while I'm here. I'll give these people my best.

That starts with a request for Paxton. I ring him through the intercom and he comes running to the door. "Yes, Mr. Taylor?"

"Paxton, call me Damian, please." I take a deep breath, because this is a reminder I've given the young man no less than two hundred times. "I need to call a staff meeting. Today, tomorrow, next week. Whatever works for everyone. Can you handle that?"

"Yes, sir. What do I reference?"

"Tell them it's for a team-building exercise."

42

ANGEL

Haunted Heart

The past few days have been a whirlwind. I've been swamped with work, spending every moment outside of business hours with Damian, and sleeping. For weeks, I've been telling myself I need to speak to Dina and allow her to share her perspective surrounding our parents' deaths. Namely, my role in their deaths. Making assumptions isn't doing either of us any good. Every time I've seen her since early September, we've been in public or surrounded by other people, so the opportunity hasn't presented itself.

I need to make the opportunity present itself.

While Genie is stopped, sniffing a skinny tree trunk placed in a small patch of dirt surrounded by brick pavers, I punch out a text to my sister.

Angel: *Can I come over tomorrow? We need to have a chat.*

Genie is on the move again, but my phone dings in response seconds later.

Dina: *Everything okay? That sounds serious.*

Angel: *All fine. I just want to chat. Some sister time.*

A few more messages to ease my sister's mind and we arrange for Dina to come to my place tomorrow as long as I have ice cream. That I can handle. The necessary conversation is the hard part.

After Genie's morning walk, I run to the store to grab some strawberry ice cream. It's Nacho's favourite, and anything I can do to get on his good side is a plus. On my way home, my phone chimes, so I assume it's Dina informing me she's arrived. But when I look down at my screen, I see a different face.

Damian: *Good morning, beautiful girlfriend.*

I take a photo of me posing with the litre of ice cream and send it to him, along with a message.

Angel: *I've already got my dairy for the day. I don't need your cheese. :p*

My phone rings, and I don't even look before answering. "Good morning."

"You don't like my cheesiness? I'm crushed."

I scan my keyring to enter my condo building but stand in the lobby so Damian doesn't get disconnected in the elevator. "I appreciate your cheese. Good morning, handsome boyfriend."

"Why are you getting ice cream at 11:30 in the morning? Big plans for the day?"

"Dina and Nacho are coming over. We're going to have a long, overdue chat."

"Oh, wow. *The* chat?"

"Yep." I exaggerate the 'P' as I rock on the heels of my leather boots. "I should get this ice cream in the freezer. Can you call me after work?"

"Of course. I might be late today."

"Okay. No worries. I don't know how late Dina will stay." I press the button on the elevator, seeing that it is on the sixth floor.

"Hey, Angel? You'll feel better after you talk to her."

"I hope so. At least I'll know." The elevator doors ding open and a middle-aged couple steps out. "Talk to you tonight."

Damian and I say a rushed goodbye as the elevator doors close.

No more than five minutes after I get the ice cream in the freezer, Dina knocks at the door. She has a key from when she lived here, but she stopped barging in after catching me in my underwear one too many times.

I shout at her to come in as I make my way to my small foyer. "Hi." I attempt to hug Dina, but Nacho voices his displeasure and stops me in my tracks. "Hello to you too, Nacho. So nice to see you're in a good mood today."

Nacho doesn't appreciate my sarcasm. Or anything about me, it seems.

Dina laughs and pats the purse containing her demon dog. "Hi. I'll let him out first. Where's Genie?"

There's a stark contrast in Genie's enthusiasm when Dina and Nacho enter versus when Damian does. Not that my sister isn't loveable, but Genie just has a special place in her heart for the man who carries her when she gets tired and lets her cool off in his air-conditioned vehicle when she gets too hot. Dina's been inside a full thirty seconds before Genie rounds the corner to see who's here.

"Hi, guard dog. I brought Nacho!"

I'm not a dog whisperer, but I'm pretty sure Genie's face says "Help me." Dina releases Nacho from the confines of his ridiculous purse and he goes tearing after Genie. I used to think she went running around because she was excited, but now I know better.

"So, what did you want to talk about?"

"Come in and get comfortable. It's nothing major. Well, I guess that depends how you look at it, but it's just a conversation we should have had a long time ago."

Dina takes tentative steps past my kitchen into the living room. She sits on the sofa and Nacho climbs up beside her, already done with tormenting Genie, who huffs and walks back to the bedroom after sending me a *look*.

"Okay, dish. I'm going crazy here." Dina twists herself to face me, earning a grumble from Nacho, who has just settled in.

"To be honest, I'm hoping you'll dish."

My beautiful sister's face scrunches. "Why me?"

Time to let it all out. I take a deep breath, steady myself and ramble out the beginning of a conversation we've neglected for too long. "Since Mom and Dad died, I've assumed you blamed me. And it's fine if you do because I blame myself, but I realize I've never given you the opportunity to really talk about it. I'm hoping you'll get everything off of your chest so we can move forward. Together."

Silence.

It would almost be better if there were crickets in the background, because Nacho's snoring is even more ominous. I'm regretting this conversation already.

While staring down at her fur baby, stroking his sleeping head, Dina finally responds after several seconds. "I didn't blame you... but I resented you."

Somehow, that feels worse. I chew my bottom lip, trying to determine how to respond.

Dina doesn't give me a chance. "I resented you because you got more time with them. Because you weren't there in those first few hours after they died and I thought I had lost you, too. Mostly, I resented you for withdrawing from me. We were best friends, then all of a sudden there was this chasm between us that I couldn't traverse."

We're nearing the nine-year anniversary of our parents' deaths and this is all news to me.

"Is there really much difference between blame and resentment?"

"There's a big difference. Mom and Dad died in an accident. That wasn't your fault, and I never thought it was. But after they died, from minutes after it happened, when you weren't there, to four years down the line when we moved in here, that entire time, it felt like my sister was in front of me, but nowhere to be found. It felt like I lost everyone."

This is where assumptions and failing to have honest conversations get you. Years lost to being a sister in action, but not in heart. All because I was too scared to hear her truth. "I'm sorry, Dina. That's stupid to even say because it doesn't fix anything, but I'm sorry for not hearing you out sooner."

Nacho grumbles something in his sleep and I laugh at the fact he's even a miserable creature in dreamland. It helps to shed some of the sombre energy surrounding us.

"If you're looking for my forgiveness to absolve you of the guilt and blame you've been carrying around, I can't give you that." Dina stares at me with a new resolve. A confidence she normally wears, but has been missing since she sat down.

"You don't forgive me?" This is the truth I was afraid to hear. Now the weight feels even heavier.

She leans forward, placing her hand on the calf of my bent leg partially tucked beneath my opposite thigh. "I have nothing to forgive you for. Yeah, I held onto some resentment because I felt like you abandoned me, but as we got older, I realized you were struggling and trying your best with the crappy hand we were dealt. I got over it." She squeezes my leg and pins me with her intense dark eyes that look just like our mother's. "The only forgiveness you need is your own. Mom and Dad wouldn't have blamed you for any of it. You think they didn't know where you were really going? They were letting you be a teenager, Angel."

"What?" I pause a moment to process this new information. "They knew?" All this time, that possibility never occurred to me.

"Of course they did. You were sixteen. Stop blaming yourself for acting like it. Okay, you lied and went over to a guy's house. So what? It had nothing to do with what killed them."

I'm in shock. Memories flash through my mind of all the times I told white lies and assumed I was getting away with it. How much did they know? Why didn't they confront me?

Then an idea strikes me, so I hop up from the couch and go into my office, rummaging through decorative boxes on my bookshelf. I grab the one I want and return to Dina. I place the box between us, careful not to disturb Nacho, and remove the lid.

Dina's eyes tear up when she sees the contents. It's my memory box full of small souvenirs from special moments of our childhood. Ticket stubs, roller coaster photos, pamphlets from provincial parks we went camping at, and as many photos as I could fit.

Forgiveness is a fickle beast. More so than the temperamental chihuahua sleeping between Dina and me. But spending several hours going through the happy memories we had with our parents, crying, laughing, and sharing those special moments goes a long way to helping me forgive myself.

I stare at our last family photo, taken at Niagara Falls in the middle of summer. Dad's Scottish ancestry and the intense sun left him with a sunburn so bad he's glowing. Dina and I were both ignorant about things like skin cancer and were embracing our natural tans. Our mom's smile was bright and reached her deep brown eyes as she looked down at us instead of at the camera. Life got really complicated shortly after this moment frozen in time. It got dark. Depressing. Hard. But it made us strong. And I think Dina and I both have become women our parents would be proud of.

All I ever wanted was to make them proud. Now, all I want is to be happy.

I t took a few days to get scheduled, but at this time next week, we have a team meeting on the books. I have between now and then to get myself in order and figure out how to win over my staff. For the time being, though, I'm immersed in finalizing the details for a new restaurant campaign when Paxton calls through the intercom. "Um… Mr. Taylor. There's someone here to see you."

"Did this person give a name, Paxton?" I don't want to interrupt my progress for someone I can reschedule.

"Mr. Taylor."

"Yes?" Is it not clear he already has my attention?

"No, his name is Mr. Taylor."

I might as well be cryogenically frozen. That lasts all of twelve seconds before rage thaws me out and my temperature stops just shy of incinerating my suit. That man is not coming into my office. Not stepping foot in the place I studied and worked for without his help. I pull myself together, stand, straighten my suit, and walk to my office door.

When I exit into Paxton's desk area, I see him. My father. Funny how the last time I saw him, he seemed like a fearless giant. A man who had the strength to defeat anyone or anything. Now, all I see is a wrinkled, greying old coward in a baggy suit who chose money over his family. I see a person who simultaneously discouraged and motivated me without being present. He gave me his skin tone and hair colour, but everything I know about being a man, I learned from my mom and brother. The people who were there for me without fail.

"Jacob, what are you doing here?"

"Hello, son. Can we talk in your office?"

His use of the term son causes my jaw to clench. "No. You won't be staying."

Paxton shifts in his leather desk chair. I don't want to undo the progress we've made over the past few days by appearing like an unfeeling jerk toward a man Paxton would assume is my family. That's the only reason I wave my father—and I use that term loosely—into my office.

I close the door behind him but don't draw the blinds. Like I said, he's not staying long. "Out with it."

Jacob sits in the chair on the opposite side of my desk, groaning in the process. Time hasn't been kind to him. He didn't deserve kindness, as far as I'm concerned. "It's been a long time, son. You've done well for yourself."

"First of all, I'm not your son. Or have you forgotten how you abandoned me and your wife to pad your bank account?" My face is growing hotter by the second as I stand on the opposite side of my desk. I look at my wall of interior windows and spot two employees strolling by, glaring into my office. I clench my fists to redirect some of my anger. "Second, we're not here to make small talk or make up for lost time. It's lost. There's no finding it again. You made your choice and I've made mine."

He blows out a ragged breath. "I know I made a mistake when I—"

"A mistake? A mistake is forgetting to put money in a parking metre or missing your highway exit. Abandoning your kid without looking back is not a mistake." My voice is getting louder by the second and a few more employees have sauntered past to take in the show. I lower my voice and continue, "You had years to reach out. Twenty-one years, to be exact."

"I know. Believe me, I regret what I did. There were so many times I wanted to come back, but I was afraid you all hated me so much. I was just… afraid."

"Well, you're right about that. We did hate you. Mom spent years crying over you. *She* was afraid to ever try again. I spent two decades trying to prove to you that it was possible to have it all. To have a career and people you love."

"I'm sorry, son."

I slam a fist on my desk. "Don't call me son! You lost that right." Of course, when I look up, a group of staffers are in the boardroom across the hall, witnessing my outburst. Again. They're going to think I need anger management, but there's a lot of context missing. Two-plus decades' worth. "Why are you here?"

"Stage four liver cancer." He looks down at an envelope in his hand that seems to have appeared out of nowhere.

I sink into my chair because now it doesn't feel right to be looming over him. Unless he came here looking for part of my liver—which, even after everything he's done, I still wouldn't refuse. "How long?"

"Found out almost a year ago. Things get put into perspective when your clock starts ticking louder each day, Damian. I screwed up and I know I did and there's no way for me to make up for that. But I want you to know I'm proud of you." He slides the envelope across my desk. It's plain white, with my first name written in a feminine scroll that doesn't belong to Jacob Taylor.

"What's this?"

"The only thing I can do to make things right. You're not wrong to hate me, but I hope you can forgive me someday."

Can I? All these years I've been so filled with hatred toward my father. Since meeting Angel, my priorities have shifted. Instead of wanting to prove to my father he was wrong, and that he could have had it all, I just want to live. I want to pursue things that will make me happy, and take care of the people I love. My father no longer has control over me. "I can't say I forgive you right now, and I'll never forget…"

Jacob nods with his crestfallen face. "I expected as much."

"But… I don't hate you anymore."

His yellow-tinged eyes appear a little brighter than ten seconds ago. "Thank you, Damian. That's more than I expected after all these years."

This man in front of me, who broke my world apart because of his own greed, I can't help but feel pity for him.

"Did you ever get married again? Have more kids?"

He shakes his head, but his yellowed eyes are watering. "I lived to work. That's all I was ever good at."

That's not entirely true. And honesty is the best policy.

"You were a good dad."

His eyes jolt wide. "You don't have to pity an old dying man. I made my choice, and now I have to die with it."

His reminder that he's dying twists my stomach. A man I believed I felt no affection for; I can't help but feel hurt all over again that I'll be forced to lose him twice when I never really had him.

"Once upon a time, you were a good dad. A good husband. None of us ever knew what we did wrong because one day we were fine, and the next you were packing your things. That's what hurt the most."

"Sorry seems so inadequate. None of you did anything wrong. It was all me." He swallows an audible gulp. "I know I lost my right to give you fatherly advice, so all I'll say is learn from my mistakes. When you have something good, don't let it go. You don't want to be staring at your hourglass, watching the grains of sand draining out, and be full of regret."

No, I don't. Even if Jacob hadn't come here today, his mistakes taught me a valuable lesson a long time ago. Despite looking across my desk at a dying man—my dying father—I can't stop the slightest hint of a smile from taking over when I think about Angel and how much she's impacted my life.

He responds with a tight smile of his own. "What about you? Married? Kids?"

Ten minutes ago, I would have told him off. But the least I can do is appease him and answer a simple question. "Not yet."

A smile creases Jacob's eyes for the first time since he entered my office. "Someday, maybe."

"Yeah. Someday."

A few seconds of silence pass between us. I don't know what to say.

Jacob eases up out of his chair with a louder groan than the one he sat down with. "Thank you for speaking to me, Damian. You've done well for yourself, but don't forget to have a life outside of these walls. Believe me when I tell you, this isn't all that matters."

He doesn't need to tell me. I don't feel like I owe him anything, but I owe it to Angel to be a better man than one carrying a chip around on his shoulder. I owe it to her to offer that forgiveness I swore I'd never have space for.

We walk to my office door, and I notice my neighbours are no longer gawking. Figures they'd look away now.

I place my hand on the handle, but before I turn it, I have one last thing to say. "I want to forgive you. This chip on my shoulder I've been wearing my entire adult life, it's done enough damage. I promise I'll try."

Making a grown man cry is a new situation for me. I'm not sure what the protocol is. Do I offer a hug? A mug of hot chocolate? A Rolex? Oh, he's already got one. I settle on the one thing six-year-old Damian never thought would happen again.

He hesitates when I step forward, like we haven't just crossed over a threshold of pent up anger and regret into new territory. I wrap my arms around him anyway.

"Thank you. I really am sorry for everything. You've given me some peace I didn't deserve."

Me too. This fifteen minute encounter hasn't healed decades' worth of residual feelings, but it's a start. The difference between me and Jacob is that I have time in front of me. I have the chance to live my life without regrets. That's what I want to do.

The silly photo I took of Damian the first day he drove me to Dina's lights up my phone as I'm flicking through the *Netflix* menu.

"Hey."

"I saw my father today."

Not what I expected. I drop the remote and sit upright. "What? Where? How?"

"I think you mean why?" There's a pause, then a deep inhale. "He's dying. He came to make peace, I guess."

That's the worst possible reason to reconnect with an absentee parent, and not how I hoped a reunion would go for Damian and his father. "I'm so sorry. How are you holding up?"

"Not sure yet. He, uh… left me some kind of letter. An envelope and I'm not sure what's in it. Are you busy?"

"No. I was just relaxing. Dina left about an hour ago."

He makes a noncommittal hum sound before he asks, "Can I stop by?"

"You don't even have to ask." After the days we both had, a relaxing evening together sounds perfect. "I'll make dinner when you get here."

A knock at my door sends Genie speeding down the hallway. We have our talk about jumping on Damian, but it's a half-hearted effort at best.

I swing the door open, and Genie surprises me by sitting like the best little smiling bully baby around. Damian steps through the door, and as soon as the door closes, Genie reverts to the wild animal I know and love.

"Hey Genie." He bends down to give her the head scratch she's desperate for without taking his eyes off of me. "Hi." His meek smile shows the emotional upheaval he's been through today.

"How are you?"

"Better now." He steps forward and wraps his arms around my waist. The second his lips land on mine, it's as if I'm absorbing all the turmoil he walked in here with, but it doesn't feel so heavy for me. It's always easier to carry for someone else, and I want to ease the weight off of him.

"I have cheap wine and discounted steak. You're in for a real treat tonight."

Damian pulls me in closer, easing my body against his, and plants another kiss on my still-tingling lips. "As long as I'm with you, I'd eat Genie's dog food."

That thought makes me laugh, but when I glance at Genie, she looks genuinely concerned. "Don't worry, girl. Your food is all yours." I grab Damian's hand and lead him into the living room, motioning for him to sit on the sofa. "I'll grab the wine and get started on dinner. You, relax."

"Let me help with something."

I tilt my head, questioning his motivations. He knows I don't like too many cooks in the kitchen, but he always helps with the wine or something. In this case, though, I'm sure it's a distraction.

"Show me what you've got."

For the next thirty minutes, we dance around each other in my tiny kitchen, working together to make the cheap steak edible. We toss together a caesar salad and make garlic butter baby potatoes to ensure we'll both need to brush our teeth before any make-out sessions commence. It takes about half of our cooking time before Damian starts laughing, but it's nice to see some of the stress from the day leave his face. We make a pretty good team.

Our conversation over dinner is complete fluff. Nothing of substance, and I can tell he's working to avoid the topic of his father's visit today, and it's for that reason I don't bring up my conversation with Dina. When we both drop our forks on our empty plates and lean back, satiated, I'm unsure if I should bring it up or wait for him.

"Apparently he has stage four liver cancer."

That solves my dilemma. I reach over to place my hand over his. "How do you feel about everything?"

He doesn't respond right away. "It is what it is, I guess. He hasn't been a part of my life for decades. I didn't need him before"—his voice breaks—"and I don't need him now."

The hurt in his voice makes it hard for me to maintain my composure.

"Just because he made the decisions he did doesn't mean this isn't hard. You're allowed to mourn the loss of the father you never had. It's okay to hurt." I grab his hand and lead him to the sofa so I can be closer to him. This is a situation that calls for a hug, not a hand-holding.

Damian slouches back on the couch. I sit beside him, turned to face him with one foot tucked underneath me.

"I wasn't enough for him. Mom wasn't. And for what? Now he's dying and all he has from his sad, pathetic life is money and a job that will replace him before the ink on his obituary dries. What good is that?"

"It's no good. You know that. He probably does too, and that's why he came to see you. He knows his time is running out, and in the end, he wanted to see you. You were always enough."

Damian swipes his one eye with his right hand before a tear falls. I take that as a sign I need to be closer. Garlic breath be damned. I settle in beside him and he drapes his arm over my shoulders.

"What am I supposed to do with this letter? I don't want to read it yet."

"That's something you could do with your mom. I mean, I'm here for you if you want me to be, but I feel like that's something you should do together."

He pats at his pants' pocket, which I'm assuming is where he has the letter. "Maybe. I don't want to open up old wounds for her. She never deserved any of it."

"I get that, but you should tell her. You didn't deserve it either."

Genie attempts to hop up onto Damian's lap, but the poor squatty girl can't get the momentum. Her failure to launch makes us both laugh. Damian bends down and grunts as he lifts her hefty body onto his thighs. She looks at him with such adoration, you can see the love in her eyes.

"Enough about my day. How did things go with Dina? I've been so distracted, I forgot to ask." Damian pets Genie with his left hand and strokes my shoulder with his right. Despite our conversation from thirty seconds ago, he looks content.

I give him an abbreviated version of what our day consisted of, including our ice cream lunch. To my surprise, he asks to see the photos I mentioned. I haven't put them away yet, so they're still tucked under my coffee table.

The first photo I pull out when I remove the lid is one of me from my grade eight graduation. I remember feeling so grown up. It was the first time I'd ever worn a gown, and shopping with my mom was one highlight of my year. I settled on a satin, dark turquoise slip dress that, looking back, was way too mature for thirteen-year-old me, but it was forty dollars on clearance and I knew my parents didn't have a lot of money, so I pretended it was my dream dress. Another occasion I lied. Good intentions or not, I still shouldn't have. That day was just as important to my mom.

Damian's hand stops moving, causing me to look over at him. "What's wrong? We don't have to look at these if it's too much."

I shake my head and explain to him where my thoughts were. He doesn't make excuses for me or tell me a little white lie is okay sometimes. He knows me better than that. The only thing he does is lean over to kiss me. Using his non-Genie hand, he pulls my head closer, deepening the kiss until my dress stress disappears.

After we separate our lips, Damian keeps his forehead pressed to mine and his eyes closed. "Have I told you lately how amazing you are?"

I've returned from my earlier guilt trip thanks to Damian's distraction. "Not recently, but I can forgive you."

"Do you feel better after talking to your sister?"

"Yeah. I do. Not saying I'm just over years of guilt I've been hauling around, but it at least feels like there's wheels on the suitcase now. It'll get easier to manage in time." I pause, not wanting to send him back to his tortured mindset from earlier, but not wanting to ignore his emotions, either. "What about you? Do you think you can ever forgive your dad?"

He drops his hand from Genie's head, who is now sound asleep on his lap, and pats at his pocket again. "I'm not sure what that forgiveness feels like, but I think I'm on my way. Ever since we visited my family, I've been trying to focus on living for the right things." He drops his other arm that he had placed back around my shoulders, and instead, takes my right hand in his left. "This feels like the right thing, Angel."

45

DAMIAN

Somebody's Somebody

It's finally the day of our staff meeting. Everyone has been busy finishing up old projects before starting new ones and today is the closest thing to a lull we'll get for a while.

As people file into the boardroom opposite my office, I walk across the hallway after I see Angel arrive. She's wearing a thick wool coat and has half her hair stuffed in a beret-style hat. Her cheeks are pink from the cold, and I'd love nothing more than to warm her up. Instead, I settle for a curt nod of acknowledgement as I enter the room.

Once I'm certain everyone is here, I begin. "Good morning. Thanks for clearing your schedules to meet with me today. I'm sure you're all wondering what this is about, but I assure you, it's nothing scary." I set down the manilla folder I carried in the room and stand at the head of the table in front of a projector screen, making eye contact with as many people as I can. Each one of them flinches under my gaze, aside from Elliot and Angel. This is going to be an uphill battle.

Paxton sends an encouraging smile my way, but I'm pretty sure he's still scared of me.

To put everyone at ease, I take a seat in the lone empty chair and lean back, resting my feet on the leg under the table.

"It seems we've gotten off on the wrong foot—a foot that didn't belong to any of us—and it's time we make it right."

The employees around the table look at each other, more terrified than before. I am horrible at this.

"What I mean to say is that I'm not the same man as Mr. Woodward. I understand I'm the new guy; I'm unfamiliar, and I've failed at expressing my intentions with you all, but that ends today." Carefully calculating my words, I take a deep breath. "Mr. Hannon and I had a chat about what the work environment was like before I arrived, and I'm sorry I didn't address it sooner. I want you all to know that isn't my style. We need to work as a team, and I value your input as much as I hope you'd value mine."

People's faces have started relaxing and, for the first time in the ten months since I took over this position, tension releases from the room.

"So I'm having Paxton distribute new informal policies and procedures. Obviously, the company has policies of their own and we have to respect those, but these are internally for our department."

I give everyone a few moments to read over the sheet of paper, and a few of them smile.

"So, what I expect from you all is to work hard while you're here. Don't waste time if you're stuck on something. Please come see me or someone else, if that's the case. My door will remain open at all times unless I'm in a meeting, so don't hesitate to stop in. And for goodness' sake, please don't be afraid of me when we run into each other in the lobby. You guys are killing me."

Every employee in the room chuckles, and I feel like an idiot for not having this conversation sooner. Why is being honest such a hard concept to grasp? I've made things difficult for me and everyone else when I could have adopted Angel's strategy and put this to rest months ago.

"Now, in the interest of being ultra cheesy"—I glance at Angel and catch her smirk—"and wanting to get to know each of you a little better, we're going to go around the room like the first day of summer camp and you're going to tell me something about yourselves that's not on your resume. I don't want to know where you went to school or what your GPA was. Trust me, I know that already. What I want to know is if you like camping or basketball. Do you have any meaningful tattoos? But for HR's sake, please don't show me. Whatever not-job related thing you want to share, I want to know it because for us to build a foundation as a team, we need to understand each other. So tell me what's important to you."

I stand from my chair, making sure I have everyone's attention; especially Angel's. My hands are shaking because I'm not sure how she's going to respond to this, but I have mentally committed to it and intend to follow through. "As you all know, my name is Damian, and I've been working at *Harbour Campaigns* for six years, though I was in the product marketing department for more than five of them."

"We don't want your resume!" Elliot shouts from across the table. Him badgering me is progress.

I laugh at his comment and reply, "I'm getting to the important part." I take a slow breath to steady my voice because I will lose all credibility if I sing these next words like a schoolgirl choir. "A few months ago, I went into a restaurant nearby, looking for lunch. That was all I expected. What I got was a salad and an introduction to our newest team member, Angel Blake. Now, to be clear, I had no part in hiring Miss Blake, so she is here by her own merit, as I'm sure you've all noticed."

"Cut to the good part." Mitchell chimes in with a huge smile on his face.

So far, so good. "Right. Well, the best part is that I fell in love with this woman, and I can't go another minute without telling her."

Myself and everyone else in the room focuses on Angel, trying to gauge her reaction. Her face is stoic. That's not the face of someone who is happy to hear a declaration of love.

"Can I speak with you for a moment, Mr. Taylor?" Angel asks, still no clarification in her expression.

The rest of the staff either gasp or snicker, and I now feel like this was the dumbest idea I've ever had. And I once jumped off my neighbour's roof into a kiddie pool. I respond with a simple nod and step toward the door. "I'll return in a moment, and I expect something juicy from all of you. You… uh… don't have to top this, though."

Angel steps out of the room in front of me, and to my surprise, reaches back to grab my hand before dragging me down the hall.

"Where are we going? My office is right there."

"I see that, but it's got glass walls. We'll have more privacy in 'the pit'."

Privacy? Is she going to slap me? Or kiss me? Tell me she hates me? My brain is sorting through a hundred different scenarios, and I'm not leaning toward any of them.

We stop in a random cubicle, which one of my staffers decorated with a few photos of her friends or family and a lot of pictures of a tuxedo cat. Angel leans back on the desk with her arms crossed. For a woman barely over five feet tall, she can be intimidating. I love that about her.

"Did you mean what you said, or are you just trying to make yourself more human to the staff to win them over?"

"What?" I step forward, placing my hands on her hips. "Angel, I'd never say something like that for any reason other than because I meant it. I've fallen hopelessly in love with you. Truer words have never left my mouth."

She stares at me with an intensity that makes me regret my decision to declare my love for her publicly. I wish I could read her thoughts. I could ask her what she's thinking, and she'd tell me, but I don't want to play with her like that. Whatever she wants to say, it needs to be because she feels inclined to say it.

She surprises me with, "Why?"

Asking that question makes me realize she doesn't see everything amazing about herself that I do. "Why do I love you?"

She nods.

"You don't make apologies for who you are or what's important to you. You're honest and trustworthy, and I, for one, appreciate that more than anything. Even more than your remarkable beauty. More than your incomparable wit and sense of humour. More than your kissable lips, and trust me, I love those a lot."

She doesn't respond with words. In a flash, she grabs the back of my neck, pulls my face to meet hers and gives me a taste of those kissable lips. Somehow, kissing Angel Blake after confessing my love for her makes her even more delectable. Kissing her now is a whole other realm of intimacy because my soul is communicating with hers.

When she pulls her head away, her cheeks are flushed like they were when she walked in from the cold, and her hair looks wild. I didn't realize I was attempting to run my hand through it until seeing the aftereffects.

"We need to get back to the meeting." Her eyes are staring down at the floor to my left.

I lift her chin to look at me, wanting to get some insight into what she's thinking, but again, she gives nothing away. "What's on your mind?" Immediately, I'm flooded with regret. "Never mind. You don't have to. I'm sorry."

"No. Don't be. I was... I was thinking I love you too, but this isn't how"—she waves her hand around gesturing to the room we're in—"or where I wanted to tell you."

My smile grows exponentially hearing those words. "I'm sorry for ruining your plans. Can you ever forgive me?"

She smirks, playfully swatting my chest. "I suppose I'll have to, since I love you and all."

I wrap my arms around her, lifting her off the ground and spinning in a circle. "You are my angel, you know that? I love you, Angel Blake."

"I love y—"

"What are you two doing out here? We've all been waiting for ten minutes." Elliot peeks his head around the corner into "the pit", catching my eyes. He tucks his head back behind a cubicle, probably feeling awkward for walking in on his boss twirling his girlfriend around.

"We're coming back now. Sorry about that." Angel slides out of my hold and walks toward Elliot, who is standing with a stupid grin on his face. Okay, maybe it's not awkwardness he's feeling.

How he feels is none of my concern, though. I can't tame my smile as I follow behind Angel and Elliot to return to the boardroom. All eyes are on us as we walk back in, but I really couldn't care less. This euphoric feeling I have can't be crushed by anything.

45

ANGEL

Love Will Find a Way

Our absence was noted, to say the least. As soon as I walk into the boardroom, the chatter halts. My face feels hot to the touch when I take my seat, which isn't remedied by Damian walking around the table, brushing his hand across my shoulders on his way to his vacated chair.

Damian dropping into his seat silences the rest of the room. "Well, now that we've got that out of the way, Meghan, would you like to go first?"

"Oh, uh… sure. First, I'd like to say that Angel has had nothing but good things to say about you, sir."

She's right. As much as I want to keep our personal and professional lives separate, after Elliot's comments last week, I was determined to make everyone see Damian wasn't the dictator they made him out to be. Granted, that was difficult over email, since this is the first day I've been back in the office, but I worked with what I had. Damian flashes me a thankful smile, which I return with a wink.

Everyone around the table continues on, explaining random facts about themselves. We hear about favourite vacation spots, why veganism is beneficial for everyone, political and religious leanings, family lives, and pets—namely

Theresa's tuxedo cat named Checkers whom she taught how to fetch. She's also single, but I'm not going to assume the facts are related.

At the end of the meeting, Damian's smile is so wide it could put Genie's to shame. Everyone takes turns walking up to him, shaking his hand, and I hear a lot of apologies that sound genuine; both from and to Damian. Everyone eventually exits the room, leaving Damian and me as the only stragglers.

"Come to my office for a minute?"

I smirk, knowing now that the meeting is over, I'm off the clock. Damian isn't. I lean in and whisper in his ear, "Only if you'll close the blinds."

I'm pretty sure I can feel his heart beat faster through his tailored suit. He swallows and I trace the bob of his Adam's apple, watching him struggle to speak.

"What do you have planned for me, Miss Blake?" His words are little more than a whisper.

As I lean in to tell him what I was thinking, a knock sounds at the open door.

"Uh, Boss. I'm sorry to bother you, but there's a man waiting on line one for you and he says it's urgent. A Mr. Cochrane." Paxton's face is redder than I've ever seen it, but after Damian's display thirty minutes ago, our private moment should hardly come as a surprise.

"I'll be right there. Thanks, Paxton."

With Paxton out of earshot, Damian whispers in my ear, "We'll finish this conversation later." He grabs my hand to lead me back to his office and instructs me to sit on his plush navy sofa under the window. He sits in his office chair, picks up the phone and presses a button. "Damian Taylor speaking."

I stare at him with a new fascination. The man I love. The man who accepts me for me. The man who slumps over in his chair and drops his face into his free hand before his shoulders start to shake.

In a few seconds, I'm standing behind him, folded over his back, wrapping my arms around him. He speaks a few more muffled words before he hangs up the receiver.

I say nothing as I squeeze him with all I can, trying to hold him together. It's not hard to guess what that phone call was about.

A few minutes later, Damian confirms it without looking up. "He's gone. My dad. He died this morning."

I note the use of the term "dad" instead of his usual "father". Father denotes someone with a biological investment in a person's life. Dad is something different. That implies a *personal* investment.

"I'm so sorry. What can I do?"

Silence. He doesn't look at me. He's breathing long, deep breaths, but he's staring at his desk without blinking.

"Damian?"

Nothing.

I run through the memories of what it felt like when my parents died. The scenario is different, but it's an enormous loss for him, nonetheless. I jump into action, not waiting for him to reply. He needs time to process his own thoughts, so that's what I'll give him.

Paxton is at his desk when I step out to speak to him. I tug Damian's office door closed behind me.

"Mr. Taylor is going to need a personal day, Paxton."

He spins in his chair with a tentative look. "In his office?"

I glance around at nothing in particular, trying to decipher Paxton's confusion. Doesn't take a genius to figure out that a short while ago Damian was confessing his love for me in front of the entire department, and now we're in his office with the blinds drawn.

I hesitate to disclose the real reason for my request, deciding even though it's not my truth to tell, basic details are necessary. I lean in closer to Paxton and whisper, "The man who just called told Damian his dad died this morning. He's still in shock, and he needs the day. But it's not my business to tell that, so please don't make it common knowledge."

Paxton's expression falls, and he nods his understanding. "I'll reschedule everything else for today." Then he scribbles something on a piece of paper. "This is my personal number. If he isn't ready to come back on Monday, let me know and I'll handle it."

There's a reason Damian has never had a bad word to say about his assistant. Even though he seemed just as terrified of Damian as everyone else, from what I've heard, he's been a stellar employee. Seeing it in action makes me have a new respect for him.

"Thank you. I'll keep you posted." I spin and place my hand on the knob, but Paxton calls my name, making me freeze.

"Tell Mr. Taylor I'm sorry for his loss, please."

I acknowledge Paxton before returning to Damian's office. When I walk back through the door, his eyes meet mine, and I notice the tears leaking down his cheeks.

He stands and walks toward me, saying nothing as he pulls me into his arms. A few seconds pass before he blows out a breath. "I thought you left me."

I pull my head back to study his face. He looks more worried than sad.

"Of course I wouldn't leave you. I was letting Paxton know that you're taking a personal day. How are you?"

"With you here, I'll be okay." He releases his grip on me and takes a step back, rubbing his hands over his face. "The letter my dad gave me…"

He doesn't continue after a few seconds, so I prompt him. "What about it?"

"Mr. Cochrane said I should read it, and when I'm ready, come into his office to sort out the estate. Apparently, I'm the executor of his will."

The past week, Damian has mentioned his father a few times, so I know he didn't have any other spouses or children beyond Laura and Damian, but still, the revelation surprises me. I can't help but feel pity for the man who gave up on having a family to pursue wealth and died before he hit retirement age.

"Do you want me to call your mom for you? Have her come with you to sort that out? Tell me whatever you need and I'll do it."

"I'm sorry for dragging you into this—"

"Nope. Before you say another word, let me make this clear." I step forward, closing the gap between us. "I'm here for you, no matter what. This is even worse timing than standing in 'the pit', but I love you, Damian. I say those words with zero hesitation and every bit of truth I've ever spoken. I love you, and I'll be by your side through this in whatever way I can."

The tears that had stopped trailing down his cheeks since I walked into his office start flowing again, but this time he doesn't swipe them away. I wrap my arms around him, wanting to put my words into action.

"I love you, Angel," he chokes out.

We stand there together for several moments, Damian occasionally hiccupping a suppressed sob, and me, trying to keep myself together. A lot is said in that silence.

I'm here for you.

I love you.

I choose you.

You can trust me.

Damian inhales a loud sniffle. "Will you come with me?"

I glance up at the tear-stained face of the man I love, feeling my heart crack a little with each droplet that rolls down his cheek. "I'll go with you anywhere."

47

DAMIAN

Casa De Mi Padre

We pull into the driveway of the small brick bungalow my mother has lived in since I was seven. It wasn't until I was older I learned the house was a sort of severance package from my father. When I found out, it made me resent him more. Thinking he could buy us off so he could go live his happy life without us. Now I know better. We got the happy life. A simple house. The rundown old car with mileage so astronomical, it became a game to see how high we could get it before it conked out for good. The love.

Angel sends me a compassionate look as she reaches over the centre console of my SUV. "If you need me to do the talking, just say the word."

If it weren't for her, I'd be so lost right now. I'm not sure she understands how much her presence means. I lift her hand and kiss her knuckles. "Thank you."

We walk to the faded burgundy door atop the concrete stoop and wait for my mom to answer. She shouts from the other side of the door that she's coming. I called her on our way here to inform her of our visit, but didn't allude to why. So when she opens the door, her stress level is obvious in her expression.

After a cursory glance at our faces, the next place she looks is Angel's stomach. If only it were happy news we were here with.

"Come in, come in. This is a nice surprise."

We enter the cramped foyer with the dull vinyl sheet flooring that's been a focal point of this space since I was a boy. We all greet each other and assure my mother we don't need any refreshments, then we seat ourselves in the living room. This room is one of the few that has been updated, so the sofa I sink into is comfortable and modern. Angel sits beside me and Mom settles into a chair on the opposite side of the coffee table.

"So, what brings you kids here?"

I glance at Angel, then back at my mom. Her eyes light up with anticipation, making me feel worse about ripping open this gaping wound that took the better part of a decade to heal.

"Jacob died this morning, Ma. He... uh... he had liver cancer."

I watch Mom's expression, which takes a moment to change as she registers what I've said. "Your father? How do you know? What happened?"

"He came to see me a week ago, and he brought me this." I hold up the plain white envelope with my name looped across it. "I thought we could open it together."

My mom doesn't shed a single tear. She grieved the loss of Jacob Taylor long ago. Much like I thought I had before he reappeared in my life, only to disappear from it again. Permanently. My emotions are not as steady as my mother's.

I hook my thumb into a gap in the envelope's seal, dragging it across to open it. I pull out the four pages that comprise what was so important, Jacob Taylor had to hand deliver it.

My voice gets stuck in my throat as I attempt to read it. I don't make it past my name before I hand it to Angel, silently begging her to read it for me.

True to her word, she obliges.

She takes a second to scan the letter before proceeding. "Damian. I know everything I have to say is coming twenty years too late. Believe me when I say there's nothing I've regretted more than leaving you and your mother. I was a selfish coward, and I don't expect you to ever forgive me. I suppose by now it's too late for that, anyway. Nothing I can say or do will make up for my mistakes, but I'm going to try. If my miserable life can make yours a little brighter, then I can die with that bit of peace."

My mom is still stone-faced, but Angel is getting emotional. I reach over, placing a hand on her knee. She gives me a small smile, then continues her reading.

"Before I do that, there's one thing I need to say. Twenty years is a long time to live alone. Now, I'm not complaining because I made my choices and I have to accept them, but you don't. Never let this life convince you that anything is more important than the people you love. I lost the right to be a father to you, but I don't want you going down the same path I did, Damian. I loved your mother, you, and Josh more than you can imagine, but my own fears, failings, and flaws drove me down a road I couldn't return from.

"I'm ashamed of how I failed you. Of how gutless I was. Of what a failure I was as a man and father. Don't feel sorry for me; I'm not saying any of this to garner sympathy. I only say it so you know that it was never about you or how much I loved you. You all deserved better, and I'm only sorry I caused so much heartache." Angel rubs her eye, but she holds herself together, which by extension, helps me maintain my composure.

Mom's facade has crumbled ever so slightly, and her eyes are glassy.

"Are you okay?" I ask her.

She nods. "I'm not sure what to think right now. He's right, that this is all coming twenty years too late. The damage has been done."

"I know, Ma. But for what it's worth, I think he knew too." I nod to Angel to continue once my mom doesn't reply.

"Use my choices as a lesson in what not to do. If you pay close enough attention to the consequences of other people's bad choices, you don't have to learn the hard way yourself. Be happy, son. At the end of your life, you'll look back and realize that was the only thing that had any real meaning. My words may not hold any value, but I love you and always have." Angel takes the first page, tucks it in behind the others, and releases a gasp.

The following pages are an abbreviated copy of my father's will. A seven-bedroom home in Rosedale, a vacation home in Antigua, a condo in Vancouver, countless investments, cars, and bank accounts flush with cash. All in all, there's over sixty million dollars' worth of assets. To be honest, it stings that this is what's left of his life. His contribution to the world. His departure from it isn't felt with immense sadness or unrelenting grief by the people he loved. It's measured with dollars and cents. What's left of him is dictated by stock and real estate markets.

"I don't want it. Any of it. It... doesn't feel right. Like it's some kind of payoff to make up for his decades of absence."

Neither my mom nor Angel respond for a moment.

"I'm going to donate it. Every penny."

Angel gives me a reassuring smile. "If that's what you want to do, I'll support that. Maybe take a few days, and when you speak with the lawyer, you can give him a decision."

"I won't change my mind. I already know a few places that are more than deserving. My time in my job has put me in front of a lot of different charities and I know which ones get neglected. His money can help them."

For the first time since we arrived, tears stream down my mother's face. "You've become the greatest man I could have ever wished for. You and your brother"—her voice breaks as she chokes out a sob and drops her face into her hands—"you've both made me so proud. Don't let this dictate any more of your life, Damian. If you want to donate this money, then I say, let's do it right."

I get up from my spot on the sofa and pull my mother up to hug her. I kiss the top of her head, feeling so grateful to have her as my family. "You could have given up on me so many times, Ma. I'm everything I am because of you." I look at Angel and nod for her to join our family hug.

She hesitates as she walks over to join us, but I don't, roping my arm around her to pull her to my side. "I love this girl, Ma. So much."

Angel blushes, but my mom looks up at me, smiling through her tears.

"Oh, honey. I knew that since before I met her. You can't even hear her name without your eyes smiling." She wraps her arm around Angel, and I stand there in the arms of two women I love most in the world, processing the major life events that have happened today.

Jacob Taylor may have run out of time to build a bridge between us, but the least I can do is make sure he redeems himself. His fortune can change a lot of lives, and right here, right now, I know there's nothing in mine that needs changing.

I've found my happiness, and I'll never let it go.

48

It took almost nine months to liquidate all of Jacob Taylor's assets and arrange everything for our fundraiser. *Harbour Campaigns'* staff pitched in during their off hours to help Damian and me put everything together. My sister, friends, and co-workers have all gone above and beyond to make this day a success.

We've rented a part of the *Exhibition Place* grounds, which is less than a kilometre from where Dina lives, and I can't help but think about how far Damian and I have come since the first day he dropped Genie and me off. Genie is even more in love with him than ever, and so am I.

He's directing volunteers, greeting people, and doing it all with Genie attached to his wrist with a bright pink leash. He claims she picked it out herself and he still can't tell her no. It's a work in progress.

After his father died, Damian approached Josh to discuss what he felt they should do with the money and Josh was in agreement with Damian's plan. Their selflessness continues to amaze me. There was enough money for Damian, Laura, and Josh all to live a lavish lifestyle. Retire, set Daisy and Dahlia up for life, buy a fancy new house and top of the line cars. But none of them want what Jacob Taylor wasted his life on, and those things only serve as a reminder of what's truly important.

"Can we go play some carnival games?" Daisy asks, tugging on my right arm.

I look at Lily and Laura, who are both standing with Dahlia a few feet away. "Let me just see if Uncle Damian needs any help with anything, then we can go, okay?"

Lily insists she'll take the girls to check out some of the many attractions we've arranged for today. I thank her with a nod, and assure Daisy I'll catch up with them shortly. Those little girls have become an integral part of my life. They remind me so much of how close Dina and I once were, and have become again since our talk many months ago.

The entire day passes in a whirlwind. I barely see Damian aside from a blur resembling him running around, doing his utmost to make this event a success. By the looks of things, his dream to turn this into an annual event could very well become reality. We're sharing proceeds in equal parts with a few different charities, and I'm confident it will make a real difference for a lot of people. A lot of families.

When things wind down and Damian stands still for more than thirty seconds, I step up beside him, instantly feeling a sense of calm in his presence. He hooks his arm around my waist and pulls me in for a kiss. Something that never gets old. He still has the ability to make my heart flutter each time our lips meet. Each time I even *think* about kissing him.

"Thank you for all of this. I couldn't have done it without you." There's a new intensity in his eyes that makes it clear he really believes that.

"This was all you. You would have pulled it off on your own." A content smile tugs at my lips as I stand wrapped in his arms, studying every tiny detail of his face. Details I memorized long ago, but can't seem to convince myself I've sufficiently committed to memory.

He hesitates for a second. "No, Angel. I guess I should have said I *wouldn't* have done it without you. I would have still been filled with so much hatred toward my father, I never would have seen the possibilities with all he left behind."

I'm not sure how to respond to that.

"My motivation before I met you was just proving to my father that he was wrong. But then you came into my life, and suddenly that didn't matter anymore. Out of everything I have, the only thing I'd hate to lose is you." Genie jumps up at his leg, which makes him chuckle. "And you, Genie. And my family, obviously. The point is, nothing else matters. I don't care where I am or what I'm doing, as long as I'm with you."

"Damian." I giggle, trying to stop myself from tearing up. "You know I love you. I'm not going anywhere."

He blows out a long breath, turning back to his brother and handing him Genie's leash. He drops to one knee, which nearly knocks me to mine.

I scan around us and everyone I know is here. The same co-workers Damian first confessed his love for me in front of, my sister, her best friend, my best friends, and Damian's family. They're all here, and all looking at me. I settle my eyes back on Damian, who is beaming like never before.

"Angel Blake, when I met you, I was a shell of a man. I knew what I wanted but couldn't achieve it because I was standing in my own way. I was lying to myself, making excuses for all the ways I fell short. But you came into my life, and just by being you, you made me face the truth. Without trying, you made me question everything about who I was and who I wanted to be."

I'm frozen in place with my hands over my mouth and nose, focused on his every word.

"As much as I've figured out since I met you, I have just as many unanswered questions I'm looking forward to answering. But the only one that really matters is if you'll be my wife. Will you marry me, Angel Blake?"

There's no part of me that hesitates. "Of course, I'll marry you."

He hops up from his kneeling position to scoop me up into his arms, lifting me like he did the first time we kissed. And he kisses me again in front of everyone, but all I can focus on is him. The way he tastes. How his muscles feel under his black fundraiser T-shirt. How I can feel him smiling against my lips.

Honesty is always the best policy, and I honestly love this man with all that I am.

THE END

If you enjoyed this book, please consider leaving a review on Amazon or the retailer's website where you purchased the book from. I love hearing from my readers.

If you'd like to hear from me, find all of my links here: linktr.ee/TiffanyAndrea.

SPECIAL THANKS

First, I want to take a moment, as I always do, to say a heartfelt thank you to my husband and kids who endlessly support and inspire me. As my girls have gotten older, they've become more interested in each of my stories (minus the kissing scenes, because… gross) and their excitement helps push me when I inevitably get to the part in each book I'm ready to give up. Thank you, my darling girls. I love you both more than you'll ever know.

Second, if you noticed the dedication in this book and aren't familiar with the term "Bookstagrammer", it's a phrase coined by book lovers on Instagram. Authors, readers, reviewers, from casual to full time. The community is based on a love for books. When I first set out to start my proofreading business, I "walked" into the community not knowing what to expect. Two women in particular, @fictionaddictionangela and @angelacairnsauthor, who were the first to really welcome me. Hence the main character's name, Angel. I appreciate you ladies and your kindness in those early days. It felt a bit like being accepted to join the cool kids at a new school.

With each of the novels in this series, I chose a musical artist to draw inspiration from to create the story. It makes the writing process so much more fun to curate a perfect playlist to go along with the book.

So, here is my ultimate playlist for Total Bull. You can find it on Spotify at linktr.ee/TiffanyAndrea.

(Please note, I do not make any claims to any of these songs. All rights belong to Christina Aguilera or the record label. I'm merely sharing my inspiration.)

Believe Me
Change
Tell Me
Fall In Line
Move It
I Come Undone*
I Hate Boys
Cease Fire
Empty Words
Come On Over
Like I Do
When You Put Your Hands On Me
Say Something
Fighter
Castle Walls
Army Of me
Obvious
Make the World Move
Make Me Happy
Light Up the Sky
Accelerate
Infatuation
I Got Trouble
Here To Stay
Get Mine, Get Yours
Blank Page

Anywhere But Here
Hurt
You Lost Me
Blessed
Deserve
Understand
Masochist
Mother
Back In the Day
Dream a Dream
By Your Side
Ain't No Other Man
Mercy On Me
The Real Thing*
Keeps Getting' Better
Haunted Heart
Reflection
All I Need
Somebody's Somebody
Love Will Find a Way
Casa De Mi Padre*
Feel This Moment

A few special mentions:
Dirrty
Genie In a Bottle
Beautiful

*Indicates song is not available on Spotify Canada at the time of publishing

You Are Enough Series:
We're All a Little Broken: Book 1 (Zara's story)
We're All a Little Overwhelmed: Book 1.5 (Zara's extended epilogue)
We're All a Little Guarded: Book 2 (Chelsea's story)
We're All a Little Tired: Book 2.5 (Chelsea's extended epilogue)
We're All a Little Scared: Book 3 (Isla's story)
We're All a Little Determined: Short Story Collection (Available free on my website)

This women's fiction series focuses on various aspects of mental health and overcoming trauma. It addresses anxiety, depression, panic disorders, miscarriage, adoption, grief and loss, racism, discrimination, and more, but in a light hearted way that will also make you laugh. The entire series is set in Muskoka/Bracebridge, Ontario.

Dear Sister, Never Again: Available free on my website as an eBook, or through Amazon as a paperback. This women's fiction novella explores the concept that DNA is not the only factor to determine family.

Suburban Watchdogs: This silly PG-13 crime comedy features four dads, three idiotic criminals, one slobbery dog, a determined cop, and a nosey nonagenarian neighbour. It's full of vigilante nonsense, terrible dad jokes, and a pursuit for justice.

Set in a small town north of the big city, these dads are not going to let criminals waltz into their neighbourhood without resistance.

A New Leash on Life Series:

This series will consist of twenty interconnected standalone romantic comedies. Some characters from Suburban Watchdogs and the You Are Enough series will have cameos or their own starring role!

Total Bull (Angel and Damian)
Ay Chihuahua (Dina and Holden)
Tell-Tail Sign (Sophie and Boyd)
The Pugly Truth (Hannah and Caleb) *Spring 2023*
Chemistry Lab (Hollis and Myer) *Summer 2023*
Pitty Party (Oscar and Frankie) *Fall 2023*

Con Artist: This standalone romantic comedy follows the story of an FBI agent tasked with investigating an art theft ring. The only thing his number one suspect makes away with, is his heart. *February 2023*.

Trip and Fall: This standalone road trip romance follows two twenty-somethings who each have a different reason for wanting to leave town and explore the countryside. One out of a sense of wonder; the other, a sense of desperation. Will they find more than the adventure they were looking for? *Summer 2023*

Sign up for my newsletter, access my website, or follow me on social media to keep up to date with new releases and sneak peeks.
Linktr.ee/TiffanyAndrea